DECEPTIVE TRUCE

BAY RIDGE ROYALS
BOOK THREE

HEATHER LONG

Deceptive Truce/Heather Long – 1st ed.

ISBN: 978-1-956264-81-4

To my coffeemaker.
Without you, I wouldn't be able to do this.
Literally.

FOREWORD

Dear Reader,

Welcome to Deceptive Truce, this is officially book 3 of the Bay Ridge Royals. If you have not read Shamelessly Loyal or Battle Lines, please set this aside and go grab those two. This series is best read in order.

All of that said, what do you *need* to know? Let's talk, previously, for the Bay Ridge Royals...

Milo Hardigan has more or less relocated to Manhattan to live with Lainey. Though they have not put any labels on their relationship, they are definitely lovers and working together to investigate King, his shell companies, and exactly what he is up to.

In the meanwhile, Lainey continues to do work for her grandfather as well as gather information on the other families. Ezra keeps intruding on her actions, particularly when she is at odds with what King wants. Late one night, Ezra shows up at her apartment and they hookup and it's revealed that after she left Milo in Shamelessly Loyal, she and Ezra had a brief affair on Ezra's family island.

Like that affair, their night ends with him leaving

abruptly and calling it a mistake. Lainey tells Milo about it, confessing she doesn't know how she feels about it all and he accepts it, with some reservations. Mostly, he doesn't want Ezra to hurt her.

Ezra also arranges for a bodyguard to accompany Lainey again, as he had during a previous conflict. As irritating as she finds it, she doesn't argue because it will make them all feel better.

Adam is continuing his campaign to get back into Lainey's good graces while also working with his new employer to take down King. In and around all of this, he and Lainey coordinate looking after their younger sister Andrea. Meanwhile, Bodhi pursues his own hunt, but finds himself drawn back to Lainey again and again.

During a masquerade at the Reed estate, a lot of truths are spilled including Adam learning about Lainey and Ezra's affair and Milo making it clear that Ezra doesn't get to hurt her. Adam keeps trying to stake his claim but Lainey refuses to yield to his controlling tendencies.

During a fencing session for Lainey to burn off some steam, she comes face to face with Adam. He knows so many of her secrets and this is just another one that he knows. Infuriated and frustrated, she focuses on Milo's birthday and arranges a special surprise for him. Unfortunately, King crashes their date with the threat of recruiting Andrea and Milo throws himself on the fire to protect her.

Probably what King planned for all along, but Milo is forced to leave Lainey behind and he goes to work for his "father."

This brings us to Deceptive Truce. Whew. For a second there, I was like wait, what happened in which book? While there are ties back to the 82nd Street Vandals (both familial and friendship), you do not have to read that series.

That said, *this* series contains some spoilers for 82nd Street Vandals, there's no way to get around that. If you do decide to check out 82nd Street Vandals, be sure to start with *Savage Vandal*.

For a little housekeeping. Bay Ridge Royals is a why choose romance with characters exploring and coming to terms with their evolving sexuality, identities, and relationships.

TWs: Mentions of SA. Kidnapping. Intimidation. Car accidents. Threats of violence. Discussion of trafficking. Smuggling. Be kind to yourself, this is a dark romance series.

Thanks for checking out Deceptive Truce, I can't wait for you to get to know them.

Happy reading.

xoxo

Heather

BAY RIDGE ROYALS

The Families
Benedict
Reed
Graham
Adley
Clifton
Marlowe
Cavendish

Main Characters
Elaine "Lainey" Benedict
Milo Hardigan
Adam Reed
Ezra Graham
Bohdi Cavendish

PROLOGUE

EZRA

MORE THAN A YEAR PRIOR...

"When does Andrea go back to school?" I'd shown up at Der Sonne at first light, hangover intact, and thank fuck the Benedict cook had the best morning-after remedies ever. She'd sat me down, fed me breakfast, then given me the hair of the dog in my coffee. It was definitely hitting the spot.

Instead of answering me, though, Lainey spared a glance up from her phone to the maid, who was clearing away plates from the breakfast table before refilling her coffee. I didn't say anything; I was just waiting it out. Once we were alone however, she cut her gaze in my direction and gave me the most baleful look.

"The maid doesn't give a shit," I reminded her. "None of them do. You're the one who cares. Not them."

"That's not the point."

I fucking loved it when she'd scold me, more for the tone of voice and the attitude than anything else. She made prim sound so damn sexy. "It is the point," I continued, soaking up the chastising look. "But we can argue about it later. How much longer is she here on break?" Because until Andrea returned to Colfax Academy, and got the hell out of New York, Lainey wasn't leaving.

And as long as she was here, she was going to have me permanently at her side. I didn't trust the king, or whatever the hell Adam was doing. He was alive—that was something—but the king had tried to have him killed. So he'd made a deal with O'Connell, and they were letting Adam "play dead" though the family hadn't acted like they knew anything.

Made sense. Lainey didn't know anything except that Adam wasn't returning her calls or messages. A complaint she'd shared with me because Andrea had asked, but she didn't have any answers for her sister.

"Tomorrow," Lainey finally relented, and I nodded. That was what I thought. "She leaves first thing in the morning. I will take her out this afternoon, then dinner tonight at Waltham Corners." She made a face. "I suppose you're going to want to come to that?"

"Yes."

"Adam's not there, so how do we explain you?" She flicked another look at me from beneath her lashes. "Unless you can reach out to him..."

As fishing attempts went, it was an excellent one.

"I spent more time at Adam's place growing up than I did at my own. I don't need an excuse to be there. Besides, Harper likes sticking it to my dad when I'm around and seeing if I'll leak any info on their latest acquisitions."

It amused me. They were supposed to be business allies, but I didn't doubt they'd knife each other in the back in a red-hot second. It also worked for me and Adam to play them off each other, so I'd keep doing it now.

Her nose wrinkled, and I leaned over to cover her hand on her coffee cup with mine. "I can't tell you where he is."

I couldn't even if I knew. He didn't want her to know, or he would have told her himself. The fact he confided in me rather than her—well, I'd always kind of reveled in that. But I wasn't in the loop this time. So I had one job, and she was sitting right next to me.

"It's fine," she said after a long moment. Her gaze held on mine for another second before she cut it away. It was so not okay. "He is old enough to make his own choices. So, dinner tonight at Waltham Corners and I'll say goodbye to her there. She will probably message me in the morning when she's on her way."

"Sounds good. Do you have anywhere else you need to be today?" Because I'd kill for a shower and a nap.

Eyebrows lifted, she shrugged. "I thought about getting together with Tally, but she messaged yesterday saying she was off to the Cayman Islands. Impulse trip."

Probably with her latest conquest. Though I rather doubted her ex would care to know she'd hooked up with his father. Wasn't sure how much Lainey knew on that, so I left it alone. Tally Marlowe was Rockston's younger sister and *his* problem. Not mine.

"Then take the day and pack your bags." If she didn't have other plans, we could make our own.

"Excuse me?"

"Pack your bags," I told her as I drained my coffee. It really was dialing back the pain in my head and easing the tension in my neck and back. "We'll head to the airport in the morning."

"Where are we going?" The question made me smile. And that's all I did, grin at her rather than answer. "Ezra?"

"Don't worry, Kotyonok," I teased, giving her ponytail a gentle tug before I pressed a kiss to the top of her head. "You're going to enjoy it."

"What am I supposed to pack?"

Better fishing attempt. But no, I wasn't telling her anything. The more information she had, the more likely she was to try and change things. I'd agreed to New York only because she worried about Andrea.

"Surprise me," I told her and when she frowned, I smiled. "Or don't. I can always surprise you. I'm gonna nap. Don't leave without telling me."

"Ezra..." she called, but I headed out of the dining room and outside toward the guest house on the far side of the open garden. Leopold Benedict didn't let anyone stay in his home. He didn't give a damn who we were. The staff had the guest house set up for us whenever anyone visited. That was where I'd slept all week.

I texted the bodyguard to let him know he was on watch until I got up. Dolion Karagiani hadn't come cheap, though he was highly recommended, reliable, dangerous, and capable of acting with extreme prejudice in defense of his clients. All things I wanted where Lainey was concerned.

∼

Twenty-four hours later...

The car took us directly to the plane at the airport. I'd kept an eye on my inbox and messages throughout the night and into this morning. Lainey was quiet, her distraction absolute. Her attention had been off since we left dinner the night before. She hated saying goodbye to her sister.

I didn't have siblings, only cousins. Most of the ones I had any kind of a relationship with were nuisances. I liked maybe one or two tops. Andrea, however, meant the world to Lainey and I didn't pretend to understand it. She was so much younger than Lainey. Almost as younger as Lainey was from me.

Me and Adam both.

So maybe I could get it. Didn't matter whether I understood it or not. She was upset, and I didn't like it.

Not at all.

"Are you trying to lull me into a false sense of security to try and get out of me where we're going?" The comment pulled a flicker of a genuine, albeit brief, smile from her.

"Feeling neglected?" It wasn't quite a tease. The drollness in the comment did entertain.

"Suspicious," I countered, and that got me another grin. "You aren't usually this cooperative. So I wanted to get a feel for how long it would last?"

Her snort was as inelegant as it was perfectly her. "Don't get attached," she informed me. "I just supposed you weren't planning on telling me anything, so why exert the energy."

"Because it's fun," I teased her. "You try to provoke me, and I tell you no and give you shit. Then you get exasperated and we go for round two."

"That sounds terribly predictable." She mused, tapping a perfectly manicured fingernail against her lower lip. "Not sure I care to be predictable."

"I would call you many things, Kotyonok," I assured her. "But I'd never say terrible."

Her soft laugh was exactly what I was going for, so I let it go. The car pulled right up to the plane. I didn't wait for our driver, letting myself out and scanning the area as I slid my sunglasses into place. When I held out my hand, I half-expected the battle to begin now. Not that she indulged me. Instead, she just slid her palm across mine and I helped her out of the car.

Without protest, she walked with me toward the steps leading up to the private plane. No arguments fell from her lips as she took the steps one at a time, with me a half-step behind her. The heels she wore did fantastic things for her figure, and as much as I wanted to enjoy the effect, I was more concerned by her cooperation.

On board, the flight attendants greeted us and took her jacket, as well as offered her a drink. Then me.

"Coffee would be lovely," was all she said as she made her way over to a seat. There, she buckled herself in and crossed one leg over the other. I watched her with a kind of morbid fascination. Not a single word of disagreement, no requests for more information, and not even a dismissive look or sharp glance.

"You shouldn't frown like that, Ezra," she murmured, as she opened her phone again. "Your face might stick."

"What are you up to?" I asked, dropping into the seat opposite hers. I could have taken the one next to her, but as it was, I just wanted to drink in the sight of her. I was missing something here and I didn't know what it was, exactly.

"Me?" She blinked at me, her eyes almost too wide, too innocent. "What do you mean?"

Then, the staff was there with the requested coffee and

also brought orange juice. "We'll be serving breakfast after takeoff. Do you have any special requests?"

"No," I told her before Lainey could answer. "I sent the requests over last night."

"Yes, Mr. Graham," she said with a polite smile before heading back to the galley.

Around us, the engines were warming up and luggage had been brought on board. Lainey had packed two suitcases. Neither was very large. She also had a single purse and was dressed business casual, which left her legs on sweet display.

"Still no questions?" I asked, catching her watching me.

"It's driving you crazy that I'm not asking, right?" She glanced down at her phone and the corner of her mouth lifted. I couldn't deny the fact that some genuine excitement threaded through me.

"So, you're torturing me on purpose." I leaned back in the seat and stretched out my legs.

"Maybe," she murmured, shutting off her phone before lifting her coffee cup for a sip. "Maybe not."

Exasperation chased delight through me as she watched me over the rim of her coffee cup. "You're going to drive me mad."

"Not a long trip."

Well... she wasn't wrong.

"And you're really not complaining."

No. I wasn't. In fact, as the outer door was sealed and locked, some of the tension tightening my muscles began to let go. It was the most relief I'd felt in months that hadn't involved alcohol.

"You're still not going to tell me anything." She finished the last by taking a sip of her coffee as if to punctuate her sentence.

"Nope," I agreed and tilted my head back so my eyes were half-closed. In a few moments, we would be taxiing on the runway, then we would take off. We would be in the air for the next sixteen hours, give or take.

Flying as far away as I could get her.

If I had my way... maybe we would never come back.

CHAPTER
ONE

LAINEY

PRESENT DAY

Rain spattered the windows of my room. Instead of closing the curtains the night before, I'd left them open so I could look out at the city lights. Well, brooded more than looked, if I were being honest. This morning, there wasn't even a trace of sunshine. The fall migrating to winter weather soaked us down in a gray, misty rain that obscured the world as it rested under a funeral shroud.

A groan tore free as I flopped onto my back. I wanted to scream, but it wouldn't do any good. Four days. It had been four, almost unbearably, *long* days since Pretty Boy threw himself on the fire for me and Andrea. After he walked out of the speakeasy, I hadn't seen or heard from him.

The lightest of knocks on the door had me shoving myself upward to sit. "I'm awake," I called. "Come in."

It was a foolish hope to think it would be Milo at the door. Yet, that imprudent and inescapable feeling bubbled up to fill my breast, only to burst when Marlene let herself in. She had a tray with her and an air of warmth and sympathy.

"Good morning," I said, summoning a smile I didn't feel and trying to square my shoulders, even if I would rather burrow back into the covers. At least they still smelled like Milo. "You didn't need to bring me breakfast."

As scolds went, mine was weak and landed without even a thud. The kindness in Marlene's eyes didn't diminish. "I brought you something light with coffee. I know you're not up for a lot, but you have appointments this afternoon."

Appointments.

I sucked back the sigh I wanted to release as Marlene set the tray over my lap and then moved to fluff the pillows behind me. She fussed around until she opened the silver domed plate with the grilled cheese sandwich. The scent struck as soon as she lifted the lid.

My half-hearted attempt at a smile turned into a real one and I met her gaze. "Your favorites. I also sliced up some pears." She touched another covered bowl. "The coffee, of course."

"Thank you, Marlene." I didn't have to struggle with gratitude. "It's perfect."

"You're a good girl. Eat, drink your coffee, and then shower. I have already arranged an appointment for you with Lydia. She will be arriving in two hours. That gives you time to finish, then a quick rinse. She's going to do your nails, give you a massage, and then style your hair."

Was I really that bad? I glanced at my hands. The color was the one I'd picked out to match my dress for his birthday. A bittersweet sigh escaped. "Did she have to change her schedule?"

"She said she had plenty of time for her favorite client." There was an admonishment lingering in those words. "Now, eat and coffee..." She glanced around my bedroom and began picking up a few items. I hadn't done much in here except stare out the window. It wasn't really that messy at all. When she picked up his t-shirt from the chair, I had to physically clamp my teeth together.

Without a word, though, she folded it up and moved it to sit on the nightstand next to his side of the bed. Then she left me alone, and I half-sagged against the pillows. I hated this helplessness scrabbling through me. I hated even more that Pretty Boy was out there, on his own, dealing with King.

Just thinking about King killed my appetite, so I cradled the mug between my palms and looked at the gray, dreary world outside. The heat chipped away at the icy shell that seemed to coat everything. Closing my eyes, I took another long breath and sipped the coffee before glancing down at the food.

Missing him was leaving this visceral ache in my chest. Everything hurt. Worse, everything made me want to cry. I wasn't this person. I was—helpless. He was out there protecting Andrea, so...it was time I got back out there and found a way to get him free. Damn Julius King.

Anger flash fired through my system. He'd been playing games with all of our lives for far too long. Ezra's words whisked out of the corner of my mind to haunt me. Adam made a deal *after* my car accident. It was the same year everything seemed to change with him.

He grew colder.

Crueler.

More controlling.

As aggravating as I found it, the fact he'd done it to protect me seemed to make it that much worse. And Ezra—he followed Adam just like he did in everything else. Did Adam know how much Ezra needed him? Turning those thoughts over, I took another bite of the sandwich. Then another. Bit by bit, until I'd eaten the whole thing. As good as it tasted, it still all turned to ash in my mouth.

"Right," I said. "Enough moping."

I drained my coffee and lifted the tray away before getting out of bed. I took a quick shower, more to rinse. I'd shower more thoroughly after I was done with my massage and hair appointment. When I came out of the bathroom, the bed was made and the tray gone.

Downstairs, I focused on going through emails and checking my schedule while I had a second cup of coffee. I reached for my phone a half-dozen times and, each time, I put it back down. The one person I really wanted to call, I shouldn't. It wouldn't be kind to make him have to ignore my call. I needed to talk to Adam and Ezra, but I needed to prepare before speaking to either.

"Lydia will be up in fifteen minutes," Marlena announced. "She just called."

"Thank you, will you bring us a pitcher of cucumber water?" As much as I'd like more coffee, I needed to hydrate.

"Absolutely, I set up the drawing room for your manicure and massage. Then, I will get your bathroom ready for hair." Approval and warmth radiated from Marlene. I'd been worrying her.

"Marlene?" I called, and she paused to look at me. "Thank you."

"You're very welcome. We'll get everything sorted. You'll see."

Yes, we would. Because I wasn't going to *wait* for something to happen. The next three hours flew by and, apparently, I needed the massage more than I realized. Lydia's care and focus helped me get out of my head, and by the time she finished blow-drying and styling my hair, I was feeling far more human.

She fussed without fussing. The woman could get a stone to talk if she put her mind to it, yet she also had the ability to be quiet. Today, I'd needed the quiet. I'd needed the time to think and to plan.

There were far more players on the board now. More than we'd even begun to identify as we looked into King's shell corporations and holdings. Ezra's admission that the Royals dated back to *before* King also got me thinking. Who or what created them? A secret society, not a gang. One that tapped those from affluent families.

But who decided who got tapped? How?

More—*how the hell had Julius King taken them over?* That answer proved elusive because I honestly had no idea how long he'd even been around. He seemed a fixture in our circle, but was that because he'd ingratiated himself? Or was he here before? How did it reconcile with Jeff Hardigan?

Long after Lydia had gone and Marlene told me she was done for the day and that she'd left dinner for me, I settled in the library at my desk and reviewed the reports. For all intents and purposes, Jeff Hardigan vanished nearly two decades before. I'd have still been a baby. Em definitely was. Milo couldn't have been more than seven.

So he took off, and what? Became Julius King and moved to New York? Began running the Royals? There had to be something that happened between leaving one life and joining another. Then there was the fact that Milo indicated they recruited Liam to take out Milo. That was one of his jobs.

That made no sense. Why would you want to eliminate your own son? Then again, nothing Julius King had done made sense, not really. Hindsight? Some of it did. His interest in Em bothered Milo a great deal, but then—King had wanted Milo to leave with him and abandon Em.

I rolled the pen between my thumb and forefinger, then began to turn it in a slow twirl. He hadn't "wanted" Em, abandoned them, but was angry with his then seven-year-old son for refusing to leave his sister and mother? No—the man seemed petty, but that seemed beyond petty.

Now, he wanted a relationship with both of the kids. Except Em didn't want him. She'd been so damn angry about him, and I could appreciate it. He mistreated her brother, and Em didn't know how to not be loyal. It was ingrained into every bone of her body. In that, she and her brother were *nothing* like their father.

The Vandals had also closed ranks around Em. As long as she didn't want to see King, he wasn't getting near her. The more I thought about it, the more the pieces of the puzzle I had didn't line up. I switched screens on the laptop and went back to the reports about his holdings. They were buried amongst shell corporations, properties, and titles hidden under a chain of various, barely there companies.

Tax shelters? Maybe. Umbrella structure? No. This was more designed to keep anyone from linking the assets. To what end, though?

That was the key. Grandfather always said if you could identify what someone wanted and what their end goal was, you could figure out everything else. So far, nothing we'd done had seemed to surprise King. Or maybe it had, and his gambit on Pretty Boy's *birthday* had been a double-edged sword.

I picked up my phone and checked the messages from Andrea. She was back at school until the winter break. I was tempted to suggest she find a friend to spend the holidays with, but I didn't think she'd want to do that. Then again, maybe she'd surprise me. It just might be better if she wasn't here.

The phone on the desk rang. There were a limited number of people who called the hardline. Among them, the desk downstairs. Lifting the handset from the cradle, I answered.

"Benedict residence." Yes, it was a residence. Maybe I should think about going back to Der Sonne. It was almost uncomfortably quiet here without Milo.

"Miss Benedict, it's George at the desk. We have a courier here to collect Mr. Hardigan's things..."

A courier.

My stomach plummeted. His things? "Mr. Hardigan's things are not ready for collection." I was proud that my voice remained perfectly even. "Inform the courier he should make an appointment."

"Of course, Miss Benedict. I'll take care of it."

"Thank you, George."

I hung up the phone and leaned back in the chair. If the courier was someone I needed to see, they'd find another way to send the message. Otherwise, they could wait. If I had to send Milo his things, no one from King's organization was coming up here.

No one.

I drummed my nails against the desk for a moment. If Milo wanted his things, I could have them taken to him. Pushing back from the desk, I logged out of the laptop and rose. I'd go through Pretty Boy's things and only put together the bare minimum. The idea of packing them made me ill, but it was also a chance to get him some information.

Think, Lainey, I told myself. Think. Plan. Get ahead of them.

There was a way to do this. I just had to figure out a way to do it that wouldn't involve *also* alerting King. As I headed for the bedroom, I had to focus very hard on calling it just *the* bedroom and not *our* bedroom.

CHAPTER
TWO

ADAM

Make friends with Milo Hardigan. That was the assignment. Make friends with the former Vandal leader, ex-con, and brother of Emersyn Sharpe. None of those were truly bad things, not even his time in prison, if I were honest. Mainly considering the circumstances surrounding *how* and *why* he ended up in prison. No, he wasn't that bad at all. The problem was he also just happened to be the guy who currently possessed Lainey's interest.

And occupied her bed.

That made me despise him. It also gave rise to more than one mental debate on how to get rid of him. He would hardly be the first man I erased from her life. Though, I normally got to them long before they got this much of a foothold. Irritation flooded me all over again.

No, it had gone down while I'd been "playing dead" and seemingly continued after I traded myself for Emersyn. I wanted to know who wished the king dead. I wanted access to that power. Only power always came at a price.

The time had already cost me Lainey.

She was the one price I wasn't willing to pay. Fine, Hardigan was in her bed now, and Ezra... I shoved the thought of Ezra Graham to the back of my mind and slammed the lid on it. On him. The last thing I needed to focus on was his admission that he'd taken her to bed.

Ezra had touched her—

Averting the destruction waiting at the end of that thought, I headed for the door. The apartment was secure and the distance to Lainey's building wasn't long. Still, I avoided exposure by going straight to the garage. Since learning I'd "survived" his little assassination attempt, Julius King had made no direct moves against me. Nor against Lainey. That had been the risk, although Emersyn's loyalty to Lainey was as fierce as Lainey's to her.

I would exploit that relationship cheerfully if it meant keeping Lainey safe. So far, I hadn't had to ask.

But that didn't mean I wouldn't.

In the parking garage located below the building, I slid into my Lexus. It wasn't the fanciest or the sleekest of vehicles. It was, however, reinforced and it offered me anonymity. The drive from my building to hers was negligible, even in late afternoon traffic and the rain. It also gave me time to drive around her building and check for any potential observers before I used the keycard to access the parking garage of her building. The Benedicts kept their cars in a private, gated area and my keycard allowed me access.

All three of the cars usually kept here were parked, and I slid into a fourth, unused slot. The cars' presence didn't automatically mean she was here. In the city, she usually favored a driver. A habit I approved of. It meant she had an escort door to door. Though Lainey had been known to go rogue and take a ride share.

Or a bus.

I shook my head as I let myself out. The interior of the car park was quite chilly with a hint of dampness. The silence echoed around me, not even the sound of another car motor intruding as I swept the area with a look. An elevator just outside the locked area took me to the lobby, or if you had a key, like I did, it took you up to her floor.

After pocketing the key back into my wallet, I leaned back against the wall of the elevator and waited out the ride. There were easily half a dozen reasons for me to come calling. I only needed one.

Waldemar wanting me to befriend Hardigan was fine, but I wasn't telling either of them that was why I'd come. The easiest excuse, the best one, was always the truth. Andrea's birthday wasn't for a few more months, but Christmas was coming. We should probably coordinate our gifts.

I'd already commissioned a new saddle for her. She was getting taller and would outgrow the one she used now soon enough. If she wanted to keep doing hunter jumpers, she was going to need the right equipment, the right horses —maybe a private stable of her own.

Der Sonne had the room for it and I could fund it. Lainey would agree, and she could talk her grandfather into it. The elevator dinged softly as it arrived on the correct floor. The thick carpet muffled my steps as I reached her door and lifted a hand to knock.

Did I have a key to her place? Yes. But it was better to only use that in the case of an emergency. It had taken my people serious *time* to make that key happen. Benedict had solid security. It was better not to risk it.

I glanced at the doorbell then knocked anyway. A camera above focused on me and I lifted my head to stare into it. Was she watching me right now? The sensation of being observed was there, but I couldn't say for sure.

After knocking and waiting again, I was about to ring the bell when the door opened and light framed her in the doorway. She looked—radiant. She'd trimmed her hair, and there were now streaks in it. The change was subtle yet unmistakable. Her nails were done in a soft lavender on the tips with a more natural base. More, there were glittering jewels on two of her nails. Her toes sported similar adornment.

Dressed in a pair of yoga pants and a long sweater, she was the picture of comfortable, beautiful, and—

There were tear tracks on her face and her eyes were red-rimmed.

"What happened?"

I flattened a hand to the door to get her back inside.

"Where is that son of a bitch?"

Hardigan might not be so bad, but I would kill him for putting that look on her face.

"What?" Her question barely pinged off me as I scanned the room, even as I closed and locked the door behind me. "Come in," she said almost belatedly, and I swept a look from her to the living room, to the open door of the library, and to the closed doors leading into the kitchen.

"Where is he?" I started forward.

"Where is who?" Lainey did not play dumb or coy. I cut a look back at her. The tear tracks were like slices digging through my skin, sinew, bone, and marrow. They were bad enough. Red-rimmed, faintly puffy eyes? I was going to make his death hurt.

"Hardigan. Where is he?"

She frowned. "He's not here."

"Where did he go?" I narrowed the gap. "When will he be back?"

"Hello, Adam," she said slowly, pinning me with those soft hazel eyes of hers. The redness seemed to turn them more green than brown. "I'm a little busy this evening and have a lot on my mind. How are you?"

The pointed look and brisk reminder did little to abate the pure fury striking sparks in my system. Someone had hurt her. That someone was not getting a chance to do it again. "I want to know where Hardigan is."

"Why?"

The question rocked me. "Does it matter?"

"At this point?" She gave a graceful shrug of her shoulders. "Yes." The answer didn't match the action and I narrowed my eyes.

"He made you cry."

Real surprise flickered across her face. "He didn't."

"No?" I gripped her biceps, turning her so that the lamplight illuminated her clearly. The tear tracks were right there. "Then why are you crying?"

"I can cry over something that isn't Pretty Boy."

"Sure," I agreed with her. "But you're not one who cries that easily, nor do you use your feelings to manipulate others. You didn't cry when you broke your arm coming off that horse. I've only ever seen you cry twice before," I reminded her. Only twice. And both times—both times, it had left me raging because once I'd been the reason.

The second time I couldn't do a damn thing about it.

She exhaled. "You should come sit down." Instead of

rejecting me or telling me I was wrong, she just pulled away and headed back to the library. The fire was on and there was tea. I needed something stronger, but she didn't offer and I wasn't going to just raid the bar. Stalking after her, I waited until she sat before I dropped onto the cushion of the ottoman facing her chair.

"Tell me." It wasn't a request, and she wrapped her fingers around her teacup. The look she shot me suggested she wasn't inclined toward answering me.

"Julius King came to see us a few days ago."

The fire in my blood went to ice. "He was *here*?"

"No," she said with the barest shake of her head before sipping her tea. "I took Pret—Milo out for his birthday. Just a fun little evening. King found us at the speakeasy."

I searched her face for explanations or ideas. "What did he want with Hardigan?" Any hints for what needed to be done.

"Nothing, and everything." That cleared up nothing. "He didn't come to see Milo, presumably, but me."

It was like pulling teeth to get her to loosen the information, but I resisted the urge to prompt her. The look in her eyes had gone distant.

"He wanted to do me the courtesy of letting me know that since you betrayed him—he would still honor his deal with you where I was concerned."

Fuck.

"But he planned to tap Andrea on her next birthday since they would still need a Reed in the Royals."

I was going to fucking kill him.

Waldemar wasn't intent on killing him at the moment, and he might be Emersyn's father, but I was done. Julius King could die.

"Milo convinced King to take him in her place."

My anger stumbled to a halt. "What?"

All at once, Lainey focused on me again, her eyes intent as she bestowed all that considerable intelligence on me while studying me. "He traded himself to protect Andrea." Against those words, I heard the soft echo of what she didn't say—that he'd done it to protect *her*.

"King went for it?" Then again, why would he take Milo for Andrea, for a Reed, unless...

Lainey's smile turned bittersweet. "I'm almost certain King came to deliver that ultimatum to specifically force Milo's hand."

It wouldn't surprise me.

"Considering he made Milo leave with him as a part of the arrangement and I haven't seen him since?" She shook her head then sighed.

A dozen different thoughts collided in my head. Not all of them kind. Fuck, most of them weren't kind. "So, he left you," was all that left my lips though, and the cool look she shot me could have wounded if it had been a knife.

"Yes, Adam," she said slowly. "Pretty Boy left me to protect *our* sister."

"From *his* father," I reminded her, and she rolled her eyes.

"That man is no more a father to him than mine is to me." The dismissive note didn't quite cover her hurt—or her worry.

Goddammit.

I reached over to cover her hand on the mug. "He knows what he's doing."

The faint frown and fresh surprise were a little humbling.

It was my turn to ask, "What?"

"You sound—almost confident."

"He's not a complete idiot." At her half-smile, I scowled. "Now what?"

"That's tantamount to a compliment from you." The humor didn't last long, however. Then the worry was back, along with the hurt.

The fact King's actions led to Hardigan leaving her should be a cause for rejoicing. It removed him from her bed, a place I didn't want him. It put him closer to King, and perhaps closer to answers. As much as I wanted Hardigan away from her, I didn't like how wounded she seemed.

Shifting my hand to her cheek, I stroked my thumb over the tear track. Despite its presence, her face was dry. Didn't mean it still didn't cause her some kind of injury. "I'm sorry," I told her. The two words came out far gruffer than I intended.

"For what?"

"If I hadn't betrayed him—" Then again, what was my betrayal? Proposing to Emersyn? It had nothing to do with him, but he hadn't seen it that way. If Liam hadn't been the guy he was, I would be dead instead of just being on the outside.

"He tried to have you killed," Lainey reminded me, not that I needed it. I'd hardly forgotten. "He did that, not you. At the end of the day, if it hadn't been you, it would have been something else. He wanted Milo. I wish I understood what for, but I'll figure it out."

The last five words poured ice back into my veins. "Lainey..."

"Don't you Lainey me," she said, then locked her gaze on mine. For a moment, the hurt retreated behind the ferociousness. The fire that she often showed me. The fire, the demand, and the pride that were so very much her. I far preferred her fiery temper to everything else. "You should have told me."

"Told you what?" How was I supposed to know he'd target Andrea? He'd avoided tapping girls. Using them as leverage? Absolutely. But tapping them to be a part of the Royals? No, none of them had been chosen. It was why I'd made my deal to keep him away from Lainey. I half-suspected that was what kept him away from Emersyn in the first place.

"Told me that you traded yourself to keep me safe."

"Who—" I didn't even know why I was asking. "Ezra."

Dammit.

THREE

LAINEY

"Yes," I said on the heels of a long, slow exhale. Not crying took actual effort. Not yelling at him took far more. Violence swirled around Adam. It agitated the air before I even opened the door. "Ezra told me about the deal you made with Julius King. The deal to keep me out of the Royals, and that you two would work for him."

Concentrating on my breathing also kept my tone even. The rage crackling around him seemed to grow even stormier as he shoved off the ottoman and stalked away. He opened and closed his fists, clenching his fingers and digging them into his palms. The demonstration of his disquiet was also very un-Adam-like. Stillness and calculation were far more his style.

He cut a glance toward me before he turned his attention to the fire in the fireplace. One hand braced against the mantle, he seemed determined to discover every secret the fireplace held—or maybe he needed the time to reconstruct his walls.

Being vulnerable was not about being comfortable.

"Are you going to say anything?" A part of me would be willing to bet he didn't know the answer to that question. He wanted to talk to me, though not about this. No, he clearly never wanted this topic brought up where I could hear it. "Or are you going to glare at the hearth until it prostrates itself in terror?"

A single huff of laughter escaped him and he pivoted to face me. "Ezra spilled his guts—and more for you already." Bitter salted those last few words. His eyes darkened to a deeper violet, almost pure purple. He was so damn angry. "What other answer do you need?"

"Why?" It seemed so small a question to encompass so much.

"You know why." Well, at least we weren't pretending about what I was asking him. That was something. "Ezra told you I made the deal to protect you."

"You haven't," I reminded him. "You changed—I didn't have all the pieces as to *why* you changed, but you changed because of that deal. Because King threatened me—"

"He reached out to prove he could hurt you, Lainey," Adam said in a voice so solemn and soft that I had to strain to hear him. He slid his hands into his pockets, then removed them again. "He—made it clear that I couldn't protect you from everything, particularly him. You were my weakness." He sighed. "You *are* my weakness. I made a deal with him, and then I cut you off; I needed you to dislike me —hate me if necessary."

"You're such an idiot," I said with a shake of my head and his expression shifted.

"Excuse me?"

"You treated me like crap. You stopped being a friend and caring, you—became dictatorial and sometimes downright cruel." A world of half-remembered hurts swirled through me. "You made it clear that I was my mother's daughter. And Ezra followed your lead."

Ezra always did.

"It was better for you to not rely on us." The way he gritted out each word made them particularly painful. "The timing could have been better. You didn't notice at first, I was away at school, or you were..."

"You followed me when I went to see Em."

"Yes, because you *risked* yourself. If King can hurt you here, he can hurt you anywhere. You were out there *alone*. Protecting you was the one thing I could do, but I couldn't do it if I didn't know where you were."

I wanted to laugh at the high-handedness, even now. He believed every word he was saying. "So, cutting me off. Treating me like a burden..."

Sometimes worse than that, but I thought I'd tucked all those little hurts away. The sting of them still being present needed to be ignored. In fact, rehashing all of this would get us nowhere.

"This conversation isn't going anywhere," I admitted and downed the rest of my tea like it was a shot of alcohol. "Milo has gone to King, whether to work for him or to live with him—I don't know. I haven't seen or spoken to him since King made his ultimatum."

"What else did Ezra tell you?"

I snorted. "Oh no, this is not interrogating Lainey time." I debated standing, but we were already challenging each other enough. "Why are you here?" Because he hadn't known about King or Pretty Boy or the threat to Andrea.

He blinked. "What?"

"Why are you here? You came over—using a security card you shouldn't have, I presume— to get up to this floor." That was something to consider with regard to access here and another point in favor of returning to Der Sonne. At the same time, I didn't want to leave the city. Just because I didn't know where Pretty Boy was right now, didn't mean I wouldn't know where he was always.

Instead of answering, Adam stared at me as though he wanted to get inside my skull and figure me out. That or the dismay was due to how I ended our other discussion. It could be both, or something else. While Adam tended to be easier for me to read, he'd never been entirely predictable.

"I came to see you," he said finally and I raised my brows.

"Me?" Fresh concern slid through my hurt feelings and I rose. "Is something else wrong?"

"I can come to see you when nothing is wrong, Lainey," he said as though insulted.

"Can and do are two different things," I pointed out. "But if that was it, well, you've seen me."

"Yes," he said, closing the gap between us once more. "I have, though I'm not ready to leave yet."

"Adam...I don't want to fight with you right now." No matter how engaging it could be at times. "I want to make another cup of tea, then get some sleep. I have a very busy day tomorrow."

"It's not even seven," he said like the time meant anything. "You're not someone who goes to bed that early."

"Would you stop telling me who I am? I think I know myself fine. I'm *tired*, Adam. I'm tired, and I have a lot to do." The world didn't stop turning just because I wanted to cry. Pretty Boy needed me thinking, not reacting. My pity party was over. "In fact, there's the door. You're very good at them so you can show yourself out."

I didn't even make it two steps before he dragged me

back against him. One arm around my middle, he locked his hand onto my bicep to keep me from slamming my right elbow back.

Fine, I got him with my left.

It hurt, but the whoosh of air leaving him was worth it. I couldn't quite stomp on his foot, but I was able to twist and drop my hand to his dick. One hard twist, and he would be screaming.

"Fuck," he muttered against my ear even as he went perfectly still.

"Let. Me. Go."

I was tired of being manhandled. I was tired of him and Ezra hauling me around and making demands, then dumping me to go do whatever. I was fucking tired.

He released my arm and I kept my grip firm. There was no mistaking the erection or the fact he was getting harder. "So pain does it for you, huh?"

"You do it for me," he countered.

I shook my head and he raised his hand to my face, but I gave him a warning squeeze and he went still again. Could he break my grip? Probably. Could I really hurt him before he did? Without a doubt.

"I told you," he said quietly. "You're mine. You've always been mine."

"Yes, I recall your rather blunt statements. But that's not how this works, Adam. I'm not my mother's daughter, you don't get to dictate to me like your father did to her, nor am I going to come running because you snap your fingers."

Surprise flickered across his face. Surprise, and maybe fresh anger. He opened his mouth but then snapped it shut again.

"Good boy," I complimented him. "Denying it does neither of us any good. You've used my relationship with her to insult me. You've used it to distance yourself. You've used it like everything else to keep me *away,* to protect me. Congratulations. You succeeded."

His chin dipped, but I wasn't buying his acquiescence.

"Now, you're going to leave, and you're going to *stop* telling me who I am and what I do."

"Or what?" The dare was right there.

"Do you really want to find out?"

The corner of his mouth kicked up. "Maybe."

It was my turn to be surprised. Or maybe shocked was a better word. "Do you really like pain that much?"

He chuckled, and then he covered my hand on his crotch. The pressure of his fingers against mine increased the sensation of me squeezing him. There was a lot to squeeze and I really *didn't* need to know that.

"I told you, I like you that much."

"Actually," I corrected him. "What you said was I was *yours.*"

"Yes," he murmured. "Same thing." He dipped his face until his nose just barely touched mine and his breath whispered against my lips. "I'm going to kiss you now."

"No," I told him. "You're not."

He sighed, locking his gaze on mine. "I told you I'd make my place."

"You've told me a lot of things over the years. I've learned to block it out." Maybe I shouldn't enjoy taking the dig but he damn well deserved it. "Like white noise. It all fades into the din."

His smile actually grew, and for the first time in I didn't know how many years, he wore an actual grin. I could barely remember the last time I'd seen him smile—for real —particularly when it was just us.

"You're going to make me earn it, aren't you?" Then he

brushed a kiss to my cheek, just at the corner of my mouth. "Make demands. Push back. Force me to chase."

"I'm not going to make you *do* anything."

"You do it by breathing," he murmured, and this time, he pressed a kiss to the other corner of my mouth. "You do it by existing."

Perhaps it was the shock of his smile or his nearness, but the idea of twisting his dick until he cried fled me. And I loosened my grip. Instead of letting me go, he kissed me. The gentleness in the kiss startled me more. It was a whisper of contact, a request, an offering.

My lips parted, and he swept in, the storm of emotion burning in my chest. From fragile like a butterfly's wings to ferocious like a tempest, he deepened the kiss until the only thing I could taste or see was him. Nearly as soon as it started, he pulled back.

Adam did.

He ended the kiss.

My heart raced and my breath came in swift pants as he studied me for a beat. When he used his thumbs to brush away the dampness on my cheeks, it hit me that I was crying.

Again.

"I'm going to take care of this," he murmured. Another kiss, this time passing so swiftly I barely registered the contact.

Then he was striding out of the library.

Take care...

Pivoting, I followed him. "Take care of what?" I called, but he was at the door and it was already open.

"All of it."

"Adam!"

The door closed behind him and I glared at it. Stalking

back into the library, I grabbed my phone and pressed his contact information. It rang three times and went to voice-mail. I gave it a beat then rang it again. It took a third call for him to answer.

"Lainey..."

"Adam, if you go off on some half-cocked plan and don't at least read me into it, don't come back. This isn't your show anymore. You aren't the only one taking risks to protect our family."

Silence greeted me.

"Did you hear me?"

I waited.

Then finally, "Yes," he said, "I hear you."

"Good." Then I hung up on him.

My hands were shaking as I sat in the chair. Whatever Adam had planned, I hadn't stopped him—merely delayed him.

We had to give Milo time, and I didn't want Adam to get killed. King had already tried to have him killed once.

I stared at my phone, switching to messages. There were a handful from friends, some from Der Sonne, and more from the next day's charity function. Nothing from Pretty Boy.

This was Em in hiding all over again, only at least I'd been able to—

I switched to the old app Em and I had used. The notifications were off, but there was a message waiting for me from an unknown contact.

One word.

Mayhem.

CHAPTER
FOUR

MILO

"Mr. King, I appreciate you taking the time to talk to us over food, but this might be easier to demonstrate how it all works if we were in a conference room." It wasn't quite a complaint, but there was a genuine worry in the kid's eyes that his glasses did nothing to hide.

The kid, in glasses, with disheveled hair, who introduced himself as Martin Bellman when he came in, and his "business" partner Broderick Canalis did not belong at a lunch with a man like Jeff Hardigan. They were too young, too fresh-faced—honestly, could Bellman even grow a beard? They were totally out of their depth. Canalis spent most of the meal fidgeting. Neither had wanted to order food, and the fact that the latter ordered a salad that he hadn't even touched also suggested he didn't want to eat.

I had to wonder if their stomachs were doing rolls. I'd gone with a basic burger and fries and ate it with my hands instead of a knife and fork. Since I was here to "observe," I was doing just that. The restaurant was nice but not high-end. It offered an illusion of wealth, although more business-like clientele rather than socialites and other members of the elite.

Missing Lainey was like missing my goddamn arm. Every thought seemed to ignite a memory or a conversation. How many times had she explained the differences? The location of a meeting was often as important as the subject of the meeting, mainly when someone else set the stage. You could learn a lot about a person's agenda via their tactics.

I understood how the game was played; we did the same in Braxton Harbor. Specific locations offered an upper hand or a chance to lull someone into a false sense of security. It could also help neutralize any potential threats by making their opportunities to challenge us even more difficult.

King was doing the same with this location. The restaurant knocked both of these guys out of their comfort zone. They wanted to do a presentation, not have a conversation. So they were already on the back foot. Their fidgeting betrayed their nervousness and their fumbling words led to more deferral to King. It was like they needed to ask his permission to have a thought.

That, I suspected, was the point. Conditioning the creative would-be entrepreneurs to lean into his every word, take his advice, and develop a deep sense of gratitude. It was truly sickening. Of course, this was the same man who recruited young teens to do his dirty work. Kids were so much easier to manipulate.

"We're having a conversation," King said. "You shouldn't have to demonstrate what your project does, you should be able to sum it up in a few words. An elevator pitch. Tell me what it is and how it will change the world."

"It's just a smart computer," Bellman said. "Like the ones you have in your phone or on your desk—"

"It's more than that," Canalis interrupted. "It's a partner for a smart computer—an AI."

"Well, AI is a misnomer, because it presupposes that it acts independently and has the ability to learn..."

"Which it does... only Butler can do much more than that."

"It *will*," Bellman took back over, but this time he glared at Canalis. "We haven't perfected it yet, but we're close."

"Butler?" King asked as though the show of friction between the two was of no consequence to him. But it was a wedging point. One of these two was the real brains behind the idea, the other was the drive to market—if I had to bet, Bellman was the one with the skills, and Canalis was the marketing. If I could see it, so could King.

That meant if he really wanted this project, he didn't need Canalis.

Probably not the position the man imagined himself in when he made the arrangements for the meeting in the first place.

"Butler—it's a work in progress," Bellman said with more than a little consciousness. "It stands for Bellman's ultra-tailored logistics and encryption root access program. The access program part just—describes it."

"What is it meant to do precisely?"

"There are AI programs that people have written to help with answering questions about a shop online or help route you to the correct person in a customer service queue. It's a lot of if, then statements. They are getting more skilled but can only do as much as they've been "programmed" to do.

Butler is meant to go further, to be coded to the individual; you set it up, you engage it, and it loads to all your devices. In a week, it should be able to match patterns and then predict them. It won't be long before it can identify and do things like sort your email or process messages. It can even identify which apps you never use or which ones you use the most, then resort to your phone screens so it's more functional. It starts with the basics, then builds until you have the perfect assistant right in your pocket."

"In a week?" The skeptical yet interested note was all it took. Bellman dove into his subject with enthusiasm. Frankly, it got a little more technical than I care for, but it seemed like a baller idea. One that could make a lot of money—and gather a great deal of information.

Somehow, I wasn't sure they'd looked at that aspect. The market data alone would be worth a fortune. By the time the nearly two-hour lunch ended and the two men shook King's hand as they left, I had a throbbing headache. I followed about sixty percent of their idea, but I couldn't really see how they planned to make all of that science fiction into reality.

Which—I supposed, was the point.

"Coffee," King said to the waitress when she came by and cleared the table. Apparently, we were not leaving yet. She nodded and hurried away, then he turned to focus on me. "Well? What did you think?"

"He's really ambitious."

"He?" King demanded, studying me with narrowed eyes.

"Bellman is ambitious in his thinking. Canalis is ambitious in his planning."

"Interesting...which will take the capital?"

I snorted. "You don't need my assessment."

"I didn't ask for that opinion. You're here to do a job, this is part of the job." A faint smirk curled his lips. "Now, which of them will take the capital?"

"Canalis would have left with it on a handshake because he doesn't care if he can deliver." I shook my head. "Bellman wants it, because he wants the opportunity, but he's not sure he can make good on everything. He's nervous since he had to do a verbal pitch, and that's not his forte. It would have been better if Canalis could have done the selling, except he doesn't know the program anywhere near as well. He leans too much on what they *want* it to do."

The waitress brought the fresh cups of coffee and King said nothing as he took a sip. His gaze seemed distant, though I didn't doubt for an instant he wasn't paying attention to everything I was doing. So I kept my expression neutral and leaned into my patience. Three years in prison had taught me to perfect both.

"What should we do next?"

"To what point?" The past few days had been an intense education in what King did when he wasn't threatening small children or bullying the heirs of the wealthy into committing crimes for him.

"The point of what?"

"The goal. Your goal is clearly not theirs. Understanding the desired outcome often provides its own roadmap to what choices should be made."

King chuckled but said nothing. Taking another sip of his coffee, he appeared thoughtful, though his expression didn't betray which direction his thoughts leaned in. "Did you believe them?"

"Bellman, yes." Bellman had been absolutely honest. Maybe painfully and to his own detriment. He didn't care about the business aspects of it, he was too preoccupied with answering "could *he* do it." That passion blinded him, even to his own partner.

"Canalis?"

"Absolutely not."

I wouldn't trust Canalis to stand in line behind me at a grocery store. King's smile grew and he rose abruptly, clapping a hand on my shoulder. "In that, we are in agreement. Good assessment, son." He seemed so pleased I wanted to vomit. Instead, I just rose as he peeled off several bills. The hundreds were all a sign of a high-roller flaunting his wealth.

At least he tipped the waitress; I guessed that was something. His men rose from their own tables. Two had been by the front door, another pair near us. There would be two more with the car.

His men always worked in pairs. No one ran solo around him. I soaked up each piece of information as the two by the door waited for the rest of us to get there. As if summoned by one of the others—and maybe they had—his car was already pulling up out front. The gray, windy day slashed at us as we stepped outside. We slid into the longer coats, the heavier material easily blocking the chill in the breeze.

Instead of heading to the car with them, I turned to look up the street. "I'm going to make my own way back."

I needed a break from him and his men.

"We have a deal," King warned and I glanced at him. His men were all on lookout, the perfect bodyguards. I didn't doubt for an instant they weren't violently aware of my every move.

"And I've honored that deal." It had been nearly a week since my birthday. A week since I'd seen Mayhem. I'd walked away from her, just like he'd asked, and I'd come to work for him. Working for him also required me to live in his home.

I was definitely not a fan.

"I will continue to honor it," I said, sliding my hands into the pockets of the wool coat. "But I need to learn the city. Best way to do that is to walk the streets and navigate them on my own. If I need a ride, I'll call." With that, I nodded to them and pivoted to walk away.

King could make it a deal. His men could shoot me. Hell, they could tackle me and drag me back. Frankly, either was a less painful option than carving out my own heart. That open wound still bled, and it didn't matter that it had grown sluggish. I had to physically force myself to keep from reaching out.

The app had been an act born out of desperation in the deep, dark hours of the night when all I wanted to do was wrap my arms around her. I'd loaded it, sent the message, then deleted it from my phone. Ivy told me the next time I loaded it and logged in, the messages would be there. I could read them; then they would auto-delete. But she had often deleted the app in between messages just to be safe.

I needed to check to see if she'd answered me. Sending that single word had been an act of economy, but it also let me tell her I was thinking about her. Maybe that wasn't fair to her, but she hated it when I tried to shield her from everything. As much as I hated the distance, King had given me an all-access pass to his business and home.

Most of it was for show at the moment. It was a test. Could I be trusted? Did I mean what I said? It was also a punishment. The petty mother fucker still hated that I didn't choose him when I was seven.

Whatever.

His obsessions were a weakness I could exploit. If it

took him down, I'd cheerfully exploit the hell out of our non-relationship. It might even be more efficient with me on the inside. As long as Mayhem and her sister stayed safe and the guys had Ivy shielded, I could do this.

When King's limo passed me, I didn't glance toward it or react. I'd been tracking the people behind me in the windows of the storefronts I passed. He'd taken all of his little lapdogs with him. If I kept walking at this pace, it would take me time to get to his place. But I needed the time.

Fuck knew I needed the distance. I'd mapped the directions earlier. So I took a left at the next city block and came face to face with Adam Reed, who straightened up from where he leaned against the building. I almost didn't recognize him. He wore an old army coat over a thick cable knit sweater and had a knit hat yanked down over his ears. He looked more like a dockworker than an heir.

"Hardigan," he said. "We need to talk."

"Now?"

"You appear to be alone."

"I'm also on a clock."

Reed scanned the road behind me then back to me. "I'll walk with you."

"Then I'm listening," I told him as he fell into step with me.

LAINEY

Wood pulled us right up to the front of the building, and Karagiani slipped out of the front passenger seat a moment before I opened the backdoor to let myself out. "Thank you, Wood."

"You're welcome," he said with a grin. "Lunchtime pickup?"

"Let's say one, but I may text for you sooner. But it won't be later." Not if I could help it.

"You got it."

The wind was bracing as I stepped out. I resisted the urge to fold my arms, and, thankfully, the cap I'd donned before leaving kept my hair from being pulled wildly. Working in the office was not my idea of fun, but I needed to go over paperwork for the accountants. Grandfather liked to have one of us review the reports *before* they submitted them.

"What specifically am I looking for?" I'd asked him the first time he gave me this task.

"For the number that doesn't fit. They tend to keep everything neat and all their categories totaled and balanced, because they know I will be reviewing them. It's the executives who don't keep one hand on the wheel who lose control."

In other words, they were less likely to try to cook the books if they knew one of the family—in this case, my grandfather or me—would be examining them. This was only the second year he'd asked me to do it on my own. The first three times, I'd done it with him in attendance.

I learned so much from those meetings. Crossing the pavement toward the doors, movement to the left caught my attention as a man pushed away from the wall and crossed to me. Karagiani cut in front of me immediately, blocking both the newcomer's access as well as my view.

"Lainey B..."

Relief cut through the tension of my morning and I touched my bodyguard's back. "He's a friend."

"Are you certain?" Karagiani didn't move from his position.

"Yes," I said even as Phillip—Bodhi, I mentally reminded myself, added, "She didn't stutter. Take a step back there like a good boy." All perfectly pleasant but there was no mistaking the threat in his voice. Karagiani went rigid in front of me, his shoulders squared.

Shaking my head, I took the lead and moved around him to find Bodhi studying Karagiani with a rather indifferent, if cold, appraisal. The glacial look in his eyes warmed when he glanced at me. "Karagiani, my friend, Mr. Cavendish. Bodhi—" That still felt odd to say. "Bodhi, this is Karagiani."

I almost added the word "good" to the description, except I wasn't sure if we'd achieved that status label, *yet*.

"He's not a friend," Bodhi said with a nod. Then he offered me an arm. "Heading inside?"

"I am," I told him, not taking his arm automatically. The gray, miserable day had grown a bit brighter with his arrival. Apparently, I needed the distraction. "I take it you would like to join me?"

The corner of his mouth kicked a little higher. His dark brown hair appeared like he'd shoved his fingers through it a few times after it had been windswept. Still, he made the disheveled look work for him, adding to his rakish air. "I suppose I could hang out here for someone else more interesting to come along, though I don't have all day."

We were going for amusing. "I see." I hummed a moment, as though turning the idea over thoughtfully. After all, I doubted he'd just shown up for no reason. Still, I didn't want to assume I was the reason either. One thing I'd learned over the years, Ph—Bodhi did as he chose and he always had a reason, whether he shared that reason or not. "I guess I can take pity on you."

"That would be kind." His perfectly straight face didn't so much as twitch with amusement. "And different."

"Not a lot of kindness in your world?"

"No," he said with a careless shrug just before I slid my hand onto his elbow. "I mean, there's kindness, and then... there's *kindness*."

"A distinct difference," I murmured and he flashed me a real smile.

"Indeed."

He opened the door and held it open before letting me precede him. While he followed me to the next door and opened it, I didn't comment on the fact he let it close in

Karagiani's face. Then again, Karagiani wasn't here to hold my doors. He'd made that perfectly clear.

Once inside the large lobby, Bodhi offered me his arm again and we headed for the executive elevators. You needed a card and a code to use them. Security nodded to me and said nothing about my escort. The ride up to the seventy-third floor passed swiftly.

One Benedict was our tower. Or one of them, anyway. It was Grandfather's crown jewel in Manhattan, with helicopter views from the George Washington Bridge to the Statue of Liberty. We leased space on the lower floors to many other companies but the sky and penthouse floors were all ours.

"Miss Benedict," Carla said as she rose. The middle-aged woman with her salt-and-pepper hair was a classic beauty. She didn't worry about the appearance of early gray; she just embraced it. Frankly, I thought it just made her even prettier. "Good morning. Accounting day?"

"Accounting day," I told her as I began to ease off my coat. Bodhi took charge of removing it and then passing it over to Carla before he took off his own. "Is everything set up for me?"

"We prepared the West End Conference room. I know you prefer the view from it. I made sure to have tech set up your computer and bring in an extra laptop if needed before we arranged the files." With a gesture, she led the way down the hall. Grandfather's office was on this floor. I had one too, though I rarely used it. He'd installed me into a smaller office right next door to his.

People needed to get used to seeing me here. While Carla had known me since I was a child, she never treated me like a kid. Bodhi followed me like a shadow, saying nothing as Carla opened the doors to let us in. There were floor-to-ceiling windows all along the side that offered a gorgeous view of the Hudson River and New Jersey beyond. The bridge, of course, was the centerpiece, but it was also too gray and dreary to make out all the details.

Still, I wasn't complaining.

"We'll be fine in here, Karagiani," I told my bodyguard. "I have no intentions of leaving until this is done." Then I glanced at Carla. "You arranged a space for him to wait in?"

"I did," she said with a smile, while hanging up our coats in the small closet. "I've also ordered lunch, all of your favorites. It will be here in a couple of hours. Should I double it?" While she didn't glance at Bodhi, I understood the request.

"Please—" I said, then glanced at Bodhi. "Unless you have any particular requests of your own."

"Is your favorite liver and onions?" The bland response made my own lips twitch.

"Would you eat it if it was?"

He stared at me a moment before shaking his head. "No."

I laughed. "Then good for you, it's not."

"Then whatever the lady is having." He nodded to Carla. "Please."

"Of course. I'm down the hall if you need me. I would suggest beginning your review with development this year."

"Noted," I said before she led Karagiani out then closed the doors, leaving me alone with Bodhi. I glanced at him. He stood next to the table, hands in his pockets as he stared at the meticulously arranged file folders. They covered the entirety of the fifteen-person conference table, except for the small area around where my desktop computer had been set. A laptop sat on a small table behind it. Everything had been plugged in and arranged.

"She wants you to read something in particular?"

Pausing to brace one hand on the back of a chair, I lifted a foot and tugged off one heel, then the other. This was going to be a long day and I didn't need heels on to read. After setting them to the side, I headed over to the espresso machine. "Coffee?"

"Only if you're getting some."

I nodded and went to work pulling the shots. "Yes, Carla always lets us know who lagged the most on getting their reports in. Doesn't mean there's something wrong, but Grandfather is very exact in his requirements. If they were that late, they may have skimped."

"Or they could have been late to do the work."

"Agreed." The pair of lattes took little to no time to make, and I found him studying me when I turned with his cup in hand. "What can I do for you, Bodhi?" I almost managed to not stumble over his name.

Almost.

"My name isn't that bad." Amusement glimmered in his expression.

"I never said it was, but—I am used to calling you Phillip."

"You may still call me Phillip." It was such a gallant offer.

"But you don't like the name." Why else use a different one? Unless he'd been disguising his identity somehow. Still, I didn't think that was it.

His fingers brushed mine as he took the oversized cup. The foam on the top was perfect and my absolute favorite part. "I don't care for it, no. But then, I share the name with my father."

I nodded. "Say no more. I can call you Bodhi, and I promise I will get used to it."

He chuckled. "I meant what I said, Lainey B, you can call me whatever you like." After one sip of his drink, he gave me an approving expression. "Good coffee."

"Marlene made sure I could pull a decent shot by the time I was fourteen. She insisted that if I was going to drink coffee like I already worked in an office, it had to be *good* coffee."

He chuckled. "I agree. One should enjoy the good things. Though, I could argue there is something to be said for sludge."

"Not something good, I hope." I meant it to be teasing, although he seemed to give it real consideration as I made my way to the head of the table. After setting my cup down, I pulled out my chair and pushed out another for him.

"I guess it depends," Bodhi said.

"On?"

"I'm trying to figure that out right now." For a moment, humor flashed through the sobriety in his eyes. "Experience, I suppose, would dictate whether the sludge could be good. Experience and desire."

"I'm fairly certain you can apply that criteria to anything." I sat down, crossing one leg over the other.

He seemed to give that more consideration before he took a seat. "Of course," he said. "You've been getting quite a bit of experience in the desire department under your belt."

"Not a topic we're going to discuss," I informed him.

"I don't need to discuss it. As long as you're happy and not being forced, you feel free to do whatever you want." It wasn't the first time he'd said something along those lines.

Then again, he'd offered some cold, practical violence the night of the masquerade.

"I appreciate that," I told him. Not that I was happy at the moment. Just thinking about the masquerade was another reminder of Milo's absence. Trying to shake off the malaise, I focused on Bodhi. "Why are you here?"

"Straight to the point. I've always liked that about you."

"You didn't like it so much when I asked you the same question the night you broke into Der Sonne." It had been in the weeks *after* the car accident. I'd had trouble sleeping and I'd crept downstairs to see if I could sneak pie from the fridge. I found Bodhi coming out of my grandfather's office.

"I didn't mind it," Bodhi admitted. "I also didn't expect to get busted by a kid." He shrugged.

"Hmm. You never did tell me why you broke in that night." We rarely discussed it, and I only brought it up now being that it was worth a reminder that we'd been keeping secrets for each other for a very long time now. I took a sip of my coffee.

"I didn't," he agreed. "As for why I'm here, I wanted to see how you were."

"Really?" I couldn't help but be skeptical.

"You have a bodyguard, Lainey B. Who's threatening you?"

Direct.

To the point.

I blew out a breath. "That's a long story."

"I have time."

"You also appear to be very busy." While he might be from the Cavendish family, he rarely appeared at functions or did so infrequently. Honestly, I never knew where I'd see him next. The fact he showed up in Braxton Harbor when I'd been there to see Em had been a surprise.

"I will *always* make time for you." He studied me. "Who is threatening you? And why the bodyguard?"

"You don't like him." It was more of a hunch than anything he'd said. But he'd mentioned him twice and his assessment on the street hadn't been friendly.

"No," he said without disassembling. "I don't. So tell me about the threat. I'll take care of it and we can get rid of him."

"We?" I raised my brows.

He nodded once. "We."

Rather than answer, I took another sip of the coffee then glanced at the stacks of folders and paperwork before focusing on him again. "It's a long story, and I have much to do."

"I have all the time in the world—" He flicked a look at the paperwork. "I can also read."

"Offering to help?"

"With whatever you need." There was directness there that sent a shiver down my spine. "Just don't ask me to do windows. I never can seem to not streak them."

Laughter bubbled up through me at the deadpan delivery. The humor helped, and I blew out some of my tension with a long exhale. "May I ask you a question first?"

He motioned for me to continue.

"What do you know about Julius King?"

CHAPTER
SIX

EZRA

The near-inaudible vibration in my pocket only reminded me that I had silenced the phone when I got to the casino so I could continue to ignore the world. The baccarat table held my attention, along with the fine glass of Bourbon I'd ordered when I sat down. It was my third or fourth, but I was just getting warmed up. The drink was smooth, the cards were hot, and I put a thousand on the player.

Doubled my money and I lifted my drink to toast the dealer as I shifted the bet to bank and moved the winnings into my pile. I had a tidy sum. I'd won more than I lost. Cool feminine fingers glided over my nape and I spared a glance at the woman who came to settle at my side.

Kandi? Kandace? Kaylee? Katherine? I didn't fucking care.

"Hey, gorgeous," she whispered breathily, rubbing her more than generous breasts against my arm. Frankly, I was more impressed with the dress that kept that pair in place since all but her nipples seemed to be on display. "Can I do something for you?"

The dealer was calling for last bets before she began to draw the cards.

Picking up a five-hundred-dollar chip, I traced it over one globe and then lifted my gaze to meet hers. "I'm going to drop this in the slot and you're going to fuck off, okay?"

The heavy-lidded eyes with their promise of passion went wide then cold. Her swollen, gloss-laden lips formed an 'O.' To make my point, I tucked the chip right into the cleavage, where the tightly bound-up breasts would hold it, and then I tapped her on the nose.

"Go away now."

Outrage seemed to vibrate right off her, but I went back to giving the table my attention. Not so much that I wasn't aware of her or the fact that a man on the far side shook his head at her and she left without another word. I played with another chip as the cards were dealt. This round went to the bank, which meant I won—again.

Baccarat. Betting on the bank on the safe, but you had to play your own chances, too. The pit boss was keeping an eye on me as I washed down another swallow, and I let the whole bet ride on the bank. And I won.

I tapped the glass for another, split the winnings, adding it to my stack before I dropped a thousand on player again and waited for the deal. The guy next to me moved on, and another took his place.

"Graham."

Fuck.

I had a really good buzz going on, the last thing I wanted was to talk to King. He placed chips on the table. My new drink arrived, along with one for him. How long had he been hanging out?

"Last bets," the dealer said, and I picked up my glass before I glanced at King. Only instead of locking gazes with him, I was treated to the presence of Milo Hardigan on his far side. The cold void in his eyes promised he wasn't any happier about this than I was. Didn't tell me shit about what the fuck he was doing here—

The dealer played out the cards and it went to the bank. Because, of course, it did. Exhaling, I jerked my focus to King. "Sir."

The single syllable didn't do much for my mood, but I managed to keep my irritation off it. Another swallow also blunted the aggravation of having Hardigan there. That asshole was everywhere...

Wait, why wasn't he with...?

"Place your bets." The dealer focused on me and I glanced down at my chips and shifted them back onto player even as King put his bet on bank. Yeah, you do that asshole.

Glancing at King again, I met his appraising stare. He wasn't paying an ounce of attention to the table. "Are you drunk?"

"Not hardly." Even my buzz faltered in the head-on collision with this pair of assholes. "What do you need?"

"For you to answer your phone," King said, the droll reminder not remotely friendly. The vibration in my pocket earlier. "But that's a... *discussion* for another day."

Bank took the next hand. He let his winnings ride, and I slid over a matching bet to player. We weren't really playing each other. It wasn't quite how this worked, but it felt like it. The mild relaxation I'd achieved sitting here had also abandoned me.

"Then what else can I do for you?" Because he wouldn't

have come looking for me if he didn't need me for something.

"You need a new partner," King answered, and it was quite possibly the last thing I ever imagined hearing from him. Maybe not the very last thing, but nearly the last. "Milo needs to learn more about being one of us."

Being one of us...

I flicked a look past King toward Hardigan. The sewer r —the asshole. There, Kotyonok, I am trying. He didn't look any happier about it than I did. The next win went to the bank. We repeated our moves. As long as King went to bet on bank, I'd bet on anything else. I didn't care if I pissed all my money away. I'd already netted a tidy sum for the evening.

"Milo has some solid ideas and his own experience, as you're aware."

Yes, I was fucking aware.

King's smirk just made me want to punch him, so I took another drink of bourbon instead. It really didn't help to water down the urge. Just gave me something to do. This time, bank lost and player won. Score a point for me. We played again, and I waited for King's instructions.

He'd get to the finer points sooner or later.

"You're going to take him under your wing. Make sure he understands the ins and outs of everything that you do. This includes contacts and negotiations."

I barely managed to stuff my incredulity. So he wanted me to take Milo with me when I went to beat clients who failed to pay, or to steal property King wanted even though the owners had refused to sell. "Everything?"

"Everything," King said. "He's going to be in charge of you someday. He can't lead if he doesn't know where every-thing is."

Right.

I needed another drink.

"You'll do this," King continued almost conversationally, "without objection or protest, because you failed to acquire the painting I wanted. I gave you a job, and you chose to let that little girl poach it out from under you." I didn't respond or look at him. "Be grateful that I am choosing to see it that way, for otherwise, I would have presumed that you helped her acquire it in absolute defiance, and you know how I feel about that."

Yes, I was very well aware.

"Excellent," King said. "I thought you would see things my way."

One more hand and it went to player, and King lost his bet. I wasn't quite back up to what I'd lost, but it was definitely on the upswing. He rose, then motioned to Milo to take his seat. "Keep the chips, son. Learn the game. Ezra plays it very well. I'll see both of you later."

I wasn't the only one who went silent in his absence. I moved the chips to bank. The bank winning was the odds on favorite. That was why the table always took a commission on the win. Still...

"You know baccarat?" He seemed more like a poker guy, although he might surprise me.

"Not really," Milo said. "Though it doesn't look that hard." He put a bet down on player. Now, he and I were in opposition. I was used to the view here.

"Do you want me to explain it?" It was the closest to offering to help him as I was going to come. I took a long swallow of bourbon and debated how many glasses I would need to regain the buzz I lost.

"Sure," Milo said. "Why don't you explain the game to me?"

I spared him a look and found the cool calculation in his eyes preferable to the cool disdain in King's.

"It's all about getting to nine," I told him. "It's not blackjack, and adding cards doesn't threaten to break the bank..."

He listened as I went over the basics. The dealer played the cards. Milo won twice. I won twice. The even split wasn't lost on me. The table was getting cold now. More players left, leaving us with the dealer.

When Milo shifted his bet from player to bank, I left mine on bank to test the waters. "You have it?" I asked and he nodded.

"Not that hard. I prefer poker, though."

Yeah, I had already figured that out.

"This isn't strategy or even odds. This is just—pure chance."

I chuckled. "That's the beauty of baccarat, elegant chaos. Hoping you can predict the cards, but how can you? There are the odds of the bank winning more often, because the bank always does. Except do you risk the player? Or the tie?"

"Tie doesn't come up often?" It was a fair question.

"Not predictably," I told him. "But it pays eight to one. The reward is quite often worth the risk."

"Huh."

We said nothing for another half-hour, varying our bets even as we continued to play. I was breaking even, losing only as much as I'd won since King joined the table. Milo was slightly up.

Slightly.

"I suppose this is a good gauge of whether or not you can learn." I'd finally gotten another drink, but I only sipped this one. "Not that I have any interest in teaching you."

"No problem. I have no interest in learning anything from you, either." The suggestion of a veiled insult amused me more than annoyed me. "Because, frankly, I don't see what you have to teach that doesn't involve betrayal and shitting on people."

The words struck, the ripples skating over me and I downed the Bourbon before I moved five thousand to tie. If I won the tie, I'd teach the son of a bitch—because he really was one and King was the bitch.

If I didn't, he could fucking flounder.

Maybe he'd get himself killed and remove himself as a problem. Lainey would be sad, but she'd get over him. She was strong.

"Last bets..."

"I thought you said a tie was a rare thing?" Milo said as he hesitated.

"That's what I said." I wasn't taking it back, either. "You playing?"

With the slightest hesitation, he put a single thousand-dollar marker on the tie. I snorted. Would he follow me into a burning building because I told him that was the lesson? That had possibilities.

The dealer played out the hands.

Six and six.

A fucking tie.

"Well done," the dealer said, smiling. Eight times my bet was going to be close to two hundred thousand. "Do you wish to continue to play, Mr. Graham?"

"No," I said slowly. I really didn't want to keep playing, but I bet against myself and now I had to pay up. "Cash me out."

"We will need to take you to the cage to cash you out, Mr. Graham."

"Yep," I said, rising and glancing at Milo, who was stacking his chips. "Leave them. They'll bring them to us."

Her table was already being closed. A concierge met us and escorted us to the cashier's cage. I handed them the numbers to wire the money to my account and told them I'd take a few thousand for spending money. Milo cashed in his chips. It was just thirty-five thousand.

I was tempted to give him shit, but I bit back the urge. My restraint was legendary, particularly because I hated biting my tongue. When we were finally done, I jerked my head toward the elevators. "Let's get food and talk."

Milo eyed me. "I don't really—"

"I don't care. He said you need to learn from me. That means where I go, so do you. What I do, so do you. And if you don't listen, well, that's on you too."

Leaving him, I headed for the elevators and he caught me up just as I hit the button.

"What the fuck are you doing with King, anyway?" I had to know.

"I thought you didn't care?"

I rolled my eyes at his response and my phone vibrated again. Since King just showed up, I pulled it out this time and stared at the name on the screen before I declined the call. I wasn't in the mood for Oksana.

Fuck, I wasn't in the mood for anyone, but here I was...

CHAPTER
SEVEN

LAINEY

MORE THAN A YEAR AGO...

The yacht sliced through the sparkling water. The scarf I'd tied around my hair snapped in the breeze. I'd gone with a one-piece bathing suit to sun myself, but I'd also applied the sunscreen before I'd climbed up on deck. Ezra sat, shirt open to the sun and dressed in shorts, but there was no mistaking his tension. For all that he *looked* relaxed, he wasn't.

While the sunglasses shielded his eyes, the weight of his gaze burned a hole between my shoulder blades. Not that I turned to look in his direction. If anything, I focused on the distance. The nearly seventeen-hour flight landed us at a private airport, where he'd hustled us into a car that took us to a port and aboard this yacht. I didn't get the time I wanted to admire the beautiful lines of the ship. She was almost pure elegance and gleamed in the morning light. I had no idea what day it was or what time, so I just enjoyed the look that reminded me of a swan before I climbed on board.

"Would you like a drink, Miss?" One of the crew had apparently come out to join us. He didn't seem much older than we were, his skin warmly tanned and his smile genuine. I didn't recognize the accent that kissed his words, but I appreciated it.

"Water is fine," I told him. "Or juice. Thank you."

"Of course." He smiled a little wider at my grin then turned his attention to Ezra. "For you, sir?"

"Same," he said. "With coffee for both of us." His tone was far less friendly and a great deal more dismissive. I shook my head.

"Yes, sir." Then the young man was gone and I turned to face Ezra.

"You don't have to be an ass."

"He doesn't need to be flirting with you," he countered. "You should definitely not encourage it."

I rolled my eyes. "Okay, if you think me smiling at someone is flirting—I weep for the women you've been hanging out with."

His smile turned thin-lipped. "You're half-dressed, with a sarong around your hips, and that's a lot of skin on display. News flash, Kotyonok, you're beautiful."

"Yet, somehow—you make that sound like an insult."

It didn't take long for the man to return with our drinks and he set up the coffees, water, *and* juice on the table where Ezra lounged. I debated just taking my drink back to the railing and ignoring Ezra, but baiting him only worsened his behavior.

"Thank you," I said, even as Ezra waved the man off.

The steward was not the problem. If anything, he'd been perfectly polite.

"Yes, Miss. Breakfast will be brought up in an hour unless you want it sooner."

Honestly, I didn't want food at all. The yacht sliced through the water almost too smoothly. Still, we hadn't eaten except for dinner before the attendants opened the bedroom for me. I'd slept in it and Ezra stayed in the main cabin.

"An hour is perfect," I assured him. Maybe it would give Ezra time to find his manners or a better mood. Either would be ideal. After he left us alone again, I caught Ezra staring at me. Or at least in my direction.

The disgruntled look on his face suggested he would rather be anywhere else. Not that it was my fault he was here. He was the one who dragged us out of town. I'd had enough time to message Grandfather to let him know I was taking a vacation and I'd be back in a few weeks. Then, I mentioned getting away with friends.

He didn't approve immediately, but he didn't order me to return home. Then again, I wasn't asking for permission. Grandfather and I worked better when we trusted each other. I said I would check in and that I would be back. He accepted it and would let me know if something changed. Course, now I had to deal with Ezra's moods and I was pretty certain the boat wasn't our final destination.

No, the Grahams owned an entire island in the South Pacific. They didn't advertise it, but it wasn't really a classified secret. Ezra and Adam had discussed it plenty of times. How, if they ever needed to run away from the whole world, this was the place to go. It was on the far side of the world and seemed lightyears away from Manhattan and all the problems there.

Adam wasn't on the island. As much as I might wish he was, whatever he was doing, he had to maintain a low profile. Well, whatever he was doing that wasn't proposing marriage to my best friend. It was and wasn't a betrayal. If anything, it had been almost sweet of him to offer protection to someone I cared about.

As much as I wanted to think he had no other ulterior motives, I was far too much of a pragmatist. Our whole world had been constructed on ulterior motives, secrets, and lies. To believe anything else was asking for disappointment.

"Drink your coffee," Ezra said, reminding me that I wasn't just sitting out here alone. He'd poured some into a cup for me and rose long enough to set it in front of me before retaking his seat.

"I'm not a dog," I reminded him and he canted his head. "What?"

"I said," I continued, crossing one leg over the other. "I'm not a dog. Stop barking orders at me."

"I would never call you a dog." He actually sounded insulted, and for some reason, that entertained me.

"No, but you would speak to me like I was. Sit, Lainey. Come with me, Lainey. Eat, Lainey. Do what you're told, Lainey." I mimicked his brisk tone, and one corner of his mouth kicked slightly higher. "I don't find it funny."

"You find it a little funny," he retorted before taking a sip of his coffee. The scent of it, coupled with the smell of the sea and the sunshine, was kind of intoxicating. It was like being far away from the world, ensconced in a bubble where we were the only occupants. It was both strangely satisfying and, at the same time, weirdly uncomfortable.

I snorted. "Why do you think that?"

"Because you didn't threaten to stab me." Now he

grinned. "The last time I insulted you, you nearly got me with that fork."

Fork?

I frowned, pausing with the coffee cup nearly to my mouth. "I—when did I nearly stab you with a fork?"

All at once, Ezra clutched at his chest. "You've forgotten? Kotyonok, how could you? That moment was so important."

What the hell was he talking about? I finally took a sip of the coffee. The blend was damn near perfect and I was ready for a second swallow as soon as I finished the first. At the same time, I kept turning the idea over in my head. When did I stab him? Or at least try to?

Shaking his head, Ezra made a mournful face. "Wow, talk about an ego check. Granted, I just asked if you knew why they said girls were a lot like shellfish..."

The minute he said the sentence, I scowled. That hadn't been all he said. He'd been drunk, and it was during the reception for Mother and Harper following their wedding. I still thought it was rather disgusting they'd barely waited a respectable amount of time to announce their engagement, much less get married, after Adam's mother died, but I'd had to go.

Even when I wanted to refuse, Grandfather was the one who said one of us needed to be there. It was probably one of the few times we'd truly disagreed. Why did I have to go and not him? While his reasoning—his appearance would suggest tacit approval while mine only said that I'd been required—was sound, I didn't like it.

"You remember now," Ezra continued as if unaware of the scab he'd ripped open. "I can see it. You're thinking about stabbing me again."

"Not everything is about you," I said. "And my aim is a

lot better now. You also don't have Adam to stop me and save you, so maybe you should consider that before you challenge me into stabbing you again."

Granted, there was no cutlery, but that didn't mean anything. Ezra grinned, a genuine, open smile with obvious enjoyment. "I promise to stand still this time," he said. "Just remember, if you bite me, I bite back."

Whether he meant that tease to be sensuous or not, it still rasped over me and I shook my head. I wasn't playing that game with him. Not here—and especially not after Pretty Boy. Some of the joy in the moment fled. Leaving Pretty Boy in Braxton Harbor had been difficult enough. Not talking to him had been even harder. I'd messaged him twice, and he'd answered neither.

The memory dried up all the relaxation I'd managed to claim, and I focused on drinking the coffee and ignoring Ezra. He noticed too, but he didn't say anything. It was another couple of hours after breakfast before he held out a hand to me.

"Come..."

I raised my eyebrows at the imperious note.

Lips pursed, he considered me, and for a brief moment, he seemed almost amused before he said, "Please, Koty-onok. Come and see the island. She really is beautiful."

That was at least better. I clasped his hand and he pulled me out of the seat. Food had helped. Coffee had helped. Ezra letting me bask in the quiet had helped. I'd packed away those complicated thoughts of Pretty Boy that aroused, and I was ready to enjoy the view he wanted to share.

The perfect blue of the skies, decorated with white wispy clouds, was the perfect canvas against which to see the island. It was still some ways in the distance but it was a splash of green with hints of color and some golden yellow that I presumed was the beach.

"Be another hour until we're close enough to take one of the tender boats up onto the beach."

"No dock?" We were still some ways out. There could just as easily be a harbor or something on the other side of the island.

"Nope," Ezra said, wrapping an arm around my shoulders. "You can take the tender in, but the yacht is too big."

That seemed odd.

"We could also land a water plane here if we had to," he admitted, and that almost sounded like a concession. "We did that once when I was a kid." Not that he ever talked about those days. "But I prefer the yacht. I like being out on the open water, and I like that island."

"You know," I said, letting myself lean on him. The water had gotten choppier, but I was adjusting my stance to adapt to the waves. "I've heard stories about the island. They always sounded a little bit like fairy tales and not the real thing."

"How so?" Real curiosity inhabited his voice.

"A private island in the South Pacific, isolated with no population except for you and your family and whatever house you have there?"

"There's caretakers," he admitted. "They live on the island, but also come and go. We pay them to take care of the property, do any maintenance, and stock it when we're on our way out. Then they leave when we arrive. They won't be back until we go. It's just a place where we can be us."

That surprised me. "It's just us?"

"Well, it will be after Captain Adamson and his crew drop us off. I need a break. You need a break. We won't get that back in Manhattan or anywhere else we can be reached by phone."

I frowned.

"How are you planning on us eating?"

"There's food," he said, chuckling. "Food. Wine. Everything we need. There's even power...we have a generator."

I just stared at him.

"What?"

"Who is going to cook the food, Ezra?" I could do some stuff. Marlene had been teaching me on and off for years, but it was all pretty basic. Not to mention, she always got all the ingredients together and walked me through proportions.

He laughed, a genuine, from the belly laugh. The sound added to the warmth of him tightening the arm around me. Then he pressed a kiss to the top of my head. I tried to not gawk at the open, almost carefree expression on his face. When had I *ever* seen Ezra look like that?

"We can do it," he said.

"You know how to cook?" I couldn't help it; the skepticism escaped despite how amused he looked.

"How hard can it be?"

It was my turn to laugh. How hard could it be? "I hope you have fire extinguishers there," I admitted and his chuckles deepened.

"Don't worry, Kotyonok."

Yeah, that terrified me. Just a little.

Then again, I must have been as crazy as he was because I was still laughing with him.

CHAPTER
EIGHT

BODHI

My eyes opened a full minute before the alarm would go off. I rarely needed to set them anymore. Old habits lingered from my days in school. Rolling out of the bed, I went into a series of push-ups. Fifty got my heart pumping. Swapping to my back, I switched to crunches. Another fifty, and a faint hint of sweat was dotting my skin.

On my feet, I strode into the bathroom, emptied my bladder, and washed my face before I brushed my teeth. I needed clothes to hit the treadmill. I preferred to sleep nude, especially when I didn't have to be on guard for everything. Running shoes in place, I turned on the half-dozen televisions surrounding the treadmill.

The water bottle I'd prepared the night before was waiting for me, and I started the warming-up jog at a three-mile-per-hour speed that I would take up to four shortly. Morning financials, gossip, entertainment, local news, and international news all played out on the screens around me.

I switched the sound on for the international news and left the others on subtitles only. My version of a morning briefing.

....stocks and futures closed up with late trading on the Nikkei...

...protests in Paris move into the fourth day...

...Standish Industries rallying following a late-day stock split yesterday and in anticipation of the investor call...

...girl band Torched announces a new multi-city international tour and album to kick off later this year with three song drops overnight. The first, Kiss Ninja, smashed the group's previous streaming record...

...Striking workers at docks in three port cities raise concerns of supply chain issues...

...local law enforcement in Vancouver, Canada, reportedly closed down an illegal hospice care facility, though only three patients were still in residence, and most of the staff appears to have fled...

I turned up the sound and focused on that story. Persons of interest were flashed across the screen, including one nurse whose name I recognized. There wasn't much on the story, though the news speculated that the facility received some kind of warning about the police raid.

While the patients who were liberated from the facility were not identified to the public, pending family notification, none were expected to survive. Hence, why they were left behind. However, penalties would be assessed for those three being abandoned. Of that, I had no doubt.

I pushed up the speed on the treadmill until I hit four miles per hour. Splitting my attention between the screens, I tried to absorb as much information as possible while pushing my body. Running was not my favorite sport, but it was a useful rehab, especially after being shot. I had most of my speed back, my heart rate was almost back in the target zone too.

An hour later, I slowed it to a walk to cool down and narrowed my focus to the gossip channel. They spent more time on celebrities than old money families. Families that made it to that channel usually faced far more problems than public rumors. Gossip was currency, but only in as much as it could be cornered and cultivated.

Even as I studied the channel's latest updates on the first family of reality television—reality television was a whole other beast. If you filmed everything, you were always on camera, how real could it be?

No, the reality was brutal behind closed doors and delivered with fists as much as with scalpels. It was the hush of stories better left untold and had nothing to do with how much lip injection you took out of your ass.

Why the fuck was that a thing?

As hypnotic as that was, I shut off the screens one by one before I drained the last of my water. After a shower, I dressed and went into the kitchen to fix breakfast. Only after I'd prepared four scrambled eggs, a half-dozen slices of bacon, two pieces of toast, and neatly sliced fruit with a huge glass of milk and cleaned up, did I take a seat at the dining table.

The coffee brewed while I ate and I opened up my email. Collin had been doing more digging for me. As much as he complained, he was good at keeping the fishing lines out there. He tested each when they got a tug. Sometimes, he threw them back; other times, he gave them a tug. When he was certain, he threw them to me.

The updates weren't anything notable. He was still tracking a handful of people, names that we'd never been able to isolate. One, I was almost sure was dead, but until I had a body in front of me—decaying corpse or not—I refused to accept the "near-certainty." No, absolute certainty was required.

Next, I switched to the business account and reviewed the latest reports from the board and the prospectus. I didn't involve myself in Cavendish if I could help it. At least not the day-to-day running of the company. The multi-level pharmaceuticals were just not my interest, except when certain patents came through.

That was why the board access was good. Collin preferred to immerse himself in the minutiae. I let him have it.

Once breakfast was done, I washed up the plate and cutlery, rinsed it before adding it to the drying rack with my glass, and poured myself a large cup of coffee. Tucking my earpiece on, I connected it via Bluetooth to my phone and then called Collin.

"Do you have cameras in here?" he answered, his tone more than a little grumpy. "I literally just walked into my office."

"You're predictable," I reminded him. "It's Friday, so you go in early to deal with all the foreign markets because they are either already closed or closing soon. You also want to be free to head to the golf course at noon."

This was not news to him.

"I may resemble that description," Collin muttered before the sound of a door closing and a beep indicated he'd locked himself in his office. "Why do I feel like you calling me so early on a Friday is a bad thing?"

"Because you're also observant." I scratched at a patch of scar tissue on my chest. After some workouts it tended to itch more than others. I'd lost some of the flexibility there following the fight. Not enough for it to matter, but enough that I noticed. "Tell me what you know about Julius King."

"I'd really rather not," Collin replied. The jangle of keys hitting a desk followed the squeak of a chair. "But because you are my favorite cousin, I'll ask why are we looking into a man most people would rather pretend didn't exist?"

"Why do they want to pretend he doesn't exist?" I had some ideas. I'd met King once upon a time myself. It had been a brief meeting. After, he left me alone and never came near me again. I hadn't thought about him in years. Normally, I didn't care now. Except Lainey B asked me a question.

Lainey B asked me a question, and Milo Hardigan had also reached out to me on a similar subject. The man was tied to PPG and to Milo. They were tied to Lainey B. Whether I cared or not, Julius King was a subject I needed to consider.

"Because he's a criminal," Collin replied, the outrage right there in his voice. "You can dress him up in fine suits and teach him which fork to use, but at his base? He's still a crook. He may not put a gun in your face to rob you these days, but he's not far from it."

Leaning back in the chair, I pulled up King's social media. He definitely didn't use it. Every profile I'd linked to him seemed run by someone else. It was all public relations, pruned to only present the best image. Publicly, he was a venture capitalist.

I snorted.

"Do we have anything invested with him?" I skipped to the next website. This one had more business links. There were ties to the Reeds, Grahams, Adleys, Harroldsons, and more.

"He's done a few soft approaches with the old man. But

you know how your father is… he doesn't like 'possibilities' and 'ideas.'"

No, he preferred concrete and substantial results. "So how much of his 'profits' come from other investors?" Ponzi schemes were hardly new business.

"You really want me to look, don't you?" Collin sounded so aggrieved and I chuckled.

"You don't like him." It wasn't a question.

"No," my cousin said. "I don't. People who get involved with him—it doesn't end well. It's not what we can prove that I take issue with… but all the rumors that we can't because the people involved are missing—or dead."

Food for thought.

"How long has he been around?"

"I don't know. I can see licenses and business filings going back almost two decades, but that's just for some of the current stuff and a few defunct—" He went quiet. Collin had found something. "You know, let me dig a little deeper and I'll build you a picture. How far you want me to take this?"

"As far as you can—then if you need me to take it the rest of the way, you tell me."

"Priority? Because our previous searches take up a lot of bandwidth."

That was a solid question. But then, Lainey B asked and I didn't like the look in her eyes when she had. "Move it up. Don't take resources off the others, just—get us more."

"Get us more," Collin grumbled. "This isn't like going to the grocery store, you know?"

"No," I told him. "That's why I have you do it."

"Asshole."

I chuckled.

"Hey," Collin said, sobering. "Thank you."

"Don't know what you're talking about."

"I know, but thank you anyway. And no, I'm not still seeing him, though I am keeping an eye out."

"Good. Keep it buttoned up. They already found one way to you." With that, I hung up the phone and drummed my fingers against the table. I didn't like what I'd seen of King so far, and I didn't like what I didn't know.

After refilling the coffee, I left the phone on the table and headed to the private office. It was accessible through my main office only if you had the correct electronic code and knew where to enter it. The bookshelf popped out, the air releasing as the pressurized door opened.

Inside, I kept a soundproof workroom for when I had to bring work home. There was also a private drain system, and a shower. Long term, it wouldn't be ideal, however it could work in a pinch, especially if I needed to lock someone down swiftly. Ignoring that room for now, I moved into the conference room where I activated the work board.

A series of names, associates, and previous positions were highlighted. Voss had been scratched off, since I was done with him. Although, thanks to him, I did have the names of two more on the medical staff. Each name included a link to more. Some were dotted because they were references only. Others were solid lines because they were direct connections.

I was rapidly running out of names on the chart. Focusing on the name in the center, I exhaled. I would get answers. It might take me the rest of my life, but I wouldn't stop until I had them. There were no new updates on the searches that were always running, so I fired up a new screen and entered Lainey B's name in the center.

If I were going to do this project, I needed to make sure I

had everything covered. Around her, I added the names of Milo Hardigan, Ezra Graham, and Adam Reed. Then I began to fill in the gaps, the families, the dates, where they crossed. In an hour, I had a network of connections and possible candidates.

Far too many tied to Julius King and there were far too many blanks around him. A beep on the laptop in the corner pulled my attention. A possible sighting. It was a few hours away. I glanced back to Lainey's name on my new chart. The lead was a day job—I could go and check it out then be back. Lainey B was perfectly capable of looking after herself.

I could also invite her to go with me.

I liked that idea more.

CHAPTER
NINE

LAINEY

"Marlene," I called as I walked into the kitchen with my nearly finished cup of coffee. "Grandfather asked me to come spend next weekend at Der Sonne. It's her birthday, so we're going to celebrate it with my grandmother." It was important to him, both of us really. I did my best to never miss the occasion. Once or twice, he'd had to request to get me from school early so we could be there. Since I wasn't currently enrolled in college courses, this wasn't an issue we needed to worry about.

At least not until next year. The plan had been only to take one year off. I had a feeling this might lead to more. I might consider taking classes independently or just at one of the local campuses here in the city. Grandfather might be persuaded because I'd initially been looking at Stanford in California, Oxford in England, and the University of St. Andrew in Scotland.

Grandfather was not a fan of my being that far away.

"I'll take care of everything," Marlene said, casting me a

smile from where she had a laptop open on the counter. She was reviewing our shopping list and the supplies as well as schedules for the cleaners. "Do you want me to pack you a weekend getaway bag? Or just an overnight one?"

I lifted my shoulders in a casual shrug. "At the moment...let's just go with an overnight bag. I have things at Der Sonne, so it's not like I will be going without." Der Sonne was my primary residence. It was the house I grew up in. Waltham Corners had only ever been a place I stayed briefly on vacations when Mother had visitation with me.

Beyond school, this apartment had very much become my home of choice.

"Would you like more coffee?" She was already heading toward the espresso maker when the landline rang. It was probably a delivery. She answered it with a brisk, "Benedict residence."

She glanced at me as I rinsed out my now-empty cup. Yes, I was treading on Marlene's territory, but she was also on the phone.

"One moment, please," she said, then put the call on hold. "Mr. Cavendish is here to see you. Does he have an appointment?"

Mr. Cavendish? I frowned. "I am presuming the younger Mr. Cavendish, yes?" Because I really didn't know his father very well at all and I'd prefer not to invite someone I didn't know up to my apartment.

Marlene picked the call up again then made a shooing motion at me to get away from the espresso machine. I grinned and retreated to where she'd left the written list for the cleaners. Specific instructions to begin changing out the curtains, pillows, and other general decor to prepare for the winter holidays. There were deep cleaning instructions, including for the guest rooms. New linens to be ordered for my room and everything changed out. As well as maintenance on the fireplaces and sconces.

A sigh escaped me. Deep cleaning instructions because Christmas was coming. Unless I planned to retreat to Der Sonne for the bulk of the holiday, we'd need to get the trees brought in and set up. It was a plan...Pretty Boy was unlikely to return by then and a long sigh escaped me.

I didn't realize I'd begun to think that far ahead. Still... I could get him a present and hang onto it. I unlocked my phone and loaded up the app I'd used to message Em. There'd been no updates since Milo's single message that read "Mayhem." But I'd answered with Pretty Boy. I wanted him to know I'd seen it.

One word made me feel better than should be possible.

"The younger Mr. Cavendish," Marlene continued, catching my eye. "Bodhi." The level of skepticism she layered over his name made me smile. I nodded once, and Marlene's expression turned almost amused as she shook her head at me. She disapproved, but she wasn't arguing. "Absolutely. Please send Mr. Cavendish up."

Biting back my own smile, I logged into the app and stared at the blank messages. The Pretty Boy comment was gone. So he'd seen it. Relief trickled into my veins. The messages were the most fragile, intangible of items, and yet there was something profoundly satisfying knowing he'd found a way to reach out to me and that he'd gotten my message.

My fingers itched to send him another message. No, that was disingenuous. I wanted to touch his face. I wanted to *see* his face. I wanted to hear his voice. The more I let my thoughts linger there, the greater the ache became. So I closed the app and pivoted when Marlene hung up the phone.

"Mr. Cavendish is on his way up." The amused disapproval in her voice made me smile. "Should I prepare him coffee as well?"

"That would be the gracious thing to do," I teased, enjoying the exasperation that sparked in her expression. "Although, to be fair, I don't know what kind of coffee he prefers so maybe offer it when he gets up here."

I was already on my way to the door. The ride up in the express elevator didn't take long. While I was dressed more casually than I would be if I were planning to head into the office, I paused to check my appearance in the mirror. My hair was pulled up and back from my face. The angora sweater offered a softer look while also keeping me warm and the yoga pants were very comfortable. I probably shouldn't have given in to the impulse to wear them, but they'd been a gift from Em.

Fuck, I needed to call her.

Better, I needed to go and see her. But I didn't think I'd be able to keep everything from her that was going on with Pretty Boy and he didn't want Em anywhere near King. Currently, I wrestled with what he needed and what she needed—and in the midst of all of that, what *I* needed.

The brisk knock on the door announced Phi—Bodhi's arrival. Bodhi. I checked the camera to be on the safe side. Currently, Karagiani wasn't here and wouldn't show up unless I indicated I was going out. Frankly, I could use the break. As if aware of my scrutiny, Bodhi glanced at the camera and a smile flirted with the corners of his mouth.

Unlike his previous drop-in at the office, he was dressed in a t-shirt, jeans, and what appeared to be a leather jacket. His dark hair was rough and askew, like he'd run his fingers through it one too many times. The intensity that was often present in his eyes didn't mask a twinkle.

It was like he wanted me to know he was absolutely up to mischief. It didn't seem to matter that he was nearly ten years older than me. There were days when I understood him better than I did anyone else in my life. Frankly, if he invited me to get into trouble, there was a solid chance I'd say yes and to hell with the consequences.

Opening the door, I grinned at him. "Good morning, Trouble. This is almost twice in the same week."

"Almost," he agreed, then swept me over from head to toe. "Going out?"

"Wasn't my plan." No, my plan was to do more research to see what else I could dig up on King. I had a line on three of his companies. Three that he *actually* owned, not ones he hid behind an enormously complicated shell game. If I knew anything about men with power, it was that they coveted and wanted to hold onto their power.

Taking it away could inflict a great deal more damage than a verbal assault or a social dismissal. While he seemed intent on developing his social capital, I wasn't as worried about that as I was *why* he wanted Pretty Boy, and what he planned to do with him.

"Good," Bodhi said, his grin growing as I pulled the door wider. "Then you're free for me to kidnap for a day or so?"

Kidnap? I raised my eyebrows.

"Excuse me." Marlene's voice sliced through the room with an almost icy demand. Bodhi winked at me before he stepped inside and looked toward the housekeeper. "I was going to prepare Miss Benedict a coffee. How do you take yours, *Mr.* Cavendish?"

"Whatever way Lainey B is having it," he said with ease. "I try not to be difficult."

"I don't believe you have to try." Disapproval hung off

every syllable. Her gaze flicked to mine as I closed the door and leaned against it. I could practically read the question in her eyes. Did I need help?

I shook my head once. "Coffee sounds wonderful, Marlene. Trouble and I will be in the library."

For his part, Bodhi laughed softly. "I like trouble."

"I know you do," I reminded him, then gave him a hip bump before I passed him. He trailed after me, stripping off his coat. And yes, my impression from the camera was confirmed. He looked more like he belonged in Braxton Harbor than here in Manhattan. Curiosity threaded through me as I pushed the doors to the library open and headed inside.

My research was still on the desk, but I left it where it was and moved over toward one of the sofas and let him decide where he was going. Instead of following me, he drifted over to the files and made no pretense out of studying them.

"Kidnap me?" I prompted when he didn't resume his earlier conversation.

"Want me to wait for coffee to get here so we don't upset the battle axe?"

"Don't call Marlene a battle axe," I scolded and he grinned without an ounce of contrition.

"Just calling her what I see. She is more than ready to go to war for you, Lainey B." Approval glowed there for a moment. "I like her."

I chuckled. "She's wonderful."

"Good."

"For that, we can wait for the coffee. Let's not scare her, shall we, Trouble?"

He offered me a half-bow with just a hint of a mocking smile before he went back to reviewing the table's contents.

I settled down to sit and crossed one leg over the other before pulling out my phone. I didn't care if he looked at my research. Knowing Bodhi, he might have answers to some of those questions that continued to elude me.

Marlene didn't keep us waiting. She delivered a pair of caramel lattes with just a hint of extra sweetness, adding the toffee nut, before she gazed between us. "Anything else?" That question was definitely for me.

"We're fine, Marlene," I promised her. "Go ahead and get on with your day. We might be here a while."

"Or not," Bodhi suggested, like the helpful little shit that he was, and I shook my head at him. "But I promise—" He even crossed his heart. "We will tell you before I steal her away."

The gimlet eye she fixed on him just made him smile wider. "Hmm. I won't be far." Yes, that was definitely a warning. She retreated to the doors then paused mid-closing them to give me another look, but I shook my head.

I really was fine, and oddly enough for the type of acquaintance Bodhi and I shared, I did trust him. I trusted him a great deal more than I did many people in our world. Maybe because in the Venn diagram of our shared experiences, we crossed over in all the places that mattered.

With just a hint of a sigh to mark her disapproval, Marlene closed the doors and left us alone. Bodhi said nothing while I sipped my coffee and he finally picked up the last file folder and carried it over to where I'd taken a seat.

"It's going to take me some time, but I'll make sure I'm her favorite," he said, taking the seat next to me and leaving the folder on his lap. "Does she have a favorite flower?"

"You want to be her favorite," I told him. "You do your own legwork."

That earned a genuine chuckle. "Challenge accepted, Lainey B. Now, tell me the truth—are you actually free today?"

"I'm not free any day," I retorted, rather enjoying this particular type of verbal sparring. "As you can see, I have some work to do."

"Yes, but it's work we can take on the road. We're too young and you're too beautiful to keep being stuck with all this stuffiness. I have a place I need to be and some work I need to do. You can come with me, help me with my job, and I'll help you with this," he said, and by this, he meant the folder he tapped. "We'll have time."

Honestly, I was intrigued. "How can I help you?"

"Well, you'll have to come with me to find out." While the teasing note in his voice didn't so much as quaver, there was a kind of raw honesty in his eyes.

"How long?"

"Two days," he said. "At the most, three. But I think two is more than sufficient. We can always revisit every twenty-four hours."

Two days. That would get us back well before the weekend.

"When do you need to be back here?" Bodhi asked and it wasn't an unfair question.

"It's not just when I need to be back, but next weekend, it's important for me to be at Der Sonne. It's my grand-mother's birthday."

"I'll make sure you're there. But that gives us plenty of time." Confidence should not be that attractive.

"I also need to reach out to Karagiani, he's supposed to go where I—"

"No," Bodhi said with a sharp shake of his head. "You

don't need him. I'll handle all bodyguard duties and I promise, I won't let you out of my sight."

Surprise filtered through me.

"You can also come armed," he said. "If you don't have a comfortable gun, I can get you one."

"I have one."

That didn't surprise him in the slightest.

"So what do you say, Lainey B? Let's take off for a few days and see what we can see?"

"Go get into trouble together?"

He grinned and raised his coffee cup.

I should say no.

I should stay here and keep researching.

Then I glanced at the folder. "You'll help with that?"

"You have my word."

Head canted, I pursed my lips. "How soon do we need to leave?"

"As soon as you're packed."

I patted his leg and rose. "Then I better go let Marlene know there's been a change of plans. "

I should stay. I should stay and do exactly what I had been doing, but I was no closer to getting Pretty Boy back. So, a change of plans and scenery were needed.

"Trouble?" I said, glancing at him from the door and he rose to his feet.

"Hmm?"

"Transport?"

He grinned. "Car." Then he raised his eyebrows. "You want to drive?"

"Depends on the car." I pushed the doors open.

"It's a stick," he warned.

It was my turn to chuckle. "I can handle a stick, Trouble."

CHAPTER
TEN

ADAM

"Mr. Reed," the manager of the Hotel De Marquis was already striding across the lobby to greet me as I stepped inside the marble-floored opulence. Hand extended, the older man with his nearly full head of silver hair donned a genuine smile.

"Claude," I said as I clasped his hand. "I told you to call me Adam."

"Old habits, Mr. Reed," he chided me with a familiar, if indulgent smile. "You will correct me because you are a good man and I will still honor you with the respect you are owed."

It was a very old argument. Then again, Claude Marius Wilson was an old and very dear friend to my mother. He earned a great deal of latitude from me. "You have a point."

"I do try," he said with a chuckle, before turning with his arm outstretched as if to say 'this way.' "Everything is ready to your specifications. I also kept all reservations under the name you preferred."

Hadleigh. An old family name from Mother's side of the family. One that she used to tell me stories about as a boy. When I preferred to distance myself from my father and uncles, I retreated to my great-grandfather's name—a man whom Mom admired so much.

"Thank you, I appreciate it." I'd called Claude just three days before. I needed a place where I could meet with Hardigan and Ezra. A place where we could be certain to not be observed, but it wouldn't be unusual for them to be. Since the hotel wasn't listed in any of my public assets, it was an excellent cover. "I'm the first to arrive?"

"You are. I thought a quick inspection would be necessary so you can assure yourself." Claude definitely knew me well.

"Absolutely."

Fifteen minutes later, I sat inside the small ballroom at a table set for only three. A buffet had been delivered and everything set before the staff vanished discreetly. There would be no witnesses to the meeting. The cameras in the room were deactivated. The valets and porters working the halls, along with a pair of maintenance men and custodians, were all security.

They would ensure that we weren't disturbed and no one got close enough to listen. Before Claude left me, the last step was to sweep the room for electronic surveillance. Claude's brother had worked in the intelligence sector for many years and he'd given him tips over the years.

Very useful tips.

Like the rest of the hotel, the ballroom more closely resembled a Renaissance palace down to the gold filigreed patterns on the edging and the classical art styles decorating the walls. It was lavish without being pretentious or overbearing. My first real "tea" had been served in this room. Mother and I spoke for hours as she made sure I could not only make polite conversation, but that I could participate like a gentleman.

The door opened, pushing aside the melancholy thoughts, and I rose to my feet as Ezra strode through. Anger radiated the air around him, turning it almost electric with the ferocity of his barely contained temper. Not that he seemed to care what weakness he put on display as he glared at me. The normal tension in his face had surrendered to a gauntness that hadn't been there before. Always a little on the wild side, Ezra had grown more reckless the last few years.

Before the door behind him could close fully, Hardigan's arrival stopped it. The man was an enigma. He didn't radiate the vibe of wealth or belonging. Frankly, he shouldn't. He *didn't* belong here. More comfortable with violence and possessing a street ethic I didn't pretend to understand, Milo Hardigan seemed intent on carving his own place. His connections, however, were undeniable. Whether I liked it or not, he was here and seemed intent upon staying. A lot of what-ifs were strung around him, questions without answers that I didn't like.

Still, Milo Hardigan could be useful to us, and he was already invested in the one part I would do anything to protect. Alliances had been forged on weaker foundations. "Gentlemen," I said, and Ezra just shot me a look so full of venom it made me frown. What the hell was wrong with him today?

"Asshole," he said and I shook my head. He yanked out a chair on the opposite side of the table. Granted, it was round so it wasn't like he was escaping some grand distance, though it was still as far away from where I was sitting as he could.

He was going to make me deal with this petty bullshit before we were going to get anything done, wasn't he?

Hardigan, by contrast, wore a far more neutral, if cautious, expression. We'd spoken briefly a few days earlier. His work for King was not a choice he would have made if not for the bold threat to Andrea and Lainey. In that, I owed him. Not a position I found comfortable to be in.

When I held out my hand to him, he eyed me with raised brows before he clasped it briefly. The handshake was precisely that: a swift greeting, easily offered, accepted, and then done. "Hardigan."

"Reed," he answered easily.

"Well, aren't you two sweet?" Ezra drawled in a tone dipped in arrogance, alcohol, and asshole. "Been making buddy buddy behind my back?"

For his part, Hardigan just scoffed. "Apparently, he's already started drinking and it's just after ten in the morning."

"It's five o'clock somewhere," Ezra countered. "If you were stuck with *you* as a partner, you'd want to drink too." The barest hint of a slur touched his words. Honestly, I'd missed it with his greeting, but Hardigan wasn't wrong.

"If you're drunk," I said, returning to the table and my coffee, "then you don't need to be here for this."

"If I was drunk," he retaliated, expression turning dark, "I wouldn't even be here. Taking the edge off isn't the same as being drunk."

"Drinking to get through the day is a problem." A discussion we'd had before.

"Well, it's a good thing you don't have to worry about it —you know, wherever the fuck it is you're sitting these days. I got a promotion—and baggage." He motioned to Hardigan. "So I think I'll do whatever the fuck I need to do."

Hardigan pulled out a chair but he didn't sit, just eyed the coffee options and poured himself a mug. "This isn't going to go far if he's gonna be like this the whole time."

"No one invited you, *Pretty Boy*," Ezra said with a smirk.

Hardigan, to his credit, didn't rise to the bait. "Actually, dick," —or maybe he did— "He did. I know why I'm here. You? Not so much."

"This isn't helping," I interrupted before Ezra could say anything and then I jammed a finger in his direction as he sat up straighter. "*You're* not helping. Stop trying to pick a fight."

"Why should I?" Ezra asked, rising to put his fists against the table. "Because *you* say so? I don't know if you've noticed *Adam*, but you're no longer part of this group. You checked your ass out to work for someone else."

I blew out a breath.

"Right," Ezra continued, his smirk growing more brittle and angry. His eyes were dark, stormy, and haunted. Goddammit. I was torn between making him dry out or knocking his ass out. We did not have time for this fucking pity party. "I forgot. It's 'need to know' and I apparently never need to know. But your new bestie is here," he said, swinging a hand toward Hardigan. "So, you two conspire like a pair of bitches and I'll eat."

A headache pulsed behind my eye and I cut a glance at Hardigan. He was staring at Ezra in disgust. This— "The point of this is to put all our cards on the table," I said, switching my attention to Ezra. "To read you into the need to know."

"Why?" Ezra demanded. "Because now *he* is involved? *Now* you want to tell me what the fuck is going on?"

Always volatile, Ezra had crossed the line from wild to out of control. The last few months had been tough, but this was… "What's going on?" I asked. "What does King have you doing that you're this on edge?"

Or was it his family?

"Oh, now you care about King." Ezra shook his head. "You know, fuck this, if you two want to plot. You plot, I have things to do."

I pinched the bridge of my nose. "Sit your ass down," I snapped and Ezra sat before he'd fully straightened. When he met my glare, hostility radiated off him like steam rising in winter.

"I think this isn't going anywhere until you two sort your shit out," Hardigan stated. He downed his coffee like it wasn't hot. "Let me know what you two come up with, and we can arrange another meeting. I have limited windows where he isn't on my ass."

"Where are you going now?" I asked. While he was right, we *needed* to have this conversation.

"Does it matter?" Hardigan challenged. "We're supposed to be doing a job." He nodded to Ezra. "I'll take care of it. You two kiss and make up or whatever the fuck it is you do. Then I'll be in touch. You can reach me the same way you did this time."

So he hadn't told Ezra about our meeting on the street. Not the easiest of meetings to arrange, but it was easier to make sure we weren't monitored or tracked. Without another word, he pivoted and stalked out.

Irritation scored deep grooves through me as I cut a look back to Ezra. His expression hadn't changed, nor did it when the door closed. Dropping back into my seat, I leaned back.

"You want to tell me what the fuck is going on with you?" Maybe I could have eased into it. But I didn't have time for his dramatics. The last few years had been weighing on me more and more. Every goddamn choice I'd made had been to protect Lainey, to protect Andrea, and to protect this prick in front of me.

"Let's see—" Ezra leaned back in his chair, spreading his hands like we were just hanging out back in our school days. "I got this promotion to Bishop for a real dick who has me juggling on four or five different fronts. My best friend bitched out from working together to fly solo and left me holding the bag with our girl—"

Our girl.

That phrase struck a match, and the dick knew it.

"Only, I can barely keep her out of anything because now she's involved with that asshole and King is noticing fucking *more and more*." The aggravation in his voice fought to disguise a real sense of fear. "That's just for starters." Now he was covering. "King brought Hardigan to heel and now he's my new partner."

Disgust curled his lip.

"I'm supposed to train him in everything, give him the keys to the kingdom. I suppose King will have him knife me in the back at some point, and he'll do it gleefully." The last he delivered with a careless shrug. "That's as good a place as any to start."

No, it wasn't. "Every word of that is a cover," I said, not bothering to sugarcoat it. "I've told you before, if you want to keep secrets from me, you can put up a billboard and say look over here. It highlights exactly where you don't want me looking."

"Right," Ezra said with a snort then knocked back some coffee before he looked around the room.

The buffet was there and he shoved away from the table to head toward it. I let him pace it out, searching for whatever it was he needed or wanted. It wouldn't take him long to realize there was no alcohol.

It wasn't until he made his way back to the table that he focused on me again. The plate had some bacon, some grilled potatoes, a couple of quiches, and a bowl of fruit. He didn't even pretend to eat it; he just shoved some of the food around before refilling his coffee. His hands were just trembling.

"Are you going to tell me why we had to have this meeting with Hardigan?" The demand was another deflection.

He'd deflected. Counter-attacked. Distracted. Now, he was back to deflection. "What's going on with your father?" I asked and he scowled.

"How's yours?" Another deflection.

"Still a dick," I replied and Ezra shrugged, some of the mutiny bleeding out of his expression. "Talk to me."

"You don't want me to talk to you," he muttered. "You just want me to be a good little bitch and say yes sir and no sir and punch me in the face when you don't like what I'm doing."

"If I didn't want you to talk to me, I wouldn't have bothered to ask." I wrestled my temper into a box and kept it locked down. The only twitch I betrayed was the light tap of my fingers against the table. "Am I happy you had sex with Lainey? No."

I wouldn't pretend otherwise.

"Am I happy she is having sex with Hardigan?" I raised my brows. "Also, no. But I'll tell you what I told her. She's mine. She's always been mine. You boys can fuck around all you want, but she is always going to be mine."

His eyes narrowed.

"Now, you're my friend, and you've been my best friend

for as long as I can remember. Tell me what the fuck is going on? Is it really about Hardigan? Or is this about Dovzhenko?"

"Doesn't matter. None of it really matters. We're never taking King down. We're stuck with the jobs we both swore we'd never do. Yesterday we were stupid, and tomorrow isn't looking any better." That wasn't deflection, that was surrender. "Fuck, I'd kill for a drink. You own this over-priced palace with its hyper-inflated art style. Can't you get me something?"

"I could," I said, but I shook my head. "But I want you sober. You need to be sober, or you're not going to remember this conversation."

He smirked. "I've already forgotten it."

"What's going on with Dovzhenko?" Because the faster he ran from that topic, the more likely it was the one plaguing him.

"It doesn't matter." Another wave off. "King wants blood on Hardigan's hands. He wants him bloodied, and he wants proof."

That didn't surprise me in the slightest. He liked having dirt on all of us. "Have you already done it?"

"No," Ezra said.

"Why not?" I raised my brows. "You don't like him, that much is clear."

Another shrug.

"Lainey wouldn't like it."

It wasn't a guess and Ezra just scowled again.

"You want to talk about her?"

"Do you?" he countered.

Neither of us said anything, seeing as we both knew the answer. "You told me that Dovzhenko was taken care of."

"You told me you were coming back and that we were taking King down together."

"I'm here," I reminded him and he locked his gaze on me. "Where are you?"

"There are days I fucking hate you," he admitted, and the corner of my mouth kicked up.

"And other days?"

Ezra sighed. "What do you want from me?"

"Tell me what's going on so I can help." Because I'd been looking away for too long. From him. From Lainey. "Talk. To. Me."

I had no idea what I expected his reaction to be, but standing up and shaking his head wasn't it. Nor was his simple response of "No" before he walked out. The door didn't slam behind him, but it might as well have.

ELEVEN

LAINEY

After securing Marlene's agreement to not let anyone know I'd left, I took the elevator down with Bodhi. While the doorman and desk security were trustworthy, I still slipped them generous tips before heading out the front doors. Instead of parking in the building, Trouble had snagged a spot down the street. I'd taken a leaf from his book and gone with jeans, a dark green turtleneck, boots that went to my mid-calf, and a leather jacket. His faint grin of approval had done so much to lift my mood that I didn't want to examine it too closely.

The air was bitter and there was a hint of snow on the breeze, but the gray clouds trying to blot out the blue skies looked more like rain—or a temper tantrum. I had a purse strung cross-body and secured under my jacket. Not that I was worried about anything; I just wanted to keep my hands free. I had also secured a gun in the purse holster. It wasn't as easily accessible as I might have liked, but it was still there.

When we got to his car though, I wanted to purr. "You have a new one..." I'd heard they were coming in but didn't think they'd arrived.

Bodhi chuckled. "Picked her up this morning. Still haven't decided if I like her or not."

The Porsche 911 Carrera Sport, with the return of the ducktail on the rear. The color was a combo of red and purple—but that was the light. She was more a copper red, but the shifting shadows and intermittent sunlight gave her a purplish cast. My palms itched to get my hands on the wheel.

"Still want to drive?" The offer sent a thrill up my spine and goosebumps rippling over my skin. I wasn't cold in the slightest despite the wind picking up. On the one hand, she was brand new. Most guys wouldn't even let their girls sit in their brand-new cars. It was like a love triangle in the making.

At the same time, I wasn't Bodhi's girl and he *was* offering. I glanced at him. "Yes." There was no point in lying about it. Everything inside of me wanted to get in that car.

He chuckled, an honest, open laugh. The rarity of it snagged my attention from his car to him as he moved around to the street side to open the driver's side door. With a light gesture, he beckoned to me. "Well, come on, Lainey B. Park yourself behind the wheel and show me how well you can handle my stick."

The innuendo was too playful to be lascivious and the spark in his eye was all challenge. To be honest, I didn't care if it was a flirt, this car— "She's sexy, I might have to change my orientation."

That earned me a snort and he went from scanning the street behind me to dipping his head nearer to mine as I stepped into the car. "Maybe she is a he—after all, that's not a strap-on in there."

Running my hand over the smoothness of the knob on the shift, I glanced up at him. "Point taken."

His grin grew. "Buckle up, Buttercup."

Buttercup. I laughed. "That better not stick," I called as he closed the door, and that just made him laugh. I snapped the seatbelt into place and some of the boulders that had collapsed inside my chest with Pretty Boy's absence eased. They weren't gone, but I could take a breath. A real one.

While Bodhi circled the car and slid into the seat next to me, I took a moment to admire the interior. The new car scent combined with something spicier and more masculine—that had to be my companion—and the leather itself was intoxicating.

"Need another minute?" The teasing comment made me stroke the steering wheel like I was petting her. Or him. Really, did the love of a good car require gender identification? Sexy was sexy.

I ran my tongue over my lower lip then grinned. "I can admire and drive at the same time."

"So can I," he said, then leaned back in his seat as I hit the starter button. The engine practically purred to life. "You need one of these in your life, Buttercup."

Yes, yes I did. "Where am I driving?" And I knew that name was gonna stick.

He touched the screen and then entered an address. It was in Philadelphia.

"Someone likes me," I murmured, checking the traffic. I also checked the other cars. It was the first time in weeks I was going somewhere without my driver and Karagiani. It was just me, Trouble, and this beautiful beast of a car.

He chuckled, and I dropped my hand to the stick, and

with one foot on the clutch and the other shifting to the gas pedal, I moved out into traffic so smoothly it was like she glided.

"Why do you say that?" Not that he was denying it.

"Two hours at least to drive? I'm buying you lunch today, Trouble, and you're going to let me."

"You got it, Buttercup. I'll let you treat me right."

I laughed and savored the way the engine hummed. She was perfect, and there was a freedom unfurling within me for every mile we crossed. It would take us a minute to get out of the city, and then we could let her open up. Until then, I planned to spend every minute edging myself in anticipation.

The drive took closer to two and a half hours, thanks to traffic in both cities. Other than fiddling with the satellite radio to find a station we both agreed on, the ride had been smooth and quiet. The weather shifted as we drove, the gray clouds grew denser, and the promise of snow seemed to grow more into a threat. Not that it diminished my enjoyment in the slightest.

The farther we got from Manhattan, the more I relaxed. Not even the hint of flurries as we drove into Philadelphia proper could diminish my mood. The directions had us ten minutes from our destination. "Thank you," I said, shooting a look at Bodhi.

He didn't say anything immediately; his attention seemed far away, and I left him alone. Whatever he had on his mind, he'd share it or not as he saw fit. "You're welcome," he said almost absently five minutes later as I left the highway and followed the direction into the suburb. I'd been to Philly a few times, but I didn't know it like I did New York or even Los Angeles.

It wasn't until we were on the street with our actual

destination that he seemed to rouse from whatever internal place he'd escaped to. "Park about a half block down."

I found a spot and parallel parked into it easily enough. I didn't need the auto control the vehicle offered. Once we were in place, I glanced at him. He didn't say anything, his gaze fixed on the distance.

Vehicle idling, I put on the safety brake and leaned back in the seat. I scanned the area, trying to identify what, if anything, we were here to see or do. Nothing leapt out as the apparent object of scrutiny. There were several medical buildings and doctor's offices. While I didn't see a hospital nearby, it didn't mean these pavilions weren't associated with one.

If I recalled the map correctly, there was a university not that far away. They could be linked to the school. A lot of medical schools relied on physicians for instructors and offered teaching environments, not only for the students but for local populations. It reduced costs and provided a service back to the community they inhabited. Still, those were just guesses.

I debated sliding my phone out, but curiosity kept my attention split between our location and my companion. He rested an elbow against the door, a hand on his jaw, but everything else about him had gone blank.

As a matter of goodwill, I gave him thirty minutes. "Are we going to be here a while?" I asked finally.

"Maybe," he replied noncommittally. "Her schedule indicates she should be making her way through this area anytime between when we got here and the next hour."

She.

"We're looking for a woman?"

That earned me a glance. "Do you really want to know?"

Interesting phrase. One that carried a lot of weight,

notably if my grandfather used it. He always replied with that when I asked a question likely to dig deeper into something I may or may not be ready to learn. It also meant that once I knew, I couldn't unknow it. So I had to be prepared for that consequence, too.

Was I ready to know? Did I really want to know?

"Do I need to know?" Not a fair response. Answering a question with a question. Then again, he started it.

"Uncertain," he said.

That gave me more food for thought and I slanted a look toward him. "You invited me to go with you."

"True," he said. "I didn't want you to be in Manhattan and me here if you needed me."

Surprise sparked through me. Not that he gave me long to examine it.

"There she is." He half-straightened in the seat.

"What are you planning to do with her?"

"Undecided."

The woman he focused on was definitely older, late forties, early fifties at the least. There was a hint of gray to her hair, but she moved with the kind of comfortable stride of someone used to being on their feet. The fact she wore scrubs under her coat told me she was medical personnel—doctor or nurse. Being on her feet would be a fact of life.

Despite being laser-focused on her, he didn't leave the car or make any moves. Canting my head toward him, I asked, "Do you want me to go and talk to her?"

Not that I had any idea what he needed from her, but he hadn't so much as taken his eyes off her once since he spotted her. Though he didn't reject my offer immediately, he finally shook his head. "It would be better for both of you if you stay in the car."

That was a non-answer. "Trouble..."

He finally looked at me. "If I can help, I will." It was an open-ended offer. I knew better than to make them. Blank checks were reserved for family and the closest of friends. It was better to not risk them on someone who might ask for more than I'd be willing to give.

Bodhi was different, though. He'd been different from the day we met, which hadn't changed in the last twelve years. Admittedly, we saw more of each other now than we had then, but still...

"I won't make you stay in the car, but if you go with me —" He sighed. "Buttercup, you have a lot on your plate already. This is my problem. Not yours."

"Are you trying to help me with my problems?"

I knew the answer to that question. Did he?

One corner of his mouth kicked up and he flicked a look out the window again. "You're going with me."

Yes, I was.

He nodded. "I go first. You stay behind me. Don't interrupt—please. I will mean every single word I say. Most threats are ineffective if you don't mean them."

I understood that.

"Don't interfere." It wasn't a request.

"If you don't want to see anything, turn around and walk out. I won't hold it against you."

Kind of him.

"Once we're in there, once you hear—"

"I can keep a secret." I shouldn't have to remind him. I'd never told anyone about him being in Der Sonne or coming out of Grandfather's office. I'd never said a word when I found him in Waltham Corners nor in the Reed business offices when I'd been there waiting for my mother.

Save for the people who already knew he'd been there, I'd never said a word about Braxton Harbor either.

I wouldn't.

He met my gaze and then nodded. "Protect yourself, Buttercup. Before you protect me."

"I'll make that call—if it comes down to it." I already had. He was one of my people. If I needed him, he'd come. "What do you need me to do?"

He cut a look back out the window. "She's going on shift. I need you to bring her to a room where I can talk to her."

"Then let's do it."

CHAPTER
TWELVE

MILO

The card with the suit indicated there was a reception following the program that evening. He didn't care if I attended the actual program, but I needed to be at the reception. I rolled my eyes. The other side of the card had the details of the Broadway play. Not a musical. He had box seats and would be there with a client. The client was more important than my appearance, so the reception would do.

Fine by me. The idea of spending even five minutes more than I absolutely had to with my sperm donor was enough to make me sick. I did *not* want to spend the time with him and I did *not* want to go to the reception. The suit was more business than evening wear. An evening reception should be at least semi-formal, or why go to a reception?

Mayhem seemed to whisper in my ear, and the phantom sensation of her wrapping her arms around me and leaning against my back battered through the barriers I had to keep erecting to keep her from occupying my thoughts twenty-four hours a day.

Would she be at the reception? She did so much for her grandfather. Or maybe she'd be at the play. She did a lot of events like that for her charities. I half-wondered if the reason she wasn't away at college was because they couldn't fit classes into her busy schedule. That kicked over some resentment for her. So much of her life was framed around what she did for others.

When did she get to do something for herself?

Rubbing a circle against my chest, I set the note down on the dresser, then eyed the suit again. The suite I'd been given was sterile, despite the dark furniture and adornments. There was no art to warm the walls. The color was cream, so it seemed almost dingy when framed by the dark wood accents. The coffin ceiling gave it a boxy feel, and the largest piece of furniture in the room was a massive four-poster bed that looked more at home in a gothic horror movie than a bedroom where you should relax.

Even the bedding was a neutral shade. Not earth tones, neutral. They were like the no comment of sheets. A snort followed by a huff of laughter escaped me. Mayhem would shred this place in her cooly, polite voice, deriding every single choice but in the most civil of terms. I hated it more because she wasn't here and at the same time, I'd cut off my own arm before I made her come to this place.

I wasn't here for comfort.

My phone buzzed and I slid it out of my back pocket. I had turned off the facial unlock and had to use my thumbprint *and* a code. I changed the code every other day. I didn't trust Jeff Hardigan *or* Julius King. The fact he used a child to get me here would have fastened the last nail to his coffin, but as far as I was concerned? He did that when he walked out on me and Ivy.

While it might seem he couldn't sink any lower, the fucker seemed to take it as a personal challenge. The name on the screen pulled a smile from me. I swiped across it to answer.

"Hang on a sec." Then I crossed over to the double doors that led outside. I didn't trust there weren't listening devices in the room. Or cameras. There were definitely cameras outside, but unless the mics were directional, the weather helped out there. "Hey, Jas," I said by way of greeting as I headed out into the damp and cold. It was days like this that made me miss the Harbor. It rained there a lot more than it did here, but today reminded me of where we'd grown up.

Then again, three years in jail made the outside taste purely sweet.

"Hey," Jasper Horan, my best friend and the first kid I met in foster care, who stuck with me all the way through and still did, never pulled his punches. While I hadn't been a fan of him dating my sister, much less all of them dating her, I also damn well knew he'd throw himself on any fire that came at her. "I'm in town."

"Manhattan?" That surprised me.

"No, Kansas City," he snarked. "Yes, Manhattan. Why the fuck would I call you from somewhere else?"

I chuckled. If I hadn't seen how soft Ivy made him, I probably wouldn't be as entertained. Still, some things didn't change, and Jasper being an ass about some stuff and abrasive about others was one of those things. "Hey, I hear they have good barbecue in Kansas City."

He laughed.

"Where in the city are you?"

"Just dropping off a delivery near—where the fuck am I?" I could almost picture him straining to look. "Near 45th and something. I had to drive through the theatre district and the big fucking square with all the flashing neon signs."

"Times Square."

"That's the place."

"There's a lot of food places down there. Can you leave the truck?"

I checked my watch. I'd been mapping my way via the subways and trains. I could get there in about forty minutes if I timed it right.

"After they're done with the offload," Jasper agreed. "Where do you want to meet? Oh, and bring your girl. I brought a present for her from Swan."

My smile died. My girl. Yeah, I'd like to bring my girl, except I tucked that away for now. Instead, I gave him a name then said I'd see him in an hour or so.

The time I'd been taking to learn the different routes paid off. I made it to the seafood chain restaurant a solid fifteen minutes before he did. Changing trains and walking a block to the next station had let me shake any possible tails.

Paranoid?

I really didn't care. I climbed the steps to get inside and took a table near the back that actually had a view of the street. The angle let me watch the door and out the window. But it kept me out of direct line of sight. Most of the guys who worked for King were not subtle in their manner or their approach.

It was like cops, you could often tell who they were by how they moved. That said, I wasn't taking any chances. When Jasper came striding toward me, following a waitress, I found a grin I'd been lacking for a while. He looked good.

He looked—happy.

I rose to greet him and got a one-armed hug before he thrust a bag at me. I eyed the bag then him.

"Told you I was bringing something for your girl." Yeah, he had. Right.

I took it and set it down in the booth before I took a seat. I waited for him to order a drink and for the waitress to leave. It was nearing lunchtime and the proximity to so many tourist spots increased the foot traffic inside and out. It was harder to observe people with so much movement, too many impediments. That said, if it impaired me spotting them, it also worked against them keeping track of me.

"You look good," I told him and he grinned.

"Healthy living," he smirked. The hint of tobacco lingering in the air around him was a counter to that, although Jas tended to smoke when he was stressed or away from Ivy. He was definitely the latter so I'd keep my opinions to myself.

"How is my sister doing?" I was eager for any knowledge he had.

"She's good," he said with an air of great satisfaction. "Real good. She's still touring and will be for a couple more months at least. But they're coming home for Christmas and a break, then another three or four-month run. In the meantime, she really wants to open that school, so we bought a couple of buildings that are side by side, and we're renovating them..."

I soaked up the knowledge. We paused only long enough to give our orders, then dove back into it. The trucking side of the business was growing. Jasper's pride was evident. They'd added a dozen new trucks and drivers.

In addition to jobs for the Network, all carefully vetted and cleared through Kellan, they were taking on more clients. Liam's company was bringing them more business.

"We're looking at adding more in the next five years, but we want to keep the growth steady and not bursting. The last thing I want to do is be on the road when Swan is home or take on too much. Every driver has to be cleared..."

That made sense to me. "You know, you're almost grounded and down to earth with these reasonable measures."

"Bite me," he said with a smile. "Anyway—that's me. What's up with you? And where's your girl?"

I sighed, then scratched at my jaw. The arrival of the food bought me a few moments, but the lack of an answer had already tipped Jasper off. His eyes narrowed, but even as he took a big bite of the fish sandwich he'd ordered, he didn't take his gaze off me.

Yeah, there was no way to sugarcoat any of this shit. "I moved in with King..." Then I plowed on, bringing him up to date with everything that happened, from the auction to the less-than-subtle threat from King regarding Andrea.

"Why aren't we just killing him?" It was a direct question and one I respected.

"Not going to lie," I said slowly, picking up a fry and half imagining it as a knife. "I've thought about it more than once. The problem is—he has his hands in everything. As much as I hate the man, he's not an idiot. He has contingencies for his contingencies. Of that—I have no doubt. He's wielding incredible control over some of the wealthiest families in this city. You don't do that by accident."

"You think if we take him out there will be a backlash we don't see coming." Not a question.

"I can't discount it. I also can't discount if that backlash wouldn't be against more than just me." If it were just me? I wouldn't care as much. "He doesn't have a problem with threatening kids or co-opting young teens into criminal enterprises. He has blackmail material and more. No—he has a lot of leverage, and I want to know what his endgame is and who is backing him."

"You need to know who is opposing him too."

We already had a lead on that. "Adam's working on that." Reed was very determined, but why wouldn't he be? King wanted Adam dead. Now, he was threatening not just Lainey but also Adam and Lainey's sister. "Look, I'm telling you this not because I want you to get involved but because you need to know if I go quiet—there's a reason for it. I'm on the inside and don't know what that's going to mean, but he runs it a lot like a gang..."

"So he's going to want to blood you," Jasper said before taking a bite. He chewed it with such fierce thoroughness, I didn't doubt he was gnashing down on the urge to hit something. After washing the bite down with a drink, he stared at me. "He's going to want to compromise you to have the material to send you *back* to jail."

"Leverage."

"Or he's going to threaten your girl."

I didn't smile. "He already cut me off from her. Walking away from her was part of the deal."

Jas's eyes narrowed. "You let him do it?"

"To protect her and her sister? Yes."

He scowled. "Swan is—"

"Not going to know about this. Not yet." As much as I wanted to keep Ivy out completely, that may not be possible. The son of a bitch was her sperm donor too, and he'd already tried making approaches with her. "He's still keeping his distance with her, right?"

"So far," Jasper said, though dislike kissed every syllable. "She is not going to like not knowing what he's doing to you or her best friend."

"I don't want her getting involved yet. Especially considering I don't know if dragging me into this isn't a trap to drag her in." I would not take Ivy down.

"I won't lie to her," Jasper said.

"I'm not asking you to lie."

"An omission *is* a lie."

It was except... "If she doesn't ask you directly, can you not tell her directly?"

"Does Liam know about this?"

"He knows some of it. But I haven't seen him since King pulled his threat on Andrea. I also haven't seen him at any Royals events. I'm kind of hoping the fact he's tied to Ivy is making King think twice about dragging him back in."

Jasper leaned back in his seat. "I don't like this."

"I don't either." I hated it. "I don't like being away from Mayhem. I don't like keeping this from Ivy. Only right now, it's the best thing for both of them."

"Your girl could tell her." Was he hoping she would?

"She could," I admitted. "But Mayhem is as protective as I am. If she doesn't see a real gain from telling Ivy, and only more threat, I don't think she will." That didn't mean she wouldn't be working on it herself. Admiration unfurled within me. I was damn glad she was on my side. Mayhem was a formidable adversary.

"You got it bad," Jasper said slowly with the barest hint of a smile. I didn't comment, but I didn't deny it. After a long moment, he sighed. "Fine, I won't *tell* her or go out of my way to tell her. But if she asks me, I'm not lying either and the guys need to know."

"If you tell Mickey..."

"He'll back your play. But of all of us, maybe he should know the most. He knew your dad, right?"

He had. Worked for him too. It was the other reason I didn't want him involved. They had history and Mickey was also with Ivy, which meant that King had a button he could push. It was just asking for trouble.

"Brief them, but keep it to *them*," I stressed.

"Tell her sooner rather than later," Jasper advised and I grimaced.

"When I think it's time," I conceded. It was the best I could do. The best I was willing to. "Is she really enjoying her tour?"

Some of the tension bled out of Jasper's expression. "Rome said she's happier than he's ever seen her in a performance. Since he's seen them all..."

Yeah. "Freedom's a good thing."

"It is," Jasper said. "Don't you forget it."

I wouldn't. I couldn't. But to keep all of them safe? Yeah, I had no problems using my freedom to secure it.

CHAPTER
THIRTEEN

LAINEY

MORE THAN A YEAR AGO...

We'd been on the island for two days and while it was beautiful and the house was exquisite—a huge bungalow style that blended in with the island's landscape, it was both too quiet and too noisy. It lacked the sounds of a city, of traffic congestion, and of the hum generated by millions living and working in close proximity. That said, the birds on the island were loud, and some even sounded like monkeys.

It was—strange. Even stranger? Ezra just keeping his distance. He appeared around mealtimes then disappeared again. When I headed down to the beach on the second day, he followed and we walked for nearly an hour. But he was keeping his own counsel. Maybe he thought if he didn't talk to me, then I couldn't ask questions. But after two days in this tropical paradise, restlessness invaded me.

My phone was useless. It couldn't even pick up a signal. As far as I could tell, there were no computers in the house. While it had an entertainment system, it was all physical media. There was a generator, too, which made sense—where *else* were we getting power?

Remote didn't begin to describe this place. It was an island in the middle of somewhere in the South Pacific—I was pretty sure it was the south side of the equator, but I didn't have a map. The yacht had left not long after we ferried to land on a tender. Now, it was just me and Ezra.

I glanced around the empty living room and then into the kitchen. Maybe just me. I retreated back up the stairs to check the other bedrooms. The fact we had plumbing and hot water was a gift. So while we were "roughing" it, we weren't. We were simply entirely out of reach.

Ezra had taken the room right next to mine. He'd put me at the end of the hall with his adjoining it. We even shared a balcony. Not that I'd seen him out there or heard from him after bed. He wasn't in his room, so I made my way to every other bedroom.

No sign of him.

Yeah, that wasn't suspicious.

Downstairs, I did a slow inspection of each room. Ezra didn't just vanish. He had to be here somewhere. Maybe down at the beach. The fact there was no way to contact the outside world didn't make sense. The Grahams might enjoy the luxury of the vacation spot, but they were hardly going to cut themselves off.

That meant there was a satellite communication room here somewhere. I debated on whether it would be here in the house or somewhere else. Surely, the staff had a different residence. The other side of the island, which wasn't that far. We just hadn't walked there.

My guess was there was a radio room somewhere here in the house. The longer I studied the layout, the more I thought it was somewhere between the kitchen and the living room. Or a basement? No, they'd want ease to get to it.

It was here. Arms folded, I headed out to the deck. If I stayed inside, I would start opening every door until I found it. I might do it yet. But Ezra brought me here for a reason. The past two days, he'd avoided me. I'd allowed it, but that stopped today.

Outside, the breeze carried the fragrant scent of florals. I'd seen orchids on one of my walks. But this was sweeter, like honeysuckle—but would that even grow here? Salt and sea air came in with the wind and I took a deep breath of it. Some of my tension melted away.

There was something peaceful about this place. Almost too peaceful. It reminded me of being at Der Sonne when I was little. In between school and having to visit my mother. Der Sonne had been the perfect retreat. Granted, the gardens there were manicured, but the herb and rose gardens weren't. My grandmother insisted they let them go wild. The only time they were pruned was for winter, otherwise—

Movement below caught my eye. Taking two steps forward, I squinted at Ezra slicing through the water. He was out past the waves—just swimming. He was insane. At the same time, anticipation curled within me. I had on a suit. The bikini was comfortable and it was more than warm enough here.

It took me only a moment to find some sandals that I could just slide on. Four steps down to the ground, I followed the short trail and the descent to the beach. Once I was out from the shade of the trees, the sun warmed me. I tugged the loose lace cover-up over my head and dropped it with the towel Ezra had left on a rock. His shoes were there too so I kicked off mine and headed down to the water.

I tracked where he was swimming, then walked out into the waves. It wasn't cold at all, so I didn't hesitate to dive into the next wave. It took some determination to swim past where the surf pushed me toward the beach. Once out there, I treaded the water to track where Ezra had gone.

He was swimming toward a sandbar, the length of his arms slicing out of the water as he swam arm over arm. I pushed myself to follow him. The exertion was what I needed. Exhilaration from chasing him, combined with the swimming itself, sanded away the worry and the restlessness.

It wasn't until he was almost to the bar that he slowed and turned. I grinned at his abrupt shake of head but I kept pushing to get to him. He was still a solid six or seven lengths ahead of me.

"Kotyonok?" Surprise turned his voice huskier and then I was there, treading water with him and I grinned.

"Boo."

He chuckled and then wrapped an arm around me to drag me closer. Our legs tangled, and it took some effort to keep us afloat.

"What are you doing out here?" Something dark and a little rough sounded in his voice. Yeah, I needed to not let him keep pushing me away.

"Chasing you." It was the truth.

He blinked. "Why?"

"Because you're running." The moment I said it, I recognized the truth in it. "You dragged me all the way out here, Ezra. Brought me halfway around the world to where it's just you and me, and you haven't stopped running since we got here."

A frown tightened his expression.

Trusting him to keep my head above water, I looped an arm around his neck and just floated while he trod the water. "Why am I here?"

"I wish you wouldn't ask me that."

Well, that was something.

"But I am asking..."

"Kotyonok..."

"You keep calling me kitten." I'd looked the word up once, sounding it out phonetically. "Talk to me, Ezra—why are we here?"

His gaze bore into mine. Our breath kept mingling and I wasn't alone in panting. Swimming took effort, my heart hammering all the while. "Fuck," he swore and before I could say a word, his mouth fused to mine and sent an electric shock to my whole system. All at once, I couldn't breathe unless he allowed it.

Buffeted by the water, we shifted closer. His hand was on my ass and mine was in his hair and then his tongue demanded entrance. A stray thought broke free.

Were we doing this?

His taste was intoxicating. Sea, coffee, and a wildness that had always been in Ezra. A wildness that was hard to miss, especially when he flashed his more abrasive edges. Then we were dunked under a wave and he hauled me up with him.

Laughter exploded out of me because it was like a hard dose of reality and at the same time, the earlier exhilaration redoubled. When our gazes connected, his wore wariness, maybe fear? The combination of emotions startled me. Did he think I was just going to reject him?

I licked my lips then reached for him. He met me halfway and this time we clung together as the next wave hit, never breaking the kiss as it thrust us toward the shore. Closer to land, he got his legs under him and dragged me up with him.

"Are we opening this door?" The provocative question looped another coil of enticement around me. Were we?

Present Day

I headed into the red-bricked medical pavilion with Bodhi. Just inside the main doors was a three-story atrium and winding stairs that led upwards. A bank of elevators were off to the left and a raised table held an index of all the offices.

"You know where she works?" If she was at work, we would have to approach her there. Bodhi moved up beside me and he skimmed the index.

"Here," he said, pointing without tapping the screen. It was a clinic on the second floor. A woman's clinic.

"Okay, let's go." We skipped the elevator and, once upstairs, I turned toward the office. It was almost lunch, but the woman had just come in so I had a feeling she was starting her day.

Once inside the clinic, I glanced at the standard waiting room with its beige chairs, orange and beige patterned carpet, and cream-colored walls that gave it that neutral, nondescript look. The television in the corner had some home fix-it show on. I didn't recognize it, but I ignored it for now.

Everything about the place gave me flashbacks to another clinic I'd had to drive Em to. A clinic where they didn't ask a lot of questions and took care of her. It wasn't the first time I'd learned something bad was happening to her—it was just the first time I realized how bad those things were.

Bodhi wanted to talk to the woman standing just beyond the glass beside a receptionist. The women were working on two different computers, but otherwise, they appeared to be alone in here.

Dismissing the curl of unease that elicited, I headed for the window and stood there until the receptionist reached up to push it open. "Good morning," she said. "Do you have an appointment?"

"No," I told her, honestly. "But we're really hoping you can help." I made a point of glancing around the empty waiting room then past them to the interior of the clinic area. No one else was visible. "You see, I might be pregnant, and we're worried because I have a heart condition. The doctors said I should never try, but we've been traveling, and it's—" My voice cracked on cue and I took a deep breath, trying to steel myself.

I had both women's attention.

"I need a pregnancy test, please. One I can pay for quietly without my insurance."

"You can get one at the grocery store," the receptionist told me gently. "Or at the pharmacy."

"We did that," Bodhi said, sliding an arm around me. "Bought all of them."

"All of them?" Now the nurse focused on us.

"Yes," Bodhi continued. "They were all positive. False positives can happen, except on a blood test."

The nurse glanced at the receptionist then at me.

"I'm sorry," I began, but Bodhi squeezed me.

"Please, we need to know. I can't lose her. The sooner we know, the sooner we can do something." The very real worry in his voice made a lump form in my throat. He rubbed his chin against my hair. "Can you help us?"

"Come on," the nurse said, relenting. A buzzer sounded, and Bodhi kissed my hair before moving to the door and holding it open for me. He caught my hand and held it as we followed the nurse down the hall. "It's lunchtime, so we're quiet right now. We can run a couple of quick tests."

"I'm going to grab food," the receptionist called. "I'll lock up on my way out."

We couldn't have timed this better. The nurse motioned us into an exam room as the external door closed. She followed us inside and headed over to the cupboards.

"Have a seat, hon, and you want to tell me your name?"

"No," Bodhi answered, closing the outer door. "She doesn't."

The nurse turned as Bodhi stared at her. "I'm sorry?"

"No," he said slowly. "You're not. We're not here for a blood test. Only information."

She frowned. "I don't appreciate—"

"Isla Cavendish," Bodhi said, there was a cord of steel in his words. "Tell me about Isla Cavendish."

All the fight went out of the nurse and the blood drained from her face. Nothing she said would ever convince me she didn't know exactly who Bodhi was talking about.

"You have five minutes to tell me everything," Bodhi said. "Then I will do something about it."

My stomach tightened, even as I held my ground. This had to do with his mother. The name tickled something in the back of my mind. Isla Cavendish was his mother.

She died a long time ago. I studied the nurse.

So, what did she have to do with it?

CHAPTER

FOURTEEN

EZRA

I dismissed Adam's message from the screen of my phone. I'd muted the sound but not the notifications because I was a glutton. There was no other explanation for why I continued to glance at his message, even as I sat through the tedium of this business lunch. Or whatever they were calling it.

King and my father were thicker than thieves at their end of the table, with guests I'd only met a couple of times previously. They were debating some art piece, or maybe it was a building. I'd checked out fifteen minutes into the lunch. After the third gin and tonic, however, I could at least listen to Mother and—fuck, I know they told me her name, but I couldn't remember it. The Mrs. went to one of the misters on the other side of the table.

"You think if we slipped away, they would notice?" My companion had been as engaged in the conversation around us as much as I was. Maybe more. She didn't have a phone out anywhere that I could see.

"Probably," I answered, talking more from the side of my mouth and using my glass to block the movement. "Just because they all look engaged with each other doesn't mean they aren't paying attention to us."

"Oh, that is true," she murmured with a long sigh. The accent kissing each of her words reminded me that she hadn't been born here. "I just find all of this..."

"*Skuchnyy*?" The Russian for boring rolled right off my tongue.

Oksana laughed, a real one and I glanced at her. There was a bit more animation in her too-solemn face. She wore the barest cosmetics, dressed demurely, and had her hair styled up in high curls that just seemed to accent how long her neck was. Not that she wasn't pretty. She was—lovely and fragile-looking.

Did they never feed her?

"Yes," she agreed, leaning toward me with an almost conspiratorial whisper. "We should not say things so loudly or they will want to do after lunch drinks."

I hated to break this to her; they were probably going to do that anyway. This club had a smoking room. I would imagine Dad was going to invite the other men up while the ladies did whatever it was they did. Was it too much to wish someone would just drive their car through the front windows or something? A gas line could break—they'd evacuate for a leak, right?

"Get an early start," I suggested. "It's what I do." It was the only way to get through these things.

"I'm not a huge fan of alcohol," she admitted, turning slightly toward me. "Mother doesn't approve."

Tilting my head toward her, I said, "Disapproval makes it taste even better. If you want a few suggestions, I can order you one or two."

Another laugh escaped her and I caught Dad's flash of an approving smile and I straightened. Yeah, charm the daughter. Right. I just met his look blandly as my phone vibrated in my pocket. Setting down my drink, I pulled it out and one look at the message had me standing.

"Excuse me, I have an emergency I need to attend to."

"Ezra?" Mother turned, reaching out a hand. "What's wrong?"

"Just business, Mother, go back to enjoying yourself. Nothing to worry about." I pressed a kiss to her cheek and then pivoted. I made a point of *not* meeting either King's gaze or my father's. I sent the message to the valet to get my car before I was three steps away. Forgotten were the table and the company as I strode out of the dining room. No sense in returning the call anywhere it might be overheard.

My car was just pulling up as I got out there. Even as I slid behind the wheel, I caught sight of one of my father's men approaching the entrance. Too late for you, Big Boy. I was already gone. I slid the fifty to the valet who made sure my car was close, while keeping my father's far away when we were here. as I pulled out of the round while leaving my tail behind.

It wasn't the first time Dad tried to sic one of his private security goons on me. They needed to work harder. Once I was clear of the club's main gates, I called Karagiani. I didn't wait for him to say anything as the call connected. "What happened?"

If someone went after Lainey...

"I can't find her," he said without preamble or excuse. My stomach dropped as icy heat skated over my skin.

"I'm sorry," I said slowly. "What did you just say?" I misheard him. Right?

"I can't find her. She slipped out earlier today. The maid covered for her, but I got someone in the building to confess that she left much earlier, but he *thought* she'd come back."

Thought...

"What the fuck am I paying you for if she is out there alone?"

"You're paying me to escort her," Karagiani returned cooly. "To take a bullet, if necessary. I am not a babysitter or a jailer. She has cooperated up until now."

And what changed that she decided to give him the slip?

"Have you checked her usual stops?"

"No, I haven't driven all over the city. I placed calls— discreetly—to one or two locations she frequented. She is not at her grandfather's office or his home unless she has told them to deny her presence." Which didn't sound all that unreasonable.

A headache pulsed behind my eye. I stared at the road in front of me. "Did you ever get a tracker on her?"

There was dead silence.

"I put a tracker on her cars," Karagiani said. "She didn't take any of them."

We needed a tracker on her. What if something happened while I was at lunch? Fuck. Where would she go? The last time we took eyes off her for any length of time, she'd gone to Braxton Harbor.

Fucking Hardigan.

"Where are you now?"

"Her building," Karagiani admitted. "Where do you want me to be?"

"Just stay there, I'll call back." Ending the call, I pulled to a stop at the red light and punched the steering wheel as

I glared out of the windshield before pressing the voice activation on the steering wheel. "Call Sewer Rat."

It rang twice. "I am not coming to the lunch."

The gruff rejection almost made me laugh. "It was boring as fuck anyway. Is Lainey with you?"

Dead silence. Then, he said, "Why?"

"It's a yes or no, Hardigan. Is Lainey there? If she is, she needs to go. Lunch was wrapping up and King's in a mood."

A chair squeaked in the background. "You worried about me?"

I snorted. "Hardly. I don't want her in his crosshairs. So if she's there, send her tight little ass on her way."

"You really have the most punchable face." It was almost conversational.

"It's a burden." I sighed. "Look, just get her out of there."

"She's not here," he said. "Not that I owe you any explanations. Not even sure why you thought she *was* here." Another beat of quiet. "Did King say something to you?"

Relief collided with frustration. As much as I didn't want her to be with him, at least if she'd been there, I would *know* and could go get her. "He says lots of shit to me."

"Why don't you be all cryptic and shit?" Hardigan retaliated and I shook my head.

"You should have stayed in Braxton Harbor," I told him. "I'll be picking you up the day after tomorrow. We have a job."

"Any details?"

"It's need to know." And I already wished I didn't know. With that, I hung up. I was halfway to Lainey's before I realized I was driving to her place. She was out there, doing whatever with...

Traffic was crawling and when I got stuck at a light, I checked Adam's messages. Did he have Lainey?

The messages were a lot of yelling at me to fucking call him.

Yeah, not in a sharing mood. He could wait. If he had Lainey, he wouldn't be yelling at me. When she was there, he couldn't seem to think about anything or anyone else. Not that I could blame him. She was intoxicating. If I was going to get drunk, being drunk on her was the way to go.

Toxic temptation. We were terrible together. I was terrible *for* her. I should never have touched her and at the same time, I didn't think I'd ever get enough. I wasn't even sorry.

Fuck that.

At her building, I let myself into the garage and headed down to the private parking area. There were enough slots in her locked garage that I could park safely.

I called Karagiani. "Any sign of her?"

"Nope," he said. "What do you want me to do?"

I wanted him to keep his eye on her and never let her take off again. "I'll be making some changes. I want you to stay with her. No more slipping off on her own. For now, I'll take over waiting for her. Head out to her grandfather's." Andrea wasn't in town, or I'd send him to the Reeds. "Just keep watch. Call me if you see her."

"She's not going to go for it."

"I didn't ask for your opinion, nor do I pay you for it. If I have to, I'll get someone else to do the job." Then I hung up on him. I pulled out a different wallet from the glove box and left my wallet and work phone inside the glove box before getting out of the car. Trackers didn't work inside there. It wasn't quite a Faraday cage, but it had been insulated to shut off electronic monitoring.

The phone I spoke to Karagiani on was using my private line and I didn't share that with King or my father. I shared it with *very* few people. It took me a moment to find the keycard access and then I headed for the elevators.

Thankfully, she hadn't changed the access. Then again, Adam and I kept these keys for a reason. If she was in the city, we always checked on her. She'd been staying here more and more. Away from her grandfather and his security. Away from the Reeds.

On her own.

I hated it.

Most of the time, I made myself forget that I had the key or the security codes. Most of the time.

When she went missing the first time, I'd staked out the apartment for three days. Then I'd gone after O'Connell. Eventually, I went to Braxton Harbor and tracked O'Connell's brother.

My gut had said I was on the right track, and I had been. Lainey was in one of the very last places she should be. On her floor, I used the keycard on the door and then entered the code. It opened up and let me in. The alarm system was armed, so I disarmed and rearmed before studying the room.

It was quiet. Only a pair of lights were on to offer a sense of welcome home. The housekeeper was absent. I kicked off my shoes before I stalked through the place. The rooms were empty. She really wasn't here.

Luggage, however, was still in her closet. The bed had been made, and everything smelled fresh and clean. Downstairs, I checked the library. It was quiet and dark. A laptop sat closed on the desk, but flipping it open only revealed a lock screen that demanded a password.

I snapped it closed again then moved to the files she

had stacked there. Flipping through them revealed an obvious hunting pattern. She was investigating King.

As much as I wanted to swear, I couldn't help the flare of pride. She was so young; it was so easy to think of her as too young for all of this. But she wasn't. She was older than when we'd gotten involved in this mess.

Didn't matter.

I needed her to stop.

We all did.

How the fuck did we make that happen *and* keep her safe?

Putting the files back, I walked out to the living room and sat down. Checking for my gun, I pulled it out and set it on the arm of the chair. She had to come back here. There was no other outcome I would accept.

She would walk through that door and I would be here.

CHAPTER
FIFTEEN

LAINEY

We'd spent the night in Philadelphia. Not because the nurse hadn't answered any questions. Far from it. She'd answered a lot. More than I was ready to hear, and it left my heart hurting for Bodhi. It also left me pondering several questions myself. Maybe too many. When we left the clinic, she'd been in tears and her apology rang in my ears.

At the car, Bodhi slid behind the driver's seat and I climbed into the passenger side. His quiet lay like a shroud over the interior of the vehicle. I wasn't sure *what* mood he was in. The fact she'd shared so much without him doing more than saying his mother's name worried me on a visceral level. How bad had it truly been? How much of it had she sanitized?

The sun had nearly set. We could easily head back to the city tonight, but he shifted gears and went downtown. I recognized the hotel as he turned into the valet line. "I already rented us a suite," he said. "Two bedrooms. We can have dinner sent up."

I considered him for a moment. Those were the first words he'd said in hours. "Do you need the time? I can get myself back if you do."

He canted his head, then glanced at me. "No, Buttercup. Just—we'll go back tomorrow, yeah? I have some research I want to do while we're here."

"Whatever you need." And I meant it. The only thing waiting for me in Manhattan was an empty bed and the frustration that I hadn't solved the problem of getting Pretty Boy back and freeing Ezra and Adam from King once and for all. I wanted all of them safe, even if the latter pair seemed intent on infuriating me. That they wanted to protect me would probably be far more sweet if it didn't involve *how* they chose to protect me.

I waited for Bodhi to deal with the valet regarding his car and the bellhops who gathered our luggage. A pair of overnight bags wasn't that much, and we could probably have taken them ourselves, but I didn't argue. Bodhi's mood was—mercurial. He'd always seemed so at ease and comfortable, whether we were at a masquerade or planning murder in the clubhouse of the Vandals.

When he placed a hand at the small of my back and guided me forward, I let him. Not fifteen minutes later, we were in the suite and dinner had been ordered. He gave me my choice of rooms, but since each of the bedrooms was identical to the other, I simply took the first one. Then he disappeared into his to shower.

I waited for the food until he returned then I went to shower and change. The yoga pants were in the suitcase, so I just pulled them back on with an oversized shirt. It was Pretty Boy's, and I didn't spend too long worrying about what it said that I wanted to wear his clothes. It was laundered, so it didn't smell like him or anything; it was just—comfort, I supposed.

The rest of our evening passed by quietly. He spent time working in a notebook and watching the movie I'd selected. It was an action film and involved spies. I had a weakness for the genre that I didn't tend to share, but for some reason the wildness of it all soothed me. The more explosions the better. A psychologist would have fun with that diagnosis.

It wasn't that late when I said, "I'm going to get some sleep, unless you need me?" I'd been careful to not intrude on his brooding.

Bodhi glanced at me and gave me a small smile. "It will be better tomorrow. I have a couple of places I want to stop at before we head back into Manhattan. Research."

"Can I help?"

"I don't know," he said, at least it was an honest answer. "I will say something if you can."

"Thank you."

I was at the bedroom door when he added, "You don't have to help, though."

"I know," I said over my shoulder. "But the offer is still there."

I could almost feel the weight of his appraisal even though I didn't turn around; I just closed the door. Bodhi didn't have to trust me with the personal information. He didn't have to involve me. Only he was, and I would honor that trust. Still, curled up in bed, I checked the messages and there was one.

My heart rebounded to slam against my ribs.

Pretty Boy: Are you safe?

I wanted to hug the phone. The message was already erasing itself. They did after being read. So I answered.

Me: Yes. Miss you.

I wrestled with the last two words, but I ultimately hit send. I did miss him.

The fact the message disappeared almost as soon as I'd hit send made me smile.

Pretty Boy: Miss you too. Stay safe, Mayhem. That's an order.

I almost laughed but instead, I just sent back: *You too.*

It disappeared and there were no more messages. I still went to sleep with a smile on my face. It wasn't hearing his voice, although it was *hearing* from him. The other messages could wait until the next day.

It was late when I woke up the next morning. Nearly nine, and I almost never slept in. Still a little groggy from too much sleep, I padded out to the sitting room. Bodhi sat on one of the sofas, his notebook in hand and the smell of coffee in the air.

"Good morning, Buttercup," he said with an actual smile. "I didn't realize you slept so late."

"I don't," I told him. "Not usually. I guess I was tired. I didn't hold you up, did I?"

"No," he said, reaching for the phone. "Coffee and breakfast?"

I wasn't sure I could eat but my stomach grumbled, deciding that. "Yes, please, I'm going to get dressed and repack my bag."

He nodded. Food, but more importantly, coffee was delivered within fifteen minutes. Thirty minutes after I'd eaten and had two cups, we were taking the elevator back to the lobby. His car awaited us and he slid the overnight bags into the slender, almost no room, trunk.

"Want to drive again?" He offered and I chuckled.

"I'm never telling you no on that." And I wasn't. The car handled like a dream. Our first stop was an art gallery. The owner was waiting for us and we were treated to a private showing for an up-and-coming artist. I didn't think this was why we were here and when Bodhi slipped away while the curator told me about some of the pieces, it confirmed it.

I let him do his research while I studied the work. The artist was fresh, raw, and very passionate. His people were —exquisite, in any case. The backgrounds seemed to blur and blend like they were all in the same place. Ultimately, the only thing that stood out was the people in them.

One reminded me of Pretty Boy, right down to the hint of a smile and the too-sober eyes.

"How much?" I asked and the curator blinked at me. "I'd like to buy a few of them."

"Well, the show opens tonight..."

"They can remain for the show and you can send them to me after." Once I made that offer, he was more than happy to tally up the total. I paid more than he asked. The gallery would get a commission, but this artist needed to keep going. He needed to see the value in his work.

And I wanted the Pretty Boy painting for myself.

By the time the tour was over, Bodhi was back and he didn't mention his absence, nor did I. Our next stop was a library. He descended into the vaults for research, and I spent some time perusing the most recent releases. Again, he didn't tell me anything and I didn't ask. Our last stop was a university. He didn't get out of the car, just stared at the admin building broodingly.

We sat there for an hour, nursing coffees we'd picked up. Then, it was time to head back to the city. On the drive back, he brought up the artist, the hotel, the city, and the weather—it had turned much colder during our sojourn in Philadelphia. The promise of snow became a reality as we left the tunnel and drove back into Manhattan proper.

Once back at my apartment, Bodhi parked on the street and got my bag out before walking me inside. "You know, I can take the elevator myself." It was only a bit of a tease, but he'd been solicitous and very focused on distracting conversation. For him or myself? I really couldn't say.

"You absolutely can," he agreed as I nodded to the doorman and the concierge at his desk. "But I promised to be your bodyguard, so I'm getting you back to your apartment safely."

I chuckled. "Thank you."

"You're welcome."

I was looking forward to and dreading being in the apartment. Except I'd heard from Pretty Boy, and that was enough to keep buoying my mood. Chuckling, I said, "Would you like some coffee before you go? Or to join me for dinner? I'm sure Marlene has left something for us..."

The words were barely out as I stepped inside and spotted Ezra in the armchair. The gun was the second thing I tracked, but my attention immediately switched back to Ezra as he surged out of the chair.

"Where the fuck have you been?" He was halfway to me when he paused. Bodhi had already slid into the room and blocked Ezra's path. "Why the fuck are you with him?"

"Where and why are none of your business," Bodhi informed him cooly. "What are you doing in her apartment?"

I didn't bother with how as I set my bag and coat to the

side. I needed to change the locks. Evidently, the liberties Adam had taken with access to my places had been shared with Ezra. "Put the gun away," I said firmly. "And be polite. I know you know how."

That dragged Ezra's angry gaze from Bodhi back to myself. "You are not allowed to just disappear."

"I'm a grown woman," I reminded him. "I have the freedom to do as I choose, with whom I choose, and how I choose. None of that is open to debate or discussion with you."

His scowl did little to hide the very real panic in his eyes. "I hired a bodyguard for you for a reason. If you leave and don't tell him or allow him to accompany you, how is he supposed to protect you?"

"I can throw him out," Bodhi offered. "If you want."

"It's fine," I said after a moment, since Ezra's gaze couldn't seem to hold onto his fury. He was upset. Genuinely. Bodhi shot me a skeptical look and I put a hand on his arm. "Truly, it's fine. He gets like this when he works himself up. You're still welcome to stay for dinner."

"No," he said slowly. "I don't really want to eat with Graham." At least he wasn't subtle about it. "And I have some work of my own to do."

"Well, you know where I am if you need help." I didn't doubt that he could handle it all on his own. He was extremely capable.

"I do." Then he pinned a look on Ezra. "Put away the gun." It was an order. "You will be respectful with her and not threaten, am I clear?"

The level of menace climbing into his tone gave me pause and Ezra's eyes narrowed.

"I would *never* hurt her."

"You might not mean to, Graham. But I've seen your

actions and the fallout from your choices. Lainey B is not someone for you to toy with." The pair stood in a stare-off for a long moment. The tension in the room ratcheted higher until Ezra blew out a breath and nodded once.

"Agreed."

"Excellent." Bodhi turned to me and gave me a searching look. I could almost hear him asking if I was sure. I nodded, and he surprised me when he pressed a kiss to my cheek before he murmured, "Put me on speed dial. I'll linger downstairs for another hour. I can stay closer if you need me."

"Thank you," I told him, and I meant it. "But I will be fine."

He didn't disagree with me, but he also didn't retract his offer. The door closed softly behind him and I turned to where Ezra had put his gun back into his holster, which lay on the table next to him. His jacket was tossed carelessly over the back of the sofa and his hair was a wreck.

"How long have you been here?" I slipped my boots off and wiggled my toes against the carpet.

"Since yesterday," he admitted. "You ignored my messages."

I had. I'd ignored everyone who wasn't Pretty Boy or Grandfather. But Grandfather hadn't messaged me. Nor had Andrea. I would have returned those. "I was busy."

"Doing what?"

"I believe none of your business was stated earlier."

Suddenly, Ezra stalked across the room to loom over me. The battle he waged against his temper played out across his face. He raised his hands to my arms, but he seemed to continue to struggle against what he wanted to do. Finally, he cupped my arms rather than grab them.

The fact he was working so diligently to control his anger had me cutting him some slack.

"You can't do this to me, Kotyonok," he whispered. "You *can't* disappear. I thought someone had taken you, or worse…"

Lifting my hands to rest against his chest, I sighed. "Ezra, what am I going to do with you?"

I shouldn't have asked because he didn't even let the last word leave my lips before he swooped his head down to kiss me. This—was a terrible idea and at the same time, the taste of him ignited a banked heat in me that had my pulse racing and my fingers digging into his shirt.

I knew better, dammit. Ezra was wild, volatile, and absolutely terrible for me.

Was that why I couldn't seem to get enough?

CHAPTER
SIXTEEN

BODHI

Leaving Lainey B behind didn't sit right, especially with Graham in her apartment. Reed and Graham had been in her orbit for a long time. Now that orbit had begun to decay. She wasn't a child for them to shuffle around. They couldn't keep locking her in her room or sending her off to school. They certainly couldn't tell her to hush.

No, their orbit had begun to decay and they were tumbling headfirst toward her. Graham's wild eyes betrayed a dangerous amount of emotion. Dangerous because the unpredictable little fuckwad always took the most catastrophic options when he wasn't tempered by Reed.

And Reed?

Fuck, I hated the Reeds. I didn't want any of them near her.

Sitting in my car, I checked the time. I told her an hour. But from the moment I walked out the door, I wanted to go back up. That was the issue with trusting someone with their own safety. You had to do it. You had to believe them.

The problem wasn't that I didn't trust her. No, I trusted Lainey B—Buttercup. A huff of laughter escaped me. I trusted Buttercup just fine. The name suited her in a bizarre way. A delicate, almost too sweet nickname for a woman who was made of steel clothed in velvet. At the clinic, she'd been amazing. She'd just—conjured a story and emotion that had me wanting to believe her as much as the nurse and receptionist had.

The nurse.

All at once, my good cheer fled and sobriety flooded me. Another glance at my watch and I pulled out a phone to call Collin.

"Hang on," he said as he answered. "I'll call you back in five." Then the call disconnected. He wasn't somewhere he could speak freely. So I waited, turning over the conversation with the nurse in my head. Unlike everyone else I had questioned so far, she hadn't tried to manufacture lies. Nor had she pretended to not know what I was talking about.

These were all points in her favor.

No, she'd paled though. Terror reflected in her eyes. Then resignation. I believed what she said because there had been no effort to come up with a lie. Defeat hung around her like a noose, but she spilled her knowledge like we were in a confessional and I was the dark priest who would set her free.

Only Buttercup's presence had managed to ease the transfer of knowledge. I left the nurse alive because there was no reason to punish her. I didn't disagree with her assessment of her youth at the time. Her youth, her inexperience, or her inability to argue with those in charge.

None of that absolved her, but the fact she didn't try to

conceal any of it? That bought her a measure of mercy.

But only a measure. If I found out she'd lied to us in any way or compromised Buttercup after the fact? Well, accidents happened.

My phone rang, and I turned it over to check the ID before answering it.

"Free now?"

"Yeah," Collin said with a long exhale. "I was also walking out of a meeting with Senior and didn't want him to notice who was on the phone."

I chuckled. My father and I didn't get along on the best of days. This was far from it. "Thank you."

"You're welcome. How was the trip?"

"Productive," I said. "She gave me three new names."

"Three?" Shock went through Collin's voice. "I thought we'd tracked everyone already."

"Apparently not, but we knew the operation had to be large." It was a fool's errand to think anything else. Collin wasn't wrong about that. "How many years have we been trying to track down everyone who worked there?"

From the lowest custodian to the head of the facility. "Too long," I admitted. It was a quest I'd begun not long after she died. I sighed.

"Maybe—maybe give me the names and let me do some work and you take a break?"

"No," I told him.

"I rather expected that. You're one man, Phillie. Just one." Collin was the only person alive that I allowed to call me that and only in private. "You are allowed to have a life outside of this."

"I have one," I told him, already done with the part of the conversation. My mother had been denied her life. Solving this was my life. After? Well, when there was an after, I would deal with it. "I need you to start the deep dives."

Collin sighed. Thankfully, my cousin didn't press the argument. That was a good thing. "Give me the names."

I recited them from memory.

"*Kaloyan*?" Surprise decorated Collin's tone.

"You know the name?"

"It's Bulgarian—and it's probably a coincidence."

"There are no coincidences," I reminded him. Not in our world. It was far too incestuous for that.

"There's a woman who's been courting your father."

Did I want to know this? I rather doubted he'd bring it up if I didn't, still I waited.

"Business court. I don't pay attention to the revolving door of models going in and out of his bed."

"Are they still getting younger?" The dry note disguised my disgust.

"Yeah, but not young enough for us to do anything about it—yet."

Good. Collin was paying attention to that. "Who is she?"

"Margareta Waldemar. The name stood out, cause it's old German—but also she has ties to some Bulgarian families and assets. She's also got business interests all over Eastern Europe."

"Tell me more." Because coincidences didn't really exist.

"She's living in Brooklyn..."

The hour mark came and went with no word from upstairs. Collin had finished his briefing, including giving me addresses. I studied the ones I'd written down then entered the first one into the GPS. At least I would be in the city for this work. Still, I glanced back at the building.

I may not trust Graham, but I did trust her. If he scratched an itch—fine. That hadn't stopped me from turning some of our resources onto digging deeper into Graham. I knew him. I'd known him for years. I'd been ahead of all of them in school, but they hadn't been quiet in how they arrived or attempted to take over the hierarchy.

Society had rules. Old money society had even more. The Reeds weren't old money by classic standards, but they'd been around long enough. The fact Adam's father married a British aristocrat had definitely helped to ease their continued ascendence. The Grahams were problematic.

Also old money, but far more came from their criminal enterprises than their legitimate businesses. The unspoken about secrets. No wonder Reed courted the Benedicts. He wanted their connections.

Was that why Adam and Ezra kept circling Lainey?

For their sakes, the answer better be no.

It took me two hours to locate the first two addresses. Another hour for the third. Collin forwarded over schedules he'd been able to pull. By evening, I pulled the Porsche up to the valet at the club. I wasn't a fan of the Bay Ridge Country Club, or any club for that matter. Still, this was where Margareta Waldemar had dinner reservations.

I wanted eyes on the woman herself. The security at her home was impressive. It wasn't just electronics. No, she'd gone old school. During my wander through earlier, I'd clocked no less than a dozen guards. There were three houses around her also, housing her security.

No one would approach that house without risk of

being seen. Interesting, and troubling. You only recruited that level of intense scrutiny when you definitely wanted to not only protect your secrets but also let *everyone* know that messing with you would be a mistake.

Rather than being frightened off, it only intrigued me. I went home, showered, added notes to my files, then changed into a suit before driving out here. The hostess frowned at me as I approached her. The dining room seemed very busy for a weekday, although no private event was listed.

"I'm sorry," she said to me. "You don't have a reservation?"

I glanced at the young woman. She was very attractive with her dark hair and dark eyes. The dress was off the rack and so were the shoes. Still, she packaged up nicely.

"I'm sorry," she repeated. "I don't have your name down and dining is only by—"

"Excuse me, Mr. Cavendish," the maître d' hustled over, shooting the pretty little girl a glare. "I'm afraid Caroline is new and doesn't understand the rules. If you'll come with me, we're adding a new table for you." He gestured for me to go ahead and hissed, "Go wait in my office," to the girl.

Not saying anything, I waited for the maître d' to move ahead of me and then followed him out to the dining room, where they were indeed setting up a small two-top for me. I spotted Waldemar seated at a table for seven on the upper platform. My table gave me a good view.

"I will have a bottle of your favorite wine sent over," the maître d' continued, kissing my ass like I'd paid him to do it specifically. "I'm sorry for the —"

"Leave her alone," I said, waving off the rest of his simpering.

"I'm sorry?"

"I said leave Caroline alone. She didn't know who I was and she meant no harm. Her job is to keep out the undesirables."

"Sir..." The maître d' appeared befuddled.

"What was your name again?" I asked as I leaned back in my seat and met his gaze.

"Gerald, sir."

"Thank you, Gerald. We appreciate your service and your attention to detail. She's new. Leave her alone. I doubt she will forget who I am after this." The girl had paled and clearly needed the job.

"Of course, sir." He snapped his fingers for the waiter. "Please enjoy your meal."

I rather doubted it but I didn't comment. I'd check to make sure *Caroline* was still here when I finished. I made a point of perusing the menu as I kept an eye on the tables around me. There was a lot of business being transacted.

Harper Reed was here, dining with the new wife—Melissa Benedict Reed. Lainey's mother was nothing like her. Where Lainey seemed genuine even when playing a role, the mother seemed—patently false. She could have been generated by AI to provide a facsimile of a person. It disturbed me.

Another table played host to Graham the senior with a woman who was definitely not his wife but would probably be joining his bed from the way she kept petting his arm. One by one, I ticked off the faces I recognized and the families. King was even here. Though he sat at a table with just two other gentlemen, neither of whom I recognized.

Like me, Waldemar spent more time surveying the room than entertaining her guests. Intrigued, I lingered for coffee and dessert. The game was shifting, and there were new players on the board.

LAINEY

The sensation of his tongue teasing mine, even as he wrapped his arms around me tightly, elicited a combination of wild emotions. Like Ezra himself, it was a stormy tide thrashing at the shore and a cool breeze on a hot day—it was the island all over again. When he kissed a path from my mouth to my ear, I closed my eyes.

"Ezra," I whispered. "I don't know if I can do this again." He locked his lips over my pulse point and there was a scrape of teeth. A promise? A warning? Both?

"I need you," he answered, and the desperation in those three words threatened to destroy me.

Fisting his hair, I yanked until he lifted his head and I forced my eyes open to meet his gaze. Kissing him was an intoxicating affair. It destroyed my reason and good sense. "What happened?" What had upset him so badly?

"You disappeared," he said, a plea that I could hardly deny. "You didn't answer your phone or your messages. You didn't take Karagiani—"

Karagiani.

I touched my tongue to my teeth. "He's reporting to you." The idea made my stomach bottom out.

"Only that you had gone and he didn't know where. That you hadn't taken your cars. I sent him to Der Sonne to wait for you there—to watch for you." Then he pressed his forehead to mine. We were standing in the middle of my sitting room, wrapped around each other. I could feel his heart beating in tandem with mine. His height forced me to lean my head back even as he pushed his thigh between mine.

The imperiousness in his manner was at complete odds with the softness in his eyes or the way his breaths still came in frantic little-offs. I spread my fingers against his chest, the rapid staccato beat of his heart worrying me. "Ezra," I said with a sigh. "I'm perfectly capable of looking after myself."

"You are also perfect," he argued. "The perfect one to threaten. Do you have any idea what losing you would do to me? To Adam? Everything—we've done everything to keep you safe." He frowned, his gaze delving into mine like he could see to my soul. "I called Milo."

Milo.

Not Sewer Rat. Not Hardigan.

"I called him," he admitted. "Warned him he should send you on your way if you were there. He wouldn't admit it—one way or the other."

My heart squeezed. I missed him so damn much.

Ezra swept his hands up to cup my face. "Don't cry, please don't cry."

Closing my eyes, I tried to block out the loss drowning me. Kisses rained down on me as Ezra pressed his lips to my eyes, cheeks, forehead, and lips. A shower of affection I wanted to burrow into. I couldn't take it when he was this sweet and caring, and at the same time...

When he lifted me right off my feet, I wrapped around him and he held me tight. "I got you," he promised. "I have you, Kotyonok. Never letting you go."

Warmth stole through me at the ferocity of both his embrace and his declaration. The longing for Milo, the trip with Bodhi, and the constant worry for all of them tore at me. There was so much I needed to do. So much I needed to make sure we did. What I did, was let Ezra hold me. When he moved toward the sofa, I stiffened.

Only he didn't slow his path, he just rubbed his hand in slow, soothing circles against my back. When he sat down, I ended up straddling his lap and I leaned back so I could look at him. The fact my cheeks were damp wasn't lost on me.

"He's all right," Ezra promised me in a low tone and I sniffed as I met his gaze. The distinct sobriety in his eyes trapped me. "He's all right. I saw him a couple of days ago." Ezra raised his hand to my hair then brushed it away from my face. With care, he smoothed down the strands. "King's partnered me with him."

That admission startled me more than anything.

"You can see him?" Hope swelled up in me swifter than I could squash the reaction. "He's really okay?"

With a sigh, he ran his hand down my back then up again. The petting motion was far more soothing than it had any right to be. "He's fine. Still an asshole. Still don't like him that much—but—physically, he's fine. No bruises or gunshot wounds."

My stomach bottomed out at the idea of injuries. "I hate that he's there."

"Yeah, me too," Ezra admitted with an almost lopsided

smile. "Though I'm gonna make a bet and say it's for totally different reasons."

I bit my lip, but it didn't stop the laughter from escaping. "Maybe," I said, settling my ass more firmly on his thighs. His erection was there, though I made a point of *not* sitting on it. Instead, I found myself playing with his hair.

"You going to tell me why you were out with Cavendish?" A bit of a testier edge coated those words.

"No," I told him, not trying to avoid the demand in his eyes.

"How am I supposed to protect you if you don't tell me what you're doing?"

"You trust me to protect myself and to make my own decisions." I didn't want to have this argument with him. At the same time, I wasn't going to just give in to his demands either. "I have to trust you to look after yourself."

He dropped his head back to lean on the sofa as he slouched. With both hands on my ass, he lifted me then set me down right against the ridge where his cock strained against his pants. "Trying to tell me I don't do a good job of that?"

"You don't," I told him and one corner of his mouth kicked upwards. "Frankly, you suck at it. You're always throwing yourself at the fire, then trying to cover me before you tell me I'm a mistake and you race away again."

His eyebrows dipped. "I'm an asshole."

"Yes," I agreed with him. "You are."

"Don't hold back," he murmured, a note of humor creeping into his voice. The press of his erection against my ass was an invitation that I wasn't sure I was ready to take just yet. Then he cupped my face with one of his hands. "I've been a bastard to you."

"Well, as the resident bastard in the equation," I said

with a lift of my shoulders. "I can't honestly argue with that assessment."

His eyes darkened. "Don't call yourself a bastard."

"It's right up there with mistake," I reminded him. Only one of those two descriptions had ever really hurt me. His grip on my face tightened. "You can be a bastard, Ezra," I reminded him. "I've always known that about you."

A harsh breath escaped him and I dipped my gaze to where he ran his tongue over his lips. They were damp, and I could practically still taste him. I made a promise to Pretty Boy...

"Where did you go?" The whip-crack of demand in his voice dragged my attention back to him, and I flicked my gaze upward. "The sadness in your eyes...the pain...where did you go?"

"I promised Pretty Boy." It was the truth.

"Promised him, what?" Ezra's voice was so rough.

"Promised him I'd talk to him before I had sex with you again."

He frowned. "He—what? Really?"

I'd never seen Ezra speechless before. It was kind of adorable. Smoothing his shirt, I resisted the urge to hold his face the way he continued to hold mine. As tight as his grip was, it wasn't cutting into my chin or my cheeks. The warmth of his hand just seemed to be cradling me but refusing to let me go.

"Yes," I answered the easiest part of that question. "Really."

"Why did you tell him?" Ezra stared at me.

"Because I won't lie to him." Then, before he could make it an issue, I added, "I'm not going to lie to you either."

Surprise flickered through his eyes.

"I may not be willing to tell you everything." Tilting my head, I tested his grip and he shifted his hand to my cheek. I let my face rest against his fingers and his palm, trusting him to not let me fall over.

Trust.

Trust was a big thing for all of us.

"The truth is, I don't share all of my secrets with anyone. Some secrets aren't mine to share. Some are just...mine."

"Like Emersyn's secrets." That wasn't a question, but it also didn't require an answer.

"I don't expect you to tell me everything, Ezra. I'll ask and you'll do the same. What I expect is respect." I blew out a breath as his eyes dropped to half-lidded and he continued to study me. "We all have a right to our secrets. But if something can hurt me, I expect you to be the one who tells me, and if I am doing something or choosing something that could hurt you—I should be the one who tells you."

"That's..." He didn't finish the thought, choosing instead to stroke my cheek and then along my jaw to my throat. "Kotyonok...you have always been fierce and strong. Protecting you has never been a choice. It's a calling."

I raised my brows.

"You're so much younger than us," he admitted. "Sometimes—it's easy to think of you as too young for any of this. Then..." As if to illustrate his point, he slid his hand to my shirt and traced one finger down the center of my chest. "Then I look at you, and I understand just how much I crave you. I just wish..."

I waited him out. This was a lot for Ezra. The sweetness in his touch beckoned to me.

"I hate that you're a part of this shit that has been on us

for so long. We were supposed to be done with this before school was over. Then college. Now we're here and we're still in it. Liam is out and Adam is trying to be out..."

"Adam isn't out," I reminded him and the exasperation in his expression made me smile.

All at once, he shook his head. "This isn't about Adam." Except it was, and we both knew that. "Or Milo."

Pride filtered through me at the use of his name.

"Or fucking Cavendish."

I bit the inside of my lip at the side eye he gave me.

"You truly won't tell me what you were doing with him today?" His brow tightened again. "Cavendish is a wild card and he's—he's dangerous, Lainey."

"I know he is." You'd have to be a fool to think of him as anything else. "I also happen to trust him." Moving my fingers to Ezra's lips, I pressed one against them to keep him quiet. "I trust him. You don't have to. But I need to know you trust me."

He bit my finger. It was more than a scrape of teeth. The nip sent a pulse straight through me and I tightened my thighs against his where I straddled him. "I trust you."

"Do you trust me with me?" Because this was important.

His groan reverberated through his chest. "You're killing me, Kotyonok."

"No, I'm not." I wouldn't be put off by this. Because it was important. "You and Adam," I continued despite the way his gaze flattened at the mention of Adam. "If you had your way, I'd be on your island." I didn't add forever, nor did I shy away from the fact that the last time we discussed his island in this room, he'd turned into a raging dick. "Deny it, if you dare."

His sigh stroked my soul. "I don't want to deny it. I

150

would put you on a plane tonight if you allowed it. I'd steal away with you and never come back." The depth of that declaration carried the power of an oath. "But you're not going to let me do that, are you?"

I swallowed around the sudden lump in my throat. "I can't—I adore you for wanting to protect me. But I can't abandon any of them—including you." The last he had to understand. "I can't."

Another groan escaped him as he wrapped his hand around my nape and dragged me closer, then his breath was a whisper against my lips. "I hate you being in the middle of it all, but I refuse to leave you here alone."

That declaration took me out at the knees and I sank into his kiss. Drinking him down like I would water in the desert. The raw hunger in the kiss had me tugging at his clothes and then we were in a tangle of them. His shirt opened and I stroked my hands over his chest, slowing where the scars had left their mark on his shoulder and his arm.

Without thinking twice about it, I pulled from his lips so I could press kisses to the damaged and mottled flesh. I hated it when they were hurt. The burns on Milo's back. The bullet scars here. Bodhi had knife wounds. And Adam...?

I had no idea about Adam, but I couldn't imagine he didn't carry wounds. Ezra jerked my shirt upward and then I threw it off as he ran his hands over my breasts, teasing my nipples through the bra. Then he tumbled me backward on the sofa to tug off my boots before he reached for my pants.

I covered his hands at the waistband, and he stilled, his gaze fixed on mine. "Don't run away this time," I said.

"I'm never leaving you again," he promised. "Not if I can

help it." Then he seemed to steel himself. "Do you need to call Hardigan?"

He didn't have to make that offer. Or ask. I licked my lips. "I can't—but I am going to tell him."

Ezra closed his eyes before he dipped his head to press his lips against my abdomen, and then he whispered, "Thank fuck, because I need you, Kotyonok."

The hell of it was, I needed him too.

CHAPTER
EIGHTEEN

EZRA

Thank fuck she said yes.

The litany played on repeat in my head. Thank fuck she said yes. I barely even got her legs bare then I was dragging her panties down. The fact she'd lasered all the hair off had struck me the first time I'd seen her nude.

The satiny softness of her body beckoned to me then just as it did now. Her legs were silk. Lithe and lean, it was easy to see her as remarkably fragile. But she was so sleek, and her muscle tone was there. I wanted to devour her.

Cupping her thighs, I lifted them up and pushed her knees toward her breasts. As much as I wanted to tease and torment the puckered nipples, the slickness of her cunt left me desperate and aching. The first stroke of my tongue along her slit filled me with the musky sweetness of her taste. She gasped, and I lifted my gaze to meet hers, where she fought her own reactions to watch me feast on her.

Her face was rich in angles, from the sharp delineation

153

and chiseled cheekbones to her almost noble nose. Her lips captivated me with their straight yet full lines that gave her cheeks a hollowed appearance. If I could sculpt, it would be her face I wanted to bring to life. "Fuck," she gasped out that single word in an explosive breath as I drew circles around her swollen clit.

She clenched her thighs, pushing at me, but I held her in place. I was a starving man and I wanted to devour her. Every stroke seemed to pull another heated sound out of her. I needed all of them. I needed to hear her come, and I wanted to taste that release and then drive her mad all over again.

My cock pulsed, hard as a stone, and I ignored it. When I sank into her, I wanted to be drunk on the taste of her. She fisted my hair, and I half-thought she was going to try to pull me away. Thank fuck all she did was press me closer as she arched her hips.

Hell, yes. That was exactly what I wanted. I licked, nipped, and sucked until her lustier screams filled the air.

"Ezra," she almost whined my name, and I needed to hear it again, so I sucked on her clit until her sobs broke on every syllable as she chanted my name. Only when she tugged on my hair did I drag my head up. My face was soaked with her. She was all I could see, smell, and taste. Her pupils were fat and dilated as she held me trapped. "Please..."

One whispered word that ripped me open and had me surging upward. I still had my goddamn pants on, but I got the belt off, then the trousers opened, and her hand slapped mine aside as she wrapped her palm around my aching cock.

The delicacy of her cool strength wrapped around me like a velvet vice and I rolled my head back as she stroked me from base to tip. But it wasn't just the strokes; it was the teasing playing over my piercings. They'd been a punishment play when I'd had them done. A punishment for wanting what I could never have.

Wanting people I could never have. One piercing for each of them. And fuck, I had one of them right now with her come all over my face and my body and soul in the palm of her hands.

The distraction let her sit up and then she was on her knees in front of me on the sofa and one of her hands feathered against the dampness of my cheek. I tilted my head down and when she pushed up to kiss me, I slammed my mouth down on hers. The fact she was licking herself from my lips turned me inside out and my cock was dribbling against her belly and her hand.

One minute we were on the sofa and the next we were on the soft shag of the carpet and I was on my back with her straddling me. "Fuck me, Kotyonok," I whispered like it was a revelation. The first time I'd had her, I'd lost my goddamn mind. I'd fucked her for two straight days and it had been agony and ecstasy, until I realized how fucked I was. We had to leave, and I had to take her back, which meant letting her go.

The next time, here in her apartment, I'd taken and taken. I wanted everything and she wouldn't give it to me. Then I'd run like a bitch, despite how much I wanted to stay.

As she dragged my cock against her cunt, soaking me down, all I could see was her. All I could *feel* was her. If she wanted me on my back or my knees or under foot, all she had to do was say the word. Then she angled my dick and sank down on me. Her gasp faded into my mouth as I swallowed her cries and she consumed mine.

Her slick sheath had been made for me. Nothing and no one had ever felt so good wrapped around me. Other experiences disintegrated into dust with just the first touch of her flesh against mine and as she began to rock her hips, it took every ounce of my control to not just blow my load right here and right now.

If her mouth was paradise, her cunt was pure heaven. The brush of her nipples against my chest had me digging my hands into the globes of her ass. I wanted to thrust myself into her deeper, but she bucked against my control. The scrape of her teeth over my lower lip left me groaning and then she pushed herself up, balancing herself with her hands on my shoulders.

All I could do was stare up at her in wonder. "You're so goddamn beautiful..."

The corners of her mouth softened as she smiled. "You feel so good."

The compliment seemed to detonate inside of me, particularly when she added a twist to her hips as she rolled them. The pace increased, and I could barely catch my breath as she took control of me. My breath was hers. My pleasure was hers. I tightened my grip on her hips as she added a bounce to her motion. Head tilted back, she was so damn gorgeous as she took me and I dropped my gaze to where my cock vanished into her.

Swallowing hard, I fisted my control.

"Ezra..." My name fell from her lips like an incantation. "Harder."

I thrust with that command, slamming upward until I was balls deep and my eyes rolled back. She moved away, and then down she came as I thrust up. We found our rhythm and every thrust pushed the air out of her. Then she fell forward, her inner muscles quivering. I surged up, locking my lips to hers as I took the reins and then rolled us over until she was flat against the carpet, her hair spread out like a goddess and I gave in to the need to drive into her.

I looped my arms beneath her and gripped her shoulders so I didn't shove her away as I pounded into her. She sucked at my tongue, dug her nails into my back, and screamed as she trembled. The clamp of her inner muscles around my cock dragged my balls up and I came. Sweat slicked my skin and hers. The kisses grew more languorous and I wanted more. I wanted to take her again.

Even as the thought took root, I shuddered and my cock twitched. It was like I kept wanting to spurt more. The thought of filling her had me longing to do it again and again.

"Never enough," I whispered in worship against her lips. "Never enough of you."

A laugh escaped her, the vibration of which had her clamping down on me and I shuddered at the sensuous contact. She slid a hand into my hair and her eyes opened to betray a dazed look that I swore was reflected on my face.

"You're still here," she said in a soft voice that slashed me with guilt. I'd stormed out before. Stormed out and left her, allowing my own bruised feelings to hurt her.

"I'm sorry," I told her, dropping kisses down on her face as I leaned my hips into hers. I was softening, slowly, and I wasn't leaving the warmth of her grasp for anything. "I never meant to hurt you."

The corners of her mouth tilted upwards. "I know," she said, as if she needed to soothe me. And I hated myself all over again. Then she was running her hands up and down my back. The petting motion settling some of the irritation with myself. "You never mean to do it...it's why I can forgive you."

She could forgive me.

Had forgiven me.

"Next time," I murmured, in between kisses, "just punch me."

Her laughter swelled up, bubbling between us as she caught my mouth in another kiss. This one was as playful as it was decadent and then I nuzzled more kisses, burrowing my way to her throat.

"I mean it," I said against her ear. "I've been told I have a very punchable face."

"I like your face." If that admission didn't totally shut me down, nothing would. "I like a lot of things about you, Ezra...even the fact you keep calling me kitten."

"Kotyonok." I smiled against her throat, savoring the salt on her skin and the steady cadence of her pulse. "It suits you. Sharp teeth and claws. Determined and wild."

"Are you calling me a beast?" The flash of danger was like a red cape to a bull.

"Yes," I agreed happily, and her laughter was its own reward. "A sexy beast. The perfect beast." I swore my cock twitched and I wanted to go stiff in the grasp of her sweet pussy. I wanted to swell and stretch her, then I wanted to fuck her all over again. "I don't speak much Russian," I admitted. "Not anymore. But you have always been my kotyonok."

Her sigh had me lifting my head.

"Am I too heavy?" I was blanketing her, and her legs were still wrapped around me. As if drawn by my aware-ness, the air was cool against my overheated flesh, but I didn't want to leave her. She'd be colder still. There was so much less of her.

"No," she told me, running a foot along the back of my

leg. "You feel good. I have been trying to forget what it is like to be held, filled, and fucked."

Because of Hardigan. Dislike kindled in me, but I smashed it flat for the moment. She didn't need to soothe me. Not when she was sharing her feelings. "You miss him."

She raised her gaze to meet mine. "Yes."

No artifice or lies. No games.

"I've missed you too."

And like Hardigan, I kept taking myself away. Unlike him, I had a choice. I could stay with her.

I had her now.

He was gone, and I was here...

"What can I do?" I said, shoving aside that nuisance of a voice that demanded I lay down my claim right here and now.

"You're doing it," she told me, smiling at my frown. "You're still here."

I really needed to be punched a lot more often. "I'm going to take you off the floor...we should shower and I want to fuck you again."

The last part slipped out, but it wasn't like I regretted the thought.

"Hmm...only if I can suck you off later." The comment made me push up onto my elbows.

"Only *if?*" I chuckled. "You want me to come between those beautiful lips then I will happily fuck your mouth as fiercely as I will fuck this cunt. I want that ass too..." I frowned. "Has he taken your ass yet?"

A hot pink flush touched her face and I swore I went hard all over again. She felt it, too, because her lips parted and her eyes widened.

"You can tell me to mind my own business," I told her, but I wanted her ass. That wasn't a lie. "But I want to take that ass and I want to be the one who has it—especially if no one else has."

Hardigan had shown her passion first. Fine. She'd given herself to him. Her call—would she give it to me?

"I don't know that I'm into that," she admitted and I held my breath. "But I'd be willing to find out."

Fuck.

The word just exploded through my mind and I was stiff as hell. Dragging her up, I held her to me and she wrapped her arms around my neck and then locked her ankles behind my ass.

"That's my sweet kitten, you keep me buried in that cunt. We're going to find out for you—one step at a time, and I'm going to play with your ass—"

The knock on the door had me ready to snarl. I half-turned, and we both stared at the door.

"No one called up." No one should be able to get up here. Her grandfather and the servants wouldn't knock.

Which was good, 'cause I didn't need her grandfather walking in here while I was buried balls deep in her. Just the thought had my dick softening.

"No..."

Another knock, then a voice I knew as well as my own called. "Open the door, Lainey..."

Goddammit.

"It's Adam," she whispered.

Yeah, I knew who it was. One look at her face answered the question before I could even ask it.

We had to answer it.

"Then we better get dressed."

I was shaking with the need for her, and she licked her lips. Whatever she was about to say died unspoken when the locks on the door turned and it opened.

CHAPTER
NINETEEN

LAINEY

The door opening spiked the adrenaline. Adam's voice on the other side of the door caused me to jump even higher. Desire crashed as apprehension sucked all the air out of my lungs. The door barely opened a quarter of an inch before Ezra pulled out of me, set me on my feet, and thrust me behind him. The trickle of cum slipping down my leg seemed to magnify as my heart slammed into my ribs.

"Wait," Ezra ordered in a commanding voice. The tension in my spine and in my gut had me holding onto him. If he was facing off with Adam, he wasn't going to do it alone.

"You're here?" Adam said, and the door hadn't been pushed in any further. It seemed a stupid question, considering Ezra had just spoken to him. Trembling seemed to take over my limbs. Ezra snagged his shirt from the floor and pushed it into my hands even as he dragged his pants back on. He scooped up his boxer briefs along with my discarded clothing.

"That would be why I said wait," Ezra replied, before he cut a look at me over his shoulder. I'd pulled his shirt on as he spoke and buttoned it up. The sleeves were too long so I had to roll them up. The heat in Ezra's eyes sent a shiver through me. He glanced from me to the stairs then back.

Did I want to escape?

It was a sweet offer, but I shook my head. I meant what I said earlier. I wasn't abandoning any of them. I sure as hell wasn't abandoning him now.

His expression softened, and he touched his fingers to my cheek before dipping his head and giving me a soft kiss. It was as light as air but so much more tangible. With that in mind, he waited until I had the second sleeve rolled up and then glanced at the clothes he was holding. I snagged them and dropped them onto the sofa, then dragged the blanket from the back over the top.

The half-smile on his lips grew and amusement danced through the sobriety in his eyes. I raked a hand through my sex hair. There was no hiding the fact we'd been having sex. The scent of it filled the room around us.

"Are you done yet?" Adam asked, and his voice had grown colder and far more stern. If I hadn't been looking directly at Ezra, I might have missed the flinch he'd almost suppressed or how his eyes flattened.

Adam being here made him nervous. Or maybe Adam arriving so soon after we had sex made him nervous. Considering how bruised he'd been after the masquerade, I had a solid idea of why.

"Yes," I said, raising my voice as I clasped Ezra's hand before he could push me behind him again. A good choice, considering Adam all but shoved the door inward. He filled the doorway like a dark cloud rolling in. His eyes were icy and I swore I could *feel* the anger filling him as he swept the room.

"Well, I see you've gotten over Hardigan's absence already." The verbal slash drew blood. "Though I can't say I approve of the replacement in your bed any more than I did his predecessor."

"Fuck off," Ezra said as he started forward, but I tightened my hold on his hand. That pulled his attention to me as Adam slammed the door and then turned the lock. Yes, we were locked in here together.

Fantastic.

"Be polite," I warned them both. It didn't matter that I could meet Adam's blazing gaze. The heat flushing my face appeared to only get worse. More, the trickle of cum on my legs had seemed to increase. I didn't shift my stance or try to rub my thighs together. I held my stance even in the face of his fury.

The black thundercloud over him seemed to darken exponentially as he took in the scene before him. If I could smell the sex, then he had to be able to and, frankly, I was wearing Ezra's shirt and nothing else. My bra was also hanging off the edge of the chair nearest Adam. It had escaped the clothing cleanup.

"What the hell are you doing?" Adam ignored my response as he zeroed in on Ezra.

"Actually," I countered before Ezra could respond. "What the hell are you doing? You just let yourself into my apartment now? It's one thing to park in the garage and to use the elevators. Who the hell said *you* got to have a key?"

Considering Ezra's presence in my apartment when I got home, he *also* had a key. As much as I adored them, no. They didn't get to do this.

"I came to check on you," Adam answered without taking his gaze off Ezra. "Someone has been looking for you all over town and at Der Sonne."

How would he know someone was looking at Der Sonne? I narrowed my eyes. "Try that again."

That finally got his attention off Ezra and onto me. I moved up to stand right next to Ezra and leaned against him. The tension vibrating through him seemed to ease.

"Ezra kicked over some rocks looking for you," Adam said. "That meant he didn't know where you were, and since he has a bodyguard on you, that concerned me."

Did it now? I raised my brows and Adam exhaled harshly. Yeah, he didn't like being called on his crap any more than Ezra did.

"Fine, neither he nor Hardigan are playing ball. When I found out no one knew where you were—"

"From who?" Two words. One question.

"Karagiani didn't tell you," Ezra added another piece of the puzzle to the mystery. "So, who do you have spying on me?"

"That's rich coming from you." All at once, Adam focused on Ezra as he crossed the room to the bar. "You thrive on spying on people. One might almost think you were a voyeur..." He paused then swept his gaze over us. The fact he lingered on my legs just annoyed me. I didn't try to cover up or hide anything.

This was *my* home.

Not his.

"Then again, you do seem intent on suicidal pursuits these days."

"Fuck off, Adam," Ezra exploded, and he released my hand as he stalked across the room to where Adam poured a drink. "No one told you to come in. No one invited you.

The last I checked, you were running your own game, your own—mission. Or whatever the hell you want to call it for the Waldemar bitch."

Waldemar.

That name rocked me. Adam set the crystal bottle of whiskey down so hard I worried he might have broken it as he spun on Ezra. "You know exactly what I'm doing and why I'm doing it. If you weren't so busy being butthurt over everything, you could be useful instead of causing *more* problems."

Ezra hit him.

I could barely even process the dispute, the reasons for it, or the content, much less how the pleasurable haze of earlier had all but dissipated in the face of Adam's rancor. But Ezra hit him.

The blow caught Adam's jaw and knocked him back. He started forward and Ezra struck him again.

I'd never seen Ezra punch Adam. Not once. Now I'd seen it twice in as many minutes. The last blow sent Adam stumbling before he caught himself and then he lunged. He slammed into Ezra and they both collided with my sofa before falling over the back of it.

Oh, for fuck's sake...

Adam's fist collided with Ezra's face—or it would have but Ezra moved and Adam's fist slammed into the carpeted floor. Something cracked and the sound seemed to echo almost too loudly in the room. I marched over to the bar and pulled open the ice bucket. It was stored where it would stay cold most of the time, but it had melted from sitting out there. I had no idea when Ezra pulled it out.

"You son of a bitch," Ezra swore. "You always treat her like a possession and that I'm trash—you don't get to do that."

The wounded note in his voice dug deep into my soul, and it drew blood. I pivoted to where they grappled and I flung the water in the ice bucket at both of them. It splashed over Ezra's heated skin and soaked Adam's shirt. They pulled apart, with Adam rolling to his feet and Ezra bouncing to his own right behind him.

"She's mine," Adam asserted the demanding claim he'd made several times now. "You *knew* that."

"So what? I can't care about her?"

"You don't get to use her to get yourself off," Adam countered, and they were back to ignoring me again.

"Use her?" Ezra laughed, but there was no humor in his voice. He ran a hand over his face and the reddened and bloody knuckles of his hand betrayed how hard he'd struck Adam. "Use her—you fucking asshole. I've never wanted to use her or you. All I've ever done for both of you is *care*."

I moved toward them as Ezra invaded Adam's space and fisted his shirt.

"All I've *ever* done is *care*. For you. For her. I'd fucking die for both of you—how do you *never* see it? How do you *never* see *me*?" Ezra glared at Adam. The air was wild with the violence surrounding them. Instead of hitting him, Ezra jerked Adam toward him and slammed his mouth against Adam's.

I froze.

Adam had his hands over Ezra's on his shirt and the pair seemed fused together in some wild tableau. I forgot how to inhale, and no sooner had they kissed than Ezra staggered back a step, jerking away from Adam as if the contact had scalded him. His eyes were frenzied, his face flushed.

"Ezra..." His name slipped out as I reached for him. Fear filled his expression as he retreated another step, then another, and then he swung around madly to stare at me. He looked from me to Adam then back. "Don't..." I pleaded with him, but it was too late. He spun for the door and opened it jerkily before vanishing as it slammed behind him.

This time, I went after him. I couldn't let him run. Not again.

Not *now*.

So many pieces were falling into place, especially the fear. I got to the door and had it open just as the ding from the elevator registered. My gaze locked onto Ezra's as he pushed the button repeatedly inside the elevator and the doors closed, cutting us off.

Heat hit my back and an arm came around my middle. "Inside," Adam said, his voice raw and gruff. He didn't wait for me to say anything or even to move before dragging me back in.

I swallowed hard, the pain in Ezra's eyes threatened to gut me.

"I have to go after him," I whispered. "We do."

"No," Adam said, pulling me inside and closing the door. I whirled, shoving him away as I faced him. "No," he repeated.

"What?" Was he insane? "Didn't you see him? Didn't you *hear* him?" Was he really that blind? "Ezra needs us."

Adam's earlier anger was gone. "I said no..." Instead of fury, there was shock. Instead of rage, there was puzzlement.

More, I swore there was redness in his cheeks.

Was he embarrassed?

I didn't get to ask, because Adam jerked me to him and kissed me.

CHAPTER
TWENTY

I sank my hands into Lainey's hair and devoured her mouth. My lips were still tingling from the kiss Ezra hit me with. My jaw ached from the bruise from his fist, and my mouth from the taste of—

Fuck. Agony exploded through me when Lainey's knee slammed into my dick. Fuck.

I staggered backwards. All the breath left my body. Fuck.

Fuck.

Fuck.

Grimacing, I doubled over and squinted up to where she glared at me with her kiss-swollen lips, flushed cheeks, and shining eyes. Wearing nothing but Ezra's shirt with his cum sliding down her legs, she'd never looked more goddamn beautiful.

"You with me again?" The damn near-dry observation pulled a pained laugh out of my breathless lungs. "I'll take that as a yes. We need to go and find Ezra. If you don't want to go, fine. I *am*."

With that, she turned to the sofa and began to pull her clothes out from under a blanket.

A blanket, really?

Fuck, I limped over to a chair to sit. The pain had helped, actually, shocking clarity back into my system.

"Lainey..."

"He's your best friend," she said, her voice notching upward in a way it only did when fear hit her. My fearless girl. She didn't panic. She didn't rant. She just—*did*. "And he just bared his soul to us and then ran. How could you stop me?"

I sighed. "Lainey..."

When she flipped through the clothes with a frenetic energy that worried me more than Ezra's outburst, I packed away the pained response.

She needed me.

"Elaine." I infused her name with every ounce of command and she whirled to face me. Pallor had sapped all the flushed color from her face. "Come here."

I'd go to her if I had to, but it was better for both of us if she did what I told her. If she *listened*. Especially with that wild look in her eyes. My girl didn't deserve this; if we broke her, we had to fix it.

I had to fix it.

"Now."

The last syllable actually galvanized her from frozen to stalking over to me. She had a pair of leggings in her hand and her panties. They were a lovely shade of lace. I tugged them from her and hauled her onto my lap.

"Adam," she said, and my name came out an aggrieved groan.

"Yes, Adam," I reminded her and ignored the throbbing from my aching cock. Damn thing was still half-hard despite how fucking well-delivered her knee had been. I wrapped her up and held her close. "Listen to me..."

"Ezra..."

"Will. Be. Fine." I stressed each word, tightening my arms around her. The trembling was coming as the adrenaline crashed. "Trust me, Lainey."

The impatient look she shot at me was way more her. "Why?"

"Because he is my best friend," I told her. "He has been since we were children. Long before there was a you. Or a you and me. Or a you and him. There was—an us. I know him. He needs to run. Until he stops running, he won't be ready to talk. If you chase him—if *I* chase him, we'll just make it worse."

Tears shimmered in her eyes as my words sank in. "Did you know?"

Did I know that he cared? I sighed. Truth or deflection?

Fuck, I shifted her so her ass was more on my thigh. As light as she was, her knees were damn deadly weapons. "Be specific," I finally said. "Did I know can refer to a lot of differe—"

She had her hand flat against my chest, just over my heart.

"Did you know he was in love with you?"

That was specific.

"I want to tell you no," I admitted. "And on some levels, it is a no."

"Except?" She raised her eyebrows and, bit by bit, lost the stiffness in her posture even as the trembling began. The room reeked of sex. It reeked of her pleasure and his. Even if I wanted to pretend to ignore it earlier—which I absolutely hadn't—I was drowning in the warm musk of it here.

Head tilted back, I said, "He's always been possessive. He's always needed me. Sometimes—needed me too much because he was unhinged. Fuck the decisions he made when I wasn't around...I would tell myself it was because of his family or our upbringing or our world—even King. I excused it. But...yeah, I think I've always known on some level."

She frowned as she stared at me. "Was that the first time he's kissed you?"

Discomfort shifted through me. The last thing I wanted to talk about was Ezra. But she was relaxing and the trembling had subsided. If I answered this question, I had to deal with it. Ezra was going to take off again if I tried to talk to him about it. "Yes," I admitted with a harsh sigh.

The lightness of her hand on my cheek pulled my gaze upward. All I wanted to do was bury myself inside of her, erase the fact that anyone else had ever touched her. That lie—that lie was a good lie to tell myself right now.

"I can't fix this for him," I warned her. "Until he's ready to talk about it, there's nothing I can do."

"Except tell me if you're going to hurt him."

That had my eyebrows raising. The ferociousness was back in her eyes.

"You want to protect him," I said slowly, turning over the nonverbal threat she'd just offered me in the frame of a demand. The first part didn't surprise me. Lainey would throw herself into the fire to protect the people she cared about. I wouldn't say love—I didn't want to think about her loving Ezra or Hardigan or anyone else. "Even from me?" That was the part that startled me.

"Adam—you are so dense sometimes. How are you so damn smart and so damn stupid in the same breath? How?"

"Thank you..."

"It wasn't a compliment." The snap of that phrase damn near made me smile. I would much rather have her yelling at me, shooting fire at me from her eyes, and challenging my every move. "Oh, you're impossible."

She planted both her hands against my chest and shoved off my lap. I could have dragged her back. Wanted to. Wanted to remove every mark they'd ever left on her. The smear of dampness she left on my thigh stilled me, though. She snagged her clothes, not seeming to care that she flashed me with her bare ass before she glanced over her shoulder.

"I'm going to change. Then we're going to find him."

"No," I told her, and that earned me an actual glare. "Go change. Clean up—then we'll talk."

"Adam." I got the stomp of the foot as she whirled to face me and I kept my expression neutral as I met her hot gaze.

"Go change, Lainey, or I'm going to strip the shirt off of you and fuck you until you cooperate with me." That was not how I wanted our first time to be, but I'd learned to live with a lot of disappointment the last few years.

I didn't flinch once from her glare. I honestly didn't know if I wanted her to just do as she was told or for her to come back at me with fire. Wanting *her* had never been a problem for me, even when she was far more taboo than Ezra could ever be.

Only she wasn't. That meant I could have what I wanted.

"I will be back down in ten minutes," she said. "Do not leave."

There she was, boiling over with the need to fight. "Good girl."

It was like striking a spark to the end of a stick of dynamite. Absolute fury filled her gaze and she marched away without another word, spine ramrod straight, and real violence crackling in the air around her.

As soon as she was gone though, I leaned forward and blew out a breath as I put both hands up to my mouth. Control only went so far, and I was shaking. I needed to get a grip on it. The fact that her kiss had in no way erased his was disturbing enough.

Ezra— "Goddammit," I swore aloud, the one brief explosion of a whispered oath before I rose and limped over to the bar. My dick still hurt. That bruise wasn't going anywhere, nor was the erection that sprouted from holding her.

So, wanting her and literally aching from it seemed to be a fitting punishment. Her question swirled around in my head as I poured myself a full measure of whiskey. I needed to anesthetize this weakness and bury it.

"Did you know he was in love with you?"

It was like she stood right behind me, her phantom arms around me as she challenged me. Always a challenge. Always pushing. Always daring.

The absolute shock in Ezra's eyes that had swallowed his anger as he retreated from me had been bad enough.

Worse had been the very real fear.

I understood why she wanted to chase him. It would have been a lie if I told her I didn't share the same conviction. Thankfully, she hadn't challenged that. Not yet, anyway. I knocked back the entire glass. The heat hit my stomach and exploded outward. One glass was not enough to numb.

Far from it.

Digging my phone out, I debated calling my security team. Ezra had been running wild for more than a year. Leaving him had been my only choice; I hadn't meant for him to dangle for so long. I'd trusted him to—

Liar.

I wasn't sure whose voice I heard that accusation in. Mine. Hers. Or his.

Maybe all of us.

I'd hoped he could handle it. Then he'd only been shoving his way into the Vandals. Liam could watch out for him there. Liam had been the one to bring him to me finally when Ezra began to spiral. When my disappearance threatened Ezra's sanity as well as security. He was bound to get himself killed.

Things were all right for a while, and then...

"How do you never see me?"

I saw him. I'd always *seen* him. I'd seen him when we'd shared women before. When he looked at me when he got himself off. I'd seen him when he followed me in everything. When he pushed me. Even when he fell in love with my girl.

I glanced at the stairs. How much of that was her, and how much of that was because I—

My phone buzzed in my palm.

My father's name appeared. I ignored and silenced it, only to let it go to voice mail. The very last thing I wanted to deal with right now was Harper Reed. Not with Ezra running around like a loose cannon, wounded and hurting.

As soon as that call ended, I messaged my security team.

Me: *Find Graham. Put a tracker on him. Stay close. Don't*

let him do anything stupid. You have my permission to intercede.

I waited only for the acknowledgement before I shoved the phone back into my pocket. Then, I poured myself another drink and packed up my feelings. If she came back ready to fight, then I needed to have all my wits about me. Touching my tongue to my lower lip, I stroked it back and forth.

I hadn't hated the kiss.

Either of them.

That—was something I needed to deal with.

Ten minutes on the nose, Lainey reappeared and I was ready for her.

"You're still here..."

I supposed I deserved the surprise in her voice. Her damp hair, lack of cosmetics as well as choice of t-shirt and denim made her seem so much younger. A reminder of just how long I'd wanted her.

"Drink?"

"I thought we were going to talk." That wasn't a no, so I poured her one.

"I thought you needed to yell a bit more."

"Don't be an ass."

I snorted, as I turned to hold out the glass to her. "Default mode."

"Why aren't we going after him?"

"Because, unlike you, Ezra doesn't regain his composure that fast. Chasing only makes him run farther. Pushing makes him do stupid things. Chances are, he's already decided to do that. So no, we wait..."

Her expression fell. "For how long?"

Probably longer than she wanted to hear. "I'll know when."

The fact she didn't throw the drink in my face was a good sign. But the worry in her eyes was back. "I promised him," she whispered. "I promised him I wouldn't abandon any of you."

Well, at least I was included in that grouping. "We're not abandoning him."

She looked at me suspiciously.

"I promise." I never gave promises I didn't intend to keep. "We're not."

CHAPTER
TWENTY-ONE

LAINEY

Despite Adam's insistence that we had to wait, I'd still messaged Ezra. More than once, though he responded to none of them. As far as I could tell, he didn't even look at them. So the last message I sent before climbing into bed—alone—was a simple one:

I promise, I'm not leaving.

After sending it, I switched to the private message app and stared at the contact with Pretty Boy. I had so much to tell him, too much that would take a novel to send and we had to keep it brief.

Me: *Miss you. E and I were together again. More to tell. Be safe.*

I debated hitting send on that. One, it seemed unfair to just drop it like a bomb. Two, I couldn't see his face. Yet, I had promised to tell him beforehand. So I followed it with another message.

Me: *You're never losing me.*

Would that be enough? I turned my head to where he'd

slept for the past few months and ached all over again. Maybe instead of changing the locks, I'd just return to Der Sonne. I had this argument with myself every night. Sleep... sleep was elusive because each time I checked my phone, there were no messages from Ezra or Pretty Boy.

We'd done more than open a door, we'd taken it off the hinges...

~

More than a year ago...

"Are we opening this door?" Ezra stared down at me, the darkness in his green eyes so utterly at odds with the sapphire waters around us. A chill raced up my spine despite the heat of the sun. Was I opening this door?

With my arms looped around his neck and my body pressed to his, there was no mistaking the erection in his trunks. I searched his face—whether for his answer or mine, I honestly wasn't sure.

"If you don't—"

"Stop," I told him before he could pull away and then his arms flexed as he dragged me to him. No space separated us from breast to chest. "Is this a trap?"

He tilted his head, his brows drawing more tightly together. The shadow of stubble on his cheeks reminded me of the scrape against my face as we kissed. It would leave a little burn. I kind of wanted that burn. It meant it happened.

"Is what a trap?" The careful way he redirected the question settled some of my disquiet.

"This—kissing you." I teased my hand against his nape without looking away from him. "The possibility of actual sex." Did heat race through me at being so blunt? Yes. Did I need to be absolutely clear? Pretty Boy had been an education and... A delightful, incomparable education whom I already missed.

Our first time, I hadn't been clear with him. That had been my choice, one he didn't care for because he hated the idea of hurting me. Here? Now? On this beach? I'd chased Ezra out into the water to talk to him. To confront him about why here? Why now? Instead, he kissed me and I'd adored it.

Adored him.

Closing his eyes, Ezra dipped his head so our foreheads rested together. "Kotyonok... what would be a trap?"

A laugh escaped me. "Answering a question with a question." My response seemed to delight him as he lifted his head to study me again. Then, without a word, he scooped me up and carried me onto the beach.

"I am capable of walking."

"I know," he said, then winked at me. "But a beautiful vision swam out into the water and stole my soul with a kiss. I can't let you escape now." He walked us up to the house, pausing only long enough under the outdoor shower to douse us both in cold water.

I shrieked as he laughed. My punch to his shoulder hurt my hand, but he was still chuckling as he glanced down at me. All squirming had done was dislodge my bikini top and reveal a perked nipple. The cold water had been brutal, a stinging wake-up call that could have dampened our desire but the look on his face promised me it hadn't.

That alone was enough to dry up all the moisture in my mouth.

Only when we'd warmed up some under the water did he set me on my feet so we could rinse off the salt. Not taking his gaze off me, he backed up a step then stripped his swim trunks down and off.

I drank in the sight of him. All tanned skin and defined muscles. He might act like a wastrel, but he'd never looked like one. His cock took me off-guard because, as thick and heavy as it was, it also sported two piercings. One through the shaft and another at the tip. The gold shined against his reddened flesh and seemed to gleam.

"Not a trap," Ezra said when I finally managed to drag my eyes up to his. "Probably shouldn't want you, Lainey. You're—"

I held my breath at the declaration.

"—perfect."

My stomach bottomed out at the raw declaration.

"So perfect—" He traced a finger around my belly button then drew it up my chest to my bikini top. "Everything about you is perfect. You know you are my favorite girl, right? The only girl for me?"

I forgot how to breathe. "You've been with plenty of girls." I didn't scoff, for I'd seen him. Seen him and Adam both. There were always girls flocking to them. Too many. "It always gave you a big ego."

The corner of his mouth quirked upward. "Were you jealous, Kotyonok?"

Taking a step back from him, I reached behind me to undo the bikini top and then I let it fall while I drank in the way his teeth clicked together and his mouth snapped shut. "You chased off so many guys that I was interested in."

"None of them were good enough for you."

"But you couldn't chase off Milo."

"He's certainly not good enough for you." Before I could challenge that insult, he dragged his caressing gaze from my breasts to my face. The heat in his eyes wasn't remotely hidden. "No one is. You deserve to be worshiped. To be adored. To be given nothing but pleasure. To live safely in the sun..."

"That sounds so lonely," I said, absorbing the description. The ties on the side of my bikini bottoms required only a single tug. Then it too slipped away and Ezra froze. I walked out of the outdoor shower and stood in the sun. I was thankful for the icier spray now because the sun's heat on my chilled skin couldn't quite compete with the raging fire in his eyes. "Too lonely."

Would he follow me? I didn't have to wait long as he stepped up behind me. His palm was flat on my abdomen as his lips caressed the shell of my ear. "You're not alone," he said as though a promise. He pressed a kiss to my shoulder. "I don't want this to be a trap for either of us, but you can tell me no. You can say no and walk away. It won't change my feelings. Might make my dick a little sore for a while—"

That last comment just made me laugh.

"My pain is funny to you." As playful as he made that mock mournful tone sound, there was an element of truth to it and I pivoted to face him. No more hiding away.

"No, your pain has never been funny to me. But you've always kept me pinned up, locked away. *Secured*." I couldn't help some of my own bitterness. "I'm not a prize—"

"That's where you're wrong, you are the greatest prize..."

I glared at him, except he didn't blink.

"I mean it," he said. "Protecting you is like breathing for me. I have to do it. So yes, you're a prize. So many covet you, yet no one deserves you. That doesn't mean I don't understand the loneliness. Occupying that place where you're in front of everyone, but no one sees you. Where you inhabit the role you have to play—"

He ran his fingers through my damp hair.

"I get it," he said. Staring up at him, I had to blink back tears. There was an openness in his eyes that I'd never seen before. An honesty. "I promise, Kotyonok. You're not alone. I'm here."

"What does that make us?" What did that make any of us? When he slipped his hand around my nape and closed the distance between us, I couldn't mistake his erection for anything else. A delicious shudder went through me and I swore my thoughts were stuttering.

"Friends with benefits?"

For some reason, that comment made me laugh, and I traced my fingers over his shoulders. "Have we ever really been friends?"

"Well, maybe we can learn," he offered, pressing a kiss to the corner of my mouth. "But let's check out the benefits package and work out the terms..."

Delight speared me. I wasn't sure if it was the business terms, or the fact he'd gotten naked to offer them. Or maybe it was all of it... I wanted to know. I wanted...

"I want you," I told him, and they were the last three words he let me speak as his mouth fused to mine.

Present Day

Waking came abruptly with the knock on the bedroom door. I put a hand out for—Ezra? Pretty Boy?

Probably both.

Not that either were there.

Another soft knock.

Scrubbing a hand over my face, I swiped away the drool from the corner of my mouth. "Yes?"

"Good morning," Marlene said as she opened the door. Sympathy creased her face as I struggled to shake off the grogginess. "Miss Marlowe is on the phone for you, and your grandfather called."

I frowned and glanced over at my cell phone. It wasn't next to the bed where it should be. It took me a moment of searching to find it under the covers. I must have gone to sleep with it in my hand.

The feeling of having just been on the island lingered. Yes, it was a dream, but it was so real. The phone was at five percent and needed to be charged.

"What did Grandfather want?"

"He asked if you could come stay out at Der Sonne this weekend. Since I thought you might have plans already, I told him I would remind you and that I was sure you would call if there were any changes."

She pushed further into the room and brought in a tray with coffee on it. There was also water and a pair of pain relievers. I wasn't entirely sure how she'd known I had a headache but I adored her for it.

"Thank you," I said again.

"Not to worry, don't forget to take Miss Marlowe's call. She is in her chipper 'get things done' mood, so I made the coffee extra strong."

I didn't laugh, though I did smile. Marlene moved over to adjust the curtains. It was still early, definitely further into the day than I thought. The sky was as dark and overcast as my mood. I plugged my cell in before I reached for the landline.

"*Bonjour*, Tally," I said with a great deal more happiness than I was feeling. I also took a sip of the coffee and nearly died. It was so strong it could shear off my esophagus. Just what the doctor ordered.

"You must have had a night to still be in bed at nearly nine in the morning," Tally teased. "Tell me, is that Mr. Hardigan still making your toes curl?"

I hadn't told her about the deal Pretty Boy had struck or the choices he'd made. Honestly, I didn't want to talk about it now. "Something like that," I murmured. "But it's much later in the day and you have wine. So tell me about what you've seen and bought?"

"Are you sitting down?" Tally said, clearly relishing the subject. I leaned back against the pillows Marlene had plumped up for me before she headed out of the room.

"Well, since I'm still in bed," I admitted. "I will say yes."

"Oooh, is he still in bed with you? I can call back if you would rather have a wake-up of a different kind." The sheer happiness radiating out of her tone would brighten even the darkest day. "Vavoom, baby."

I snorted a laugh, inelegant sound and all. "You know I don't kiss and tell."

"Well, darling, that's the point. He kisses and I tell." She sounded like she was grinning. "Fine, fine. If he's there, good morning." She blew a kiss. "Now, I have found the *perfect* dress for you for the Fire and Ice Ball."

Fire and Ice...

"Yes, I know, you've been so busy *working* and being responsible, that one of us has to make sure the important things are taken care of—and oh, Lainey, it's so pretty and *so* perfect for you. Say yes. I have your measurements, and I doubt it will need any tailoring, but I'll be back in the city in time for Christmas at Mother's—you're with me for at least one night of that, don't forget, and I will pout if your paramour tries to steal you away. But that's then and this is for New Year's, so say yes to the dress."

"You already bought it, didn't you?"

Tally laughed. "If you hate it, I'm sure I'll look fabulous in it, though I make a much better ice princess. You're the queen of fire."

Queen of Fire.

"When do I get to see it?"

That launched her into another tale and one I appreciated even as I checked my cell phone. No messages from Pretty Boy or Ezra. Nothing from Trouble either.

Only one from Adam with a time and a note to *be ready*.

Imperious ass.

"Are you listening?" Tally asked abruptly, as if trying to catch me out.

"Yes, I heard all about Viscount Mon De Canteur's fine accent and even finer tongue. Promise me you aren't eloping with some broke aristocrat."

"Absolutely not," Tally said with a sniff. "He's got a wonderful wine collection, a very talented tongue, and has been great company this week. However, he wants a wife, and if I go for an aristocrat, they need to be a count or maybe a duke at least. There are still German princes, right?"

"Does he know you're not on the market?"

"Oh, I think that's half of my appeal. He's determined to *convince* me." She laughed. "It doesn't matter. He's something to fill my time until I'm home. Anyway..."

To fill the time. Tally lived her life the way she wanted and I adored that for her. I stole a glimpse at my phone again. I was surrounded by people who cared and I'd never felt more alone.

TWENTY-TWO

MILO

"Gentlemen," King said as he rose to welcome the pair to the breakfast table. "This is my new assistant, Milo." He clapped me on the shoulder and I said nothing. "Don't mind him, he's just here to observe."

He gripped their hands briefly in greeting and didn't bother introducing either man to me. Not that I needed to be introduced. He'd given me files on each of them. The tall man with the thinning reddish-blond hair and receding hairline worked in the governor's office. The second man, with his smooth bald head and bushy beard, actually worked in the Attorney General's office.

Neither were faces for their respective employers, yet both had access and information. These were invaluable in areas of business, legitimate or otherwise. So far, King had a *lot* of legitimate business interests. Diversify and invest, you never know where change will come and we need to be in a position to take advantage of it when it does.

It was what I used to tell Jasper. Never put everything in one area. Make sure we could spread it out. Protecting our assets also gave us revenue if one area faltered. It had left the Vandals vulnerable for a time, but we'd focused and built. Now—now they were well and truly established.

Ivy invested in them and that helped. But they brought their own skills and talents to the table. The fact King saw things similarly irked me. It flat-out pissed me off.

"More coffee," King said to the waiter, who hurried over to add place settings for our guests. They weren't specifically here for breakfast though had "seen" King across the room and decided to stop and "chat." A lot of effort to put on a pantomime for others to see.

Letting their conversation wash over me, I sipped my coffee and scanned the room. They were all acting very informal, yet not friendly. Just familiar faces catching up. So who was the show for? The diner was a little more high-end. Most of the customers were dressed for the office. Not everyone had on expensive suits, but they wore them.

The bell over the door jingled merrily as people came and went. They'd been doing a brisk business since just after sunrise. Crowded with people in a hurry, the din of conversation rose and fell. It would be challenging to pick out any conversations beyond segments of words here and there. I couldn't even make out the people sitting at the table directly behind me, other than a constant drone of male voices and the occasional, softer-toned feminine one.

Unless the table was wired for sound, it would be damn hard to be overheard here. Maybe if someone could read lips, I supposed. That gave me food for thought. Even as I scanned the room, their conversation never shifted from the most banal subjects. This was either a test or a code.

I really didn't think King would court these guys for no

reason. He had an agenda. So did they. Someone was scratching someone else's balls, I just wasn't sure who or—

A familiar face stood out from the sea of them and I frowned as I jerked my gaze back to where I'd been skimming. Something had set off an internal alarm. Then, a man near the door moved, and I locked onto him.

I knew him.

We'd never exchanged names. Frankly, I hadn't wanted his and he undoubtedly knew mine. He was on his phone, comfortably unaware of the room around us. Rather than stare, I just kept him in my periphery. The door opened, and a blonde strolled in, laughing. Her voice carried over the others with the apology for being late.

The man in question turned to her with a smile and he pressed a kiss to her cheek. Everything in his manner was paternal and protective. In fact, he stopped ignoring the room around him now that his daughter had arrived. His daughter. The girl who'd been attacked. He'd asked me to deal with her rapist.

And I had.

With prejudice.

Then I'd ended up in solitary for fighting but not for killing. Whatever strings he'd pulled kept my sentence from being longer. It just meant it was lonelier for a time. Seeing the happy laughing face on that girl and his own warm smile.

Yeah. Worth it.

Men who attacked women were garbage.

They should be taken out as such.

It was at that moment that he noticed me. Surprise creased his face, briefly followed by the faintest of frowns. The guy had nothing to worry about from me. He paid for the favor he'd asked for, and frankly, based on what he'd told me, I'd have done it for free. I flicked a look to his daughter and raised my eyebrows once.

He nodded but shifted her in the line so she was on his other side and away from me. No, I got it. I nodded to him and then took a sip of my coffee before deliberately returning my attention to the table in front of me. I hadn't lost track of the conversation, but I didn't need King to notice that I'd wandered.

Still, I kept track of the man and his daughter as they waited to pick up their food. One of the men with us though, also noticed him and said, "Excuse me, that's Edward Standish and I just want a quick word."

Edward Standish.

The name didn't mean anything, but I filed it away. As soon as the man from the governor's office excused himself, John Mancini from the Attorney General's office leaned forward. He shot me a look then to King.

"You can speak in front of him," was all King said as though to acknowledge the unspoken question.

"He's never going to play," Mancini stated. "Nering is not a guy who likes to be beholden to anyone. He'd rather be the one who collects the favors."

It wasn't an unfair assessment.

"What is his relationship with Standish?"

Mancini shrugged. "No idea, probably buttering him up for campaign money. His father used to be a strong supporter of the governor. He's less politically active and doesn't seem to be leaning that way at all."

King nodded slowly. "He asked for this breakfast. He can make his own decisions. If he's not in, he's not in. That means we find someone else."

Mancini sighed, the sound so resigned it almost made me laugh. Despite what he'd said about Nering, I had no doubt that the description would also apply to him. King was undoubtedly aware, but Mancini offered no arguments or disputes to the charge. He was well and truly on the hook.

"Thank you," Nering said as he returned to the table. "Sorry for that interruption. Where were we?"

Where we were was another two and a half cups of coffee before they wrapped up their "meeting" and the two men left. King leaned back in his chair, unhappiness enveloping him. It wasn't even the lack of expression that gave him away, it was the absolute lack of zeal. King gloated.

It was one of his weaknesses. When he got his way, when he won—he gloated. It was like he couldn't help himself. Anything else was a loss. He was not happy.

"Let's go," he said, leaving a few bills on the table. There was no tip this time, and we'd had that table for hours. I dropped a fifty atop his pile of bills. That waitress had been running her ass off and she'd never made us wait.

If King noticed my action, he didn't say anything. The cash he'd left me with was for on-the-road money, and once upon a time, it would have felt like a fortune. While I would happily use my own cash to pay the bills, I was fine with using his for this.

His bodyguards had been inside for a while but eventually left their table. One stood out in the cold reading a newspaper and the other had moved to a stool at the counter. They both fell in as we stepped out into the icy cold air.

I adjusted my coat as we walked the half-block to where the driver waited for us. Always a different vehicle. He had at least a dozen that I'd clocked so far and there was no pattern as to which ones he requested. At least none that I'd determined.

The man lived with an air of paranoia around him. Cars were never left alone when we were out. The driver, and sometimes a guard, stayed with them. From limos to sedans to SUVs, the only commonality his vehicles seemed to share was that they were all a uniform black. That was it.

Though his men weren't the chattiest lot, none of them so much as breathed a word on the way to the car. I guess I wasn't the only one who could read his mood. Once we were in the backseat, he closed the privacy window between us and the driver as well as the guard.

As soon as we were alone, he said, "I want you to pay a visit to Nering's son. He's at NYU. Living the good life—he needs a reminder that life isn't a party. His father should understand that making things run smoother also goes the other way."

"How much damage?" I wasn't going to go shake down some damn freshman, especially since I didn't give a shit who his father was.

"You can decide when you meet him. Just make sure he's breathing." Irritation scraped over every single one of his words. "Make sure Ezra goes with you. He has some experience in delivering messages."

I'd rather cut off my own toes. But sure, why not... The flash of the message from Mayhem that morning sliced across my vision.

They'd been together again.

She'd told me.

Then she'd followed it up with the assurance she wasn't leaving me.

I wanted to hate him, mainly because he got to see her and I didn't. I also needed to message her later and—

"How do you know Standish?"

I refocused on King. "The guy back at the diner?" I had the name now and clearly heard Nering say it. So there was no reason to play dumb on that.

"Yes. You were looking at him." King stared at me.

I shrugged. "Was looking at the hot blonde with him. A little too buttoned down for my taste, but she was certainly a stunner." Just talking about another woman was anathema, much less talking about her like she was meat.

King snorted. "I can always reach out to him."

I frowned. "For what?"

"The blonde. She was with him. Perhaps he'd like to share."

My stomach rolled. "I'm good. Thanks." If I needed a woman, I had Mayhem. There was no one else I preferred.

"You should learn to enjoy life more. There's a party coming up after Christmas. My tailor will get you sorted out with a suit."

I didn't respond because I didn't care.

"And if you need to scratch an itch, I have a few places you can use..."

"Right, when I want your commentary or assistance on my sex life, I'll be dead. And they'll need to be a necrophiliac. What else is on the agenda for the day?" Because I wasn't having any more of this conversation.

King shook his head. "Meetings. I want you to sit down with some of the lawyers. You used to be good with the law; I want you to understand how our contracts and negotiations department works."

So much better than sex.

"I have to make some arrangements. Call Ezra and have him meet you at the building in Midtown. You can discuss arrangements for Nering Jr."

"And you will be?"

"Making plans, Son, making plans. The holidays are coming..." Then he seemed to grow quiet, almost thoughtful. "What should I send your sister?"

The words "your head on a platter" were right there, though I kept them locked down. "Not sure there's much she wants or needs."

"Girls always need something. Considering her life, she's had a lot... still..." He tapped two fingers to his chin. "See if you can find out if there's something she'd really like."

"You're supposed to be leaving her alone." And I shouldn't have to remind him of that.

"I have been," King informed me. "I've not called her, and I've trusted O'Connell's word that she is fine. But I have a few Christmases to make up for. No time like the present to start."

I didn't roll my eyes, but I thought about it.

The silence grew thicker.

"What about you?" King asked. "What would you like for Christmas?"

Thankfully, his phone ringing meant I didn't have to answer that. Because what I wanted was him dead and me back with Mayhem. That was definitely a gift I would be okay with giving myself.

CHAPTER
TWENTY-THREE

LAINEY

T hanksgiving week was already here. It seemed insane that we were on the cusp of Christmas. A tree had been delivered to the apartment. Marlene said it came from Grandfather, which didn't surprise me. He preferred the holidays at Der Sonne and I would make my way out there. I'd also have to go to Waltham Corners to see Andrea, though—now that I was thinking about it, she hadn't messaged her Christmas plans. She'd gone home with friends for Thanksgiving rather than come back here, which—that suited me fine.

My car was due within the hour and I was ready to go. I'd messaged Karagiani that I was going out today and he was waiting for me downstairs. I just didn't want him in the apartment. Despite the thick alpine blue spruce standing in the library awaiting festive trimming and a smaller pine occupying the living room, it all felt so cold and empty.

It had been a week since the night Ezra and Adam both

ended up here. A week since Ezra had seemed to open up and bare his soul, promising to not leave—then he kissed Adam and fled. He'd not returned a single message or call. I was tempted to call over to Harrows Park. If he didn't want to be found—that would be a mistake.

Adam had answered messages in curt form. Pretty Boy? I'd gotten one message from him but it buoyed me.

Pretty Boy: *Not losing me.*

It may not seem like much to anyone else... To me? It was everything. I tugged on the red boots I'd chosen. They were calf-skin suede and soft. They were perfectly matched to the turtleneck red dress I'd selected. Marlene had set up my leather coat on the hook by the door and I'd grab my bag from the desk when it was time.

The phone for downstairs rang just as I checked my watch. Wood was here. That meant it was time to go. Closing my eyes, I took a deep breath, squared my shoulders, and rose. Ten minutes later, the elevator doors parted to reveal Adam waiting for me. He was dressed in a navy dark Tom Ford suit and duster. The formality of his choice didn't surprise me.

He knew what today was.

"What are you doing here?" I asked, even if I already knew the answer. Since I wasn't a little girl or afraid of confrontation, I stepped right out of the elevator. I pulled the gloves from my pocket to tug them on to save myself from him grabbing my hand.

"You're too smart to ask that question," he told me with a hint of a smile. "But I thought it would be nice if you had company, at least there and back. Maybe after—you'll let me take you to dinner."

Tilting my head, I studied him as he fell into step with me. Karagiani waited by the doors. Outside, it had actually begun to snow. That was going to make the drive longer, depending on how the weather held up.

"You know my grandfather's not a fan," I reminded him, though I didn't argue as he held the door for me, nor when he cut Karagiani off from walking with me. Wood hopped out to open the rear door of the car.

"Then it's a good thing I'm not planning to take him out to dinner." Adam waited for me to get in and the door closed before he circled the car to get in the other side. That put Karagiani up front with Wood.

"This just started, Miss Benedict," Wood told me over his shoulder. "We'll arrive just on time." There were bundles of fresh carnations sitting on the opposite seat. He'd brought the larger SUV limo. The flowers were probably why he cut his arrival so close.

"Not a worry at all, Wood. I messaged Grandfather that we were leaving when I was in the elevator." We always timed our arrival so neither of us had to wait. We also worked diligently to make sure we weren't late.

As Wood pulled out into traffic, Adam reached out with a gloved hand and left it palm up—an offer. He didn't say anything or offer any sympathy. Just waited. I despised the weakness in me that wanted to take that comfort. The last few days had been truly difficult.

However... "Have you heard from Ezra?"

He sighed. "No. He's avoiding me."

"Me too," I admitted then put my hand in his. He closed his fingers around mine and the heartfelt squeeze helped much more than I wanted to admit. Maybe too much. Adam in a gentle, caring mood had never been good for me. It relaxed my guard and made me want to forget.

We couldn't afford to forget.

Still, the drive passed in relative peace.

Adam didn't press his luck, nor did he do more than hold my hand. The snow continued to fall. It was a little on the wet side. It clung to grass and bushes, but not the roads. Course, they'd probably already treated the roads. The drive seemed to take forever, yet it wasn't that congested once we left the city. All too soon, we were passing the wrought iron gates of Harmony Springs, a private facility in the Hudson River Valley.

In the summer, it was lush with green trees and colorful flowers. The high walls around the facility were designed to protect the privacy of the residents as much as their serenity. Security here was top-notch. A sigh escaped me as Wood spoke to the gate guard before following the long drive toward the Victorian buildings in the distance.

While the snow had only begun in the city, it was thick on the ground here. Curated almost like a holiday card. Grandfather's car waited in the loop of the drive and Wood pulled up behind.

"Stay in the car," I told Karagiani and Wood. I allowed Karagiani to accompany us, except he wasn't going in. His presence would only upset my grandmother. Wood didn't need to worry. Adam was out before I could tell him to do the same. I swore the man was impossible.

Grandfather stepped out of his car and spotted Adam as he opened my door. Taking a deep breath, I braced myself. Saying Grandfather wasn't a fan was an understatement. He disliked all of the Reeds. I didn't think he'd singled out Adam for any special dislike, but considering the stern look he directed at him right now—maybe I was wrong.

I gathered up the carnations and stepped out with Adam cupping my elbow as though to balance me. He met my warning glance with a faint smile. "Don't worry," he soothed in a low voice. "I can handle him."

That was not the point. "You can't come in."

"I know," he continued, before pivoting to face Grandfather at his approach. "Mr. Benedict."

Grandfather stared at him. "Reed." The frost in his gaze melted when he glanced at me. "You brought her favorites."

"Of course I did," I told him. "I even brought extra so you can take them in too."

He patted his pocket with a faint chuckle. "Don't worry, darling girl. I have that all taken care of." He flicked a look to Adam. "You can go. I'll get her back to the city."

"I don't mind waiting, sir," Adam addressed him in the single most polite tone I'd ever heard him use. "Not to mention it's her car." Then he pressed a kiss to my cheek. Ass. The devilment in his eyes said he knew it too. "Take your time."

"Ignore him," I said to Grandfather, being that today was about my grandmother. I didn't glance back, although I could see Adam leaning against the side of the car as Grandfather and I ascended the steps. The front doors were glass and reflective.

"I'm surprised you invited him," Grandfather said by way of a scolding as he opened the door and I glanced at him.

"Adam tends to invite himself. He wanted to keep me company on the drive." That was all I wanted to discuss on this subject. "How are you?"

"Well enough," Grandfather said. One of the receptionists rose at our arrival, her kind smile growing. "Hello, Margary, how is she doing today?"

"Mrs. Benedict is in a fine mood today, sir," she said, accepting his coat, then waited as he helped me out of mine. It took a little maneuvering with the flowers. "We've taken her out to the atrium. The birds are singing and it's quite warm. She loves it out there, particularly after a good snowfall. Lunch will be brought out to you as soon as you're settled."

"Thank you."

Then we were off. We knew Harmony Springs very well. Too well. We made this pilgrimage three times a year for the last four years. It was not where Grandfather wanted her, but it was the best thing for her. Even with the staff and a nurse, she'd struggled at Der Sonne. Struggled with the passage of time.

Struggled with the memories.

The atrium wasn't that far, and it was a perfectly lovely, almost bucolic greenhouse that offered year-round flowers, happy little parakeets that the residents enjoyed, and a safe environment where she wasn't at risk for a fall. The staff here were very discreet, allowing her the illusion of privacy, though she had an escort to and from.

As we pushed out through the doors, Grandfather was striding forward and leaving me behind. Not that I minded. He came monthly at first, then every other month. He still maintained their anniversary, Valentine's, and the day he proposed, in addition to her birthday and Christmas.

"Allegra," he called as he approached her. Her silky white hair had been done up in braids and crowned her head. She also wore a lovely yellow dress. It was her favorite color. Hence, the yellow carnations. Though seated at the white table, already set for lunch, she rose and turned at the sound of her name.

Slowing to a stop, I drank in the radiant smile that lit up her face. It was a good day. She didn't always remember. Sometimes, she recognized him, but the changes in his appearance puzzled her. Leopold wasn't an old man, he was her feisty fiancé determined to marry her before her father could put a stop to it. She was an independent woman who made him wait because she wanted a bit of a job and a chance to prove herself.

Their relationship was something I'd always admired and adored. They genuinely *liked* each other. Grandfather worshiped the ground she walked on. His only wish had ever been to make her happy. In turn, she adored him but said it was her job to make him work for it because he was too damn good at everything. She kept him humble and he kept her happy.

Tears burned in my eyes.

"Leopold," she said as he swept her in for a hug and then a kiss. It was a very good day. Her laughter enveloped me in the gossamer strings of childhood. Grandmother—my nana—taught me all about being a lady but never once let me believe that I couldn't do anything I set my mind to. She'd raised competition horses and competed in them for a time. Even started a handful of smaller businesses and often provided startup money to women looking to build their own.

An angel investor.

Grandmother was still smiling when she looked past him to me, and her eyes warmed. My heart fisted as I began striding toward them. "Oh, you brought my favorites."

"I heard a rumor," I teased. Grandfather beamed as I brought the carnations over.

"Oh, Leopold, what did we do to have such a wonderful daughter," Grandmother said, then hugged me. "I've missed you so much, Melissa."

For the briefest of moments, Grandfather's face fell, and his smile flickered away. I understood. It wasn't the first time she'd mistaken me for Mother. I rather doubted it would be the last.

Melissa should come to see her, except she never had and I didn't think Grandfather would allow it now. Especially since she married Harper. Shoving all that aside, I kept my smile firm as I leaned away from my grandmother's fragile, almost waiflike vision. She'd always been a woman of such presence. Dementia had whittled away at her, but she was still in there.

The woman who loved us was right there.

"I've missed you too, Mother," I whispered and her smile brightened even further.

"Come on, girls," Grandfather said. "Let's get these carnations set up and have lunch. We have a special treat for you..."

"Oh, is it a cake?" Grandmother laughed like she was a girl, and I held onto my mood with both hands. We were here for her. "You're going to spoil me."

"That's the idea," I said, with every effort at cheerfulness. "Sugar, frosting, and chocolate. What could be better?"

She matched my smile and touched my cheek as we took our seats. "Having you here to share it with."

Yes, that definitely made it better. I might cry later, but right now, she only got smiles and laughter.

It was her birthday, and we would make the most of it.

CHAPTER
TWENTY-FOUR

EZRA

I t was early. Too early. Especially since I hadn't slept the night before. I hadn't slept in the last three days. Not really.

Fuck, I probably hadn't slept well in months. The last night I slept decently, I'd been on the island. She'd been right there, curled up next to me. No one was taking her away. No one was baring their soul.

And I hadn't fucked up the best friendship I'd ever had.

Shoving off the bed, I threw on clothes and headed down to the gym. Harrow's Corners was a monster of a house, cold, impersonal, and laid out like a castle. It belonged to another time and certainly not to Long Island. But here we were. The marble-floored hallways and the painfully white columns offered the chilliest of welcomes as I left my room and headed for one of the numerous back stairs.

Staff weren't permitted to use any of the main staircases or family entrances. I'd learned from a young age if I wanted to avoid my father I just followed the staff around. They never went into a room he occupied and would always wait patiently until he finished. Dad, his father, and his father before him, were all firm believers in a clear delineation between the upstairs and the downstairs.

We should never see the staff nor hear from them, unless it was through the butler who headed up the entirety of the staff, or the senior cook who negotiated the menus with Mother. That was it. Everyone else? They didn't exist. Unless they failed to do their jobs, in which case they were fired.

While I would drift behind them or use their routes to avoid the family, I never made the mistake of fooling myself that they were my friends. Especially not the attractive ones. The inability to trust others came directly from my father. He made a point of having the staff inform on me, in front of me, regularly.

They were employees. *His* employees. Not mine. They would never take my side. They were not to be confided in unless I wanted him to know things. Still, I jogged down the darkened corridor to the gym. I needed to get an apartment in the city. I just—had never bothered. When I was there, I crashed at Adam's or sometimes at one of the clubs. Other times, we were on the road and I didn't need to worry about it.

In my late twenties, and I still lived with my parents.

Maybe it was time to change that too.

I hit the door to the gym and pushed inward. The lights came on as I stepped inside. It smelled of too many cleaning products and lemon. A gym should smell like sweat and dust and people—this was almost too sanitized. Too empty.

Kind of like my life.

203

I headed straight for the treadmill and fired it up to begin the warm-up. I wanted to run. I needed a brutal-paced, long run that would push me. Push me until I dropped. My phone vibrated as I reached for the remote to turn on the music.

Adam's face appeared on the screen. I turned the music up to something hard and pulsing. It drowned out the vibration as I set the phone in the cradle. The rhythm pounded from the walls, shaking the equipment and thrumming in my veins. After four rings, Adam's call went to voicemail.

It flickered to life with his face again, and I dipped my gaze to stare at it before shaking my head.

Nope.

I forced my eyes up and locked them on myself in the mirror. He'd get distracted soon. He'd taken to calling three to four times a day. I didn't answer. I didn't want to answer.

I had no idea what to say.

Slipping like that had been fucking inexcusable. If I was lucky, he'd forget that it happened and wouldn't cut me off. Or maybe he'd knock one of my teeth out for touching him. That might work. It wasn't like we hadn't fought before. Hell, he'd beaten the shit out of me just a month earlier, or was it two months? Fuck, I'd half-forgotten when. They kind of bled together.

It was over my kotyo—

I cut that line of thought off with a grimace. Because even as I increased the pace to three point eight on my way to four miles per hour, I could see the pain in her eyes. The pain and the confusion as I let the elevator doors cut us off. I'd promised to not leave and then Adam ruined everything by letting himself in.

Couldn't he have just let us have that one night?

Closing my eyes, I shook my head and hit the controls to force myself to go faster. Maybe I didn't deserve good things. Maybe I *never* deserved Lainey. But it didn't change me wanting her. Didn't change me wanting him—

"Fuck." The word exploded out of me. No matter how fast I ran, I couldn't seem to escape the bad fucking choices I'd made. Hitting the stop button, I shoved myself off the treadmill and walked away from it *and* my phone. Across the room, the punching bags were waiting.

Wrapping my hands up swiftly, I started working my arms and fists, pouring my frustration into striking the bag. While I couldn't hear it, I could see the screen on my phone still lighting up. Goddammit, Adam spent months ignoring me, and now, he wouldn't let it go.

Course, I'd never kissed him before.

I almost missed my next strike and stumbled, then gripped the bag in an effort to get my breathing under control while not slamming my head against the bag. Why had I done that? I'd just had Lainey coming apart in my arms. She'd let me have her wholly and seemed on board with more, and then—

Adam.

It was always fucking Adam Reed. He walked in like he owned everything. The apartment. Her. Me. He wanted answers. He wanted to dictate the terms. And then...

The music changed, and I fought to keep my focus, but it wasn't working. By the time the music cut off abruptly and pulled me out of the zone, my arms were spaghetti, my fists were bloodied to the point they soaked through the wraps, and sweat stung my eyes.

I pivoted to face Durham. My father's right-hand man.

The fixer.

I fucking hated him.

"What?" I demanded, my breath coming in explosive pants. While he might be my father's pitbull, he was still *staff* and that meant he didn't get to decide to interrupt me. That was my call, *not* his.

"Your father sent me."

Or Dad's.

Fuck.

"Then spit it out," I told him. "I'm busy."

The man gave me the most dismissive of looks. Durham didn't pretend that he worked for me. No, he worked for my father, which meant he presented himself as someone higher, more important, and that I should answer to him.

He could go get fucked.

"Your father requires your presence at a meeting."

"No shit," I said, making no attempt to disguise my disdainful tone as I walked over to a water bottle that had been left for me. See, most of the staff knew their place and I'd been on a good track to working the edge off my temper. "He always requires my presence. Just send me a reminder for my calendar. Or better yet, talk to my secretary."

I had one. I never spoke to him. I didn't want to see him or hear from him. His job was my calendar, and that was it. He made excuses, sent regards, and good wishes, updated meetings, and otherwise fucked off at the office.

It was a good arrangement.

One I preferred.

"The meeting is today."

Of course, it was. I just stared at Durham, then raised my eyebrows.

"In thirty minutes, your father expects you to be showered, dressed presentably, and be in attendance." The clipped tone was far from impersonal. In fact, it positively dripped with disdain and irritation.

Asshole.

When he continued to stand there, I sneered. "Is that the whole of the message?"

"Yes," Durham said, his expression rippling with dislike. Right back at you.

"Then get the fuck out."

The man drew himself up, shoulders back, nostrils flared, and the dislike intensified in his eyes. Yeah, he didn't even try to hide it. Right back at you, Dick-Face.

"Did I stutter?" I said before he could finish inhaling a breath.

"Do you have a message for Mr. Graham, the senior?" Durham demanded.

"No, shitstain. I don't. You did your lapdog duty, now get the fuck out and put the music back on."

And I'd stand here all day until he did as he was told. He thought he could speak to *me* like that? No. The only person in this house allowed to take that tone with me *was* my father. Eyes incensed, Durham looked like he was going to make the mistake that others had attempted in the past.

They were gone and I was still here—and I knew how to deal with a body. My father had people to do it. I'd had to do it myself.

Maybe my expression made it clear because Durham withdrew a step and nodded. "I'll inform your father that I delivered the message."

Whatever. I gave him a dismissive wave and the door closed behind him. Prick failed to turn the music back on. As tempting as it would be to force him back to do what he was told, I didn't *want* to see him. I checked my watch. Thirty minutes until an appointment?

That seemed last minute, even for my father. I downed

more water, spilling some over my sweaty face before I retrieved my phone.

There was an appointment on the schedule. For lunch.

Which was in ninety minutes, not thirty.

Fine.

My phone rang again. Adam was like a pitbull with a bone. I sent it to voicemail then messaged him.

Busy. Will see you soon. Party coming up.

It was a month away, but he had to remember what it was like. With that, I silenced Adam's notifications.

Not quite the coward's path but close to it. I just— needed time to figure this out. And I needed him to forget. Then we could go back to normal.

Lainey's messages waited for me.

The last one yanked at me.

Call me. Come find me. Whatever you need. Just let me know you're all right.

I didn't deserve either of them.

Soon.

It was the only message I fired back to her, and then I made myself scroll away from her messages. I didn't silence them. There was an update from Karagiani; he was with her today at—

Fuck.

The date hit me.

I really was a piece of shit.

Walking out of the gym, I returned to my room to shower, wash the blood off my hands, and get dressed. When I descended to the dining room—on time—I met Durham's dislike with a faint smirk. I wasn't late.

The lunch also wasn't just with my father.

Oksana was there, along with my mother, her parents, and a few others.

Fuck.

Fuck.

Fuck.

"You have responsibilities," my father said from behind me. His voice was soft, though pitched perfectly. I couldn't miss a single word. "The Fire and Ice Ball is coming up. There is an investor's meeting this month. The annual Christmas pageant. You will make yourself available for all of it."

"Or what?" I asked, more out of a bored habit than genuine defiance. It didn't matter how much I didn't want to be involved. I didn't betray that to him because it made it a thousand times worse.

"Do you require a refresher?" Father asked as he moved past me. "I can make arrangements."

He didn't wait for my response, just continued into the dining room where our company rose to greet him and there was a warm and cheerful note. Everyone was so very happy to see everyone else.

Resentment soured through me. I caught the eye of one of the footmen. "Inform my mother of my apologies. I need five minutes." I touched a hand to my phone, drawing it out. "Short call, and I will be in directly."

"Yes, sir," the footman said before stepping in. I walked away from the dining room and pulled up a contact I rarely used but who would answer if they were available. It went to voicemail.

Dammit.

"Dominic," I said as soon as there was a beep. "We need a meeting. ASAP. If you're out of the country, message me, I'll send the jet. You need to be in New York, yesterday." With that, I ended the call and stared along the hallway with its combination of fine art and ancient artifacts. There were even suits of armor.

The way out seemed to be that way, but it wasn't. No, there was no way out but through.

I checked my phone to turn off the sound for notifications in case my cousin got back to me. Dominic Walsh was the lucky one. Our mothers were sisters, but his life got to go in a vastly different direction.

That said—when I'd needed him before, he'd come through for me.

As much as I didn't want to drag him into this, I might have no other choice. Putting the phone away, I pivoted on my heel, pasted on my politest smile and strode into the dining room.

It was time to get the latest farce over.

CHAPTER
TWENTY-FIVE

LAINEY

The week following my grandmother's birthday flew by. I spent Thanksgiving at Tally's, at least part of it, and I picked up my Fire and Ice dress from her now that she was back from Paris before I went to have dinner with my grandfather. I stayed at Der Sonne for the rest of the weekend. Adam must have been tracking me —or maybe it was Karagiani, but once I was at Der Sonne, I dismissed him. Grandfather had security. I didn't plan to go be social. Still, I was down at the stables getting ready to ride when Adam arrived.

I'd just begun tightening the cinch on Rosalind, the ten-year-old Friesian mare, who remained one of my absolute favorites in the stables. She was also the granddaughter of one of my grandmother's favorite mares, Sassy Sparks. Sassy was almost thirty years old and retired. She got to live a happy, fat, and sassy spoiled life these days. But we had four of her offspring and Rosalind had been a present to me the day she'd been born.

"Mind company?" Adam asked as he strode down the barn aisle. Like me, he was already kitted out in riding gear and a heavier coat. It had snowed, but it wasn't that deep. It was just going to be chilly. I'd put Rosalind's boots on.

"What would you do if I said yes, I minded?" I asked, securing the strap before I stroked her shoulder. Rosalind lipped at my shoulder and I chuckled at her. "You get treats after the exercise, ma'am. Not before."

"Try to change your mind," Adam offered. The dry remark actually made me smile for real. "Then probably follow you."

I snorted. That sounded about right. "Well, at least you're honest."

"Just wanted to spend time with you." The raw honesty under the declaration made his case for him more than the words themselves.

Tilting my head, I studied him as he reached a hand up to stroke Rosalind's face. But his gaze wasn't on the mare, it was on me.

"Tommy," I called out to one of the grooms. "Has Pippi been out today?"

"No, Miss Lainey. She's on the schedule for this afternoon."

The corners of Adam's mouth tilted.

"Could you get her ready for Mr. Adam?" At the request, Adam put a hand over mine.

"Just point me to her, Tommy," he said. "I'll saddle her up myself."

I raised my eyebrows and his grin grew.

"If I'm going to ride the lady, the least I can do is let her get to know me first." The blunt remark, no matter how charmingly delivered, dared me not to laugh and I was having a hard time containing my humor. Not that I didn't get the reference.

"You have a point, Mr. Adam," I teased. His startling blue-violet eyes practically danced with his own entertainment.

"I do try, Miss Lainey," he murmured, then dipped his head. The fact he halted just millimeters from my lips gave me a choice. The tease of his breath over my lips was an invitation, and I had to swallow the groan that wanted to escape as I closed that distance.

His lips were warm, soft. The flick of his tongue against me had my mouth opening to welcome him. There was something sweet and inviting about the invasion that unlocked a warmth in my chest that had been absent for too long. We seemed suspended there for the longest moment, but a stomp from Rosalind had me pulling back.

The moment of my retreat, he pulled back then his smile made my heart squeeze. Adam Reed knew exactly how to infuriate me; the fact he could also still charm me was unsettling. He touched his gloved fingers to the corner of my mouth before he winked. "Wait for me."

Then he strode away and I leaned into Rosalind's side. She huffed as I rubbed my cheek against her silky coat. "We can do this," I murmured. "Right?"

She turned her head to look at me and I grinned. She wanted treats. Spoiled baby. My beautiful, spoiled baby.

Ten minutes later, I was settled on Rosalind's back and Adam had just mounted Pippi. The seven-year-old chestnut mare was a thoroughbred and shire cross. One of my grandmother's last "investments" before her condition began to rob her of the enjoyment she took in the horses.

A love that Andrea seemed to share even more than I

did. Sadness curled through me. Andrea was never going to know our Nana the way I did. That—was even sadder.

"Hey," Adam said as he brought the eager mare up to us. Despite her age, Pippi was an energetic mare. She was also restless. I hadn't been spending as much time with them. "What's wrong?"

"Nothing I want to talk about," I said rather than just dismiss it. "More life things we can't change."

He studied me for a beat. "We going soft or hard?"

I considered him then looked out over the land. There were a lot of good trails we could take. The property was extensive. "Warm up, then hard. Rosalind needs a workout, and Pippi there needs the edge off."

"Will you let me take you to lunch after?"

"You trying to get on my good side?" I dared him.

"Maybe," he said, letting Pippi circle us as she danced with eagerness. "Or maybe I'm testing how far you'll let me go since I plan to take you to the ball for New Year's."

Surprise spiked through me. "The Fire and Ice Ball?" That was at Ezra's...

"Yes," Adam said. "You're going on my arm. I insist."

"You do, huh?"

I pursed my lips as I studied him.

"Yes, but we'll start with this ride and then maybe lunch..." The element of challenge was back in his voice. "I think I can be persuasive."

So did I. That said... "Trying to get to know me again, Adam?" I picked up his challenge.

"Reminding us both that we know each other." The verbal parry took me back to our fencing.

"True..." I gathered Rosalind's reins. "Maybe if you're a good boy, I'll give you another shot at disarming me."

He wanted to throw down a challenge? I'd offer one of

my own. The curve of his delicious lips told me he hadn't missed a step.

"Try to keep up," I told him, waiting for them to be turned away as I gave Rosalind a gentle kick and took off at a relaxed trot. We weren't racing, yet.

Soon though.

"You're never going to lose me," he called from behind and I gave into the temptation to grin.

As promised, I didn't lose him. We spent our morning riding, and then I invited him up to the house to shower and change. Grandfather was *not* thrilled to see him, but he seemed to keep most of his objections to himself. Most. Whatever he said to Adam when I wasn't there, Adam chose not to share.

I couldn't make Grandfather like him. Half the time, I wasn't even sure I liked him. Still, Adam took me out to lunch and then drove me back to the city. It was a little early, but I had things to do. He'd eyed the dress bag when one of the valets brought it down with my bags, but I just gave him an enigmatic smile.

The drive back was—nice. Almost peaceful. He even played Christmas music. "Do you remember," I mused, "the first time you took me to Rockefeller Center to ice skate?"

He glanced over at me. "You were six. Imperious and determined, but also upset." His voice gentled. "Your mother forgot you were coming for the week and she'd gone off with Dad."

My grandfather had taken my grandmother on a cruise. I'd gotten out of school early, so Em and I had come back to the city and she'd been swept back to her place and Tally to her parents. I'd found myself sitting in that huge penthouse apartment alone.

"Your mother came into the city," I said slowly. "I think it was only the second time I met her."

"The butler called out to Waltham Corners," Adam said, not shying away from it. "Dad and Melissa were somewhere in Europe on a spontaneous trip." Disgust filtered through the words. "Mom found out you were there by herself and went to look after you."

"I adored your mother," I admitted. "She was —amazing."

Adam's sigh echoed my own. "She was." No arguments from him. "Ezra and I were already on break, and we'd been using the penthouse to party."

"Oh my god." I'd forgotten that. "You brought the party back to the apartment..."

The corner of his mouth kicked up higher as a chuckle escaped. "Adam Stuart Fitz James Reed, what do you think you are doing?" The callback to his mother's incredibly polite, yet *very* stern tone, made me laugh. I clapped a hand over my mouth. "Oh, she was—vexed." Amusement curled through his words as he shook his head.

"She made them all leave." I'd been sitting on the sofa with her as she showed me how to do some needlework. She found it soothing. The memory was right there, along with the hints of her perfume. "Except Ezra, then she went with you both into the kitchen..."

"We had to wait while she sorted you out and then we had to explain ourselves." Adam laughed. "Needless to say, she was not pleased. Ezra got the boot back to Long Island, and I spent the rest of the week on Lainey duty."

I tilted my head to look at him. "So I was your punishment?"

"I was fifteen." It wasn't an excuse. "You were almost seven."

I waited.

"And yes, that was my penance. Not my punishment." He reached a hand over to steal mine, bringing it back over to rest on his thigh where he covered my hand with his. "I didn't mind having to look after you—but I was a little sour that I got busted by my mother 'cause yours..."

"Flaked," I offered up. "Again."

"Pretty much." The rough sympathy was in his voice. "She was a terrible mother."

"Yes," I said with a slow nod. "She was. But I liked the time with you and with your mom." It had become a much more festive vacation. "Though, I shouldn't have eaten so many chestnuts."

That brought out another laugh. "I tried to warn you."

Yes, he had. Still...

"What brought up Rockefeller Center?" He traced his fingers along the back of my hand. We were getting close and I hadn't invited him up. I wasn't going to, either. The day had been—good. I kind of wanted to keep it there.

"Just...sometimes you remind me of when you used to be so kind and sweet. Before you became such an asshole."

"Harsh," he commented. "But accurate."

"I don't like the asshole," I admitted, cutting a look at him and studying his profile. He'd hurt me so much over the years. The whiplash of his changing motives and advances left me dizzy.

I also didn't like to be vulnerable. Especially now.

"Not overly fond of him myself," he admitted. "Working on that."

Then we were there. He pulled up to the front of my

building and one of the doormen was already coming over to open my door.

"Lainey?" He caught my hand before I could step out. "Let me take you to dinner later this week?"

"Let me think about it?"

He met my gaze, and I could almost see him biting his tongue. It had to hurt. "Call me." That wasn't a request.

I leaned over and kissed his cheek, then the corner of his mouth and pulled away before he could drag me into a real kiss. "I'll think about it."

Then I was climbing out and the doorman helped me collect my things. Adam idled at the curb until I was inside. I collected my mail, and there was a note waiting for me. With the bag over my arm and the case next to me, I took the elevator up.

I slit open the envelope to find the note in a familiar pen.

I know I'm being difficult and I promised not to run. I will see you soon. I promise. In the meantime, I dropped off a present for you. Call it a peace offering.

Ezra.

I was still turning that over in my head as I headed to my apartment door, but it opened before I could, and a familiar, *very* welcome figure filled the door. The dress bag fell along with the mail and my suitcase as I dashed forward, all decorum forgotten.

"Pretty Boy..."

TWENTY-SIX

MILO

The holiday weekend passed in a haze of meetings and meals at so many different locations that I found myself *hating* so-called fine cuisine. As it was, when Saturday morning dawned and King summoned me to breakfast—where Ezra sat waiting for me—I was ready to just say fuck it all and flip a table.

After Mayhem's last message, Ezra fucking Graham was not high on my list of people I wanted to see. Not when *he* still got to see her and King didn't seem to give a shit. Or maybe he enjoyed the irony. Maybe he enjoyed sticking it to me. That meant *not* reacting to his presence. I never thought that the time I spent in jail would pay off in any appreciable fucking way.

Controlling my expressions required minimal effort these days. I poured my own coffee before I made my way over to the table. King kept staff, but they didn't generally serve breakfast and I preferred that.

"Not hungry?" King asked when I took a seat.

"No." Any appetite I might have had fled with Ezra's presence. "What's up?"

King eyed me as he washed down a bite of food with his coffee, then just shook his head as if he couldn't be bothered. "Change of plans for the weekend. You and Ezra are heading out this morning. You'll be working with him for the next three days. He has the assignment, and he is the lead. You will do as you're told."

Ezra didn't hide his smirk fast enough as he took a drink then glanced at his watch. "If you aren't eating, then you can get packed and we'll go."

"What do I need?" If we were going to push forward with this farce. Might as well take it all the way.

"Casual," Ezra said, then gave me a studying look. "One suit, daytime, not evening. If we end up needing something formal, we can grab it on the go."

Fine. I downed another mouthful of coffee. My blasé attitude didn't seem to allay any of King's natural suspicions, or so it seemed.

"That's it?" King said as I stood.

I met his gaze with a shrug. "Are you planning on giving me more information?"

His eyes narrowed. Not fun to be called on your bullshit, was it.

"Then I guess that's it. I'll get packed. See you in three days." Pivoting on my heel, I strode out. The sound of his voice carried, but not the content. He wasn't speaking to me this time. No doubt, he wanted Ezra to make the next three days extra unpleasant.

Sounded like a plan.

Fifteen minutes later, I was waiting by the front door when Ezra finally emerged from the dining room. He gave me a bored look as he snagged his coat from the footman who had been standing there waiting with them since I came down. I'd offered to hold them, but the man seemed to think being a doorstop was his job.

Ezra shot me an enigmatic look as he shrugged his jacket on and then he nodded to the footman who opened the door. His car sat idling, steam rising from the muffler as it warmed the interior. I didn't let the footman or the valet take my suitcase. It was an overnight bag and one suit bag. I was more than capable. I set both in the trunk before I climbed into the passenger seat.

"Put your phone in airplane mode." With that, Ezra hit the gas and followed the horseshoe to the drive. There was more security on the grounds. Even with the snow and the lack of guests at the house, King was always surrounded. You'd think he lived in the Corleone compound like some kind of godfather than he did in a fancy mansion in King's Point—the name wasn't lost on me. It really defied what I knew about him—or remembered.

Despite weeks spent in his company and going to meetings, all I'd gathered together was he used his investments to leverage money. That he, in turn, used to leverage control. All of it had allowed him to wedge his way into this upper level of society, where he then wielded more influence.

The Bay Ridge Royals weren't a "gang." That was what King said, Ezra said, all of them—even Liam had indicated that at one point. But if it walked like a gang and exacted restitution like a gang, it was a gang.

So what changed their secret society first? The society or King? And how the fuck did he manage to get control? That defied all logic.

"Are you planning on saying anything?" Ezra asked after he spent ten minutes getting us back on the road for Manhattan. King's Point wasn't near the other Bay Ridge families. Close, but definitely one would have to make an effort to travel between them. So he wasn't "naturally" a part of their crowd.

I thought I'd let my silence answer for me. Mayhem told me. She kept me in the loop and she kept her promises. On the other hand, I owed Ezra nothing; if this persisted, I might give into the urge to smash his face into his steering wheel.

So, better to hold my own peace.

"Right, well, I thought you might want to know what we're doing this weekend and why King basically kicked you out for the next few days."

I studied the landscape as Ezra accelerated onto the highway. He drove like he was running from the cops. The car continued to gain speed as he weaved in and out of traffic. This wasn't Nascar, but I supposed he could afford the tickets.

"You know, Ezra," Ezra continued, as though mimicking my voice—badly. "I am curious. Why did he bring you all the way out here so early in the morning? I thought we had other assignments."

"Well," Ezra flipped roles, resuming the part of himself. "King has a girl that he doesn't want anyone to know he has. Now, I know because this isn't the first time he's shut everything down and sent everyone away. Only his security will be on site and they will be very discreet."

"Huh." The prick deepened his voice as though I were some kind of a caveman. "Why does he think we'll care who tickles his balls?"

The less I thought of the man's balls, the better.

"'Cause she's a weakness," Ezra answered himself with a smirk. "I tried a couple of times, when I thought he was setting up a date—but he's cagey. Doesn't want anyone to know, which means—"

"She's someone powerful or related to one of the families. If it was just a hookup or a call girl, he wouldn't care." Look at that he got me talking.

Ezra snapped his fingers. "Exactly. You don't give other people leverage over yourself unless you can't help it. Whoever this is, the plan wasn't to get together today. Something changed."

I frowned. "I haven't seen him 'date' at all. Business meals. The occasional drink…" Yet none of those women had earned more than a passing or professional glance from him.

"Well, I've arranged my share of assignations. He called me at the ass crack of dawn this morning and told me to get over there and pick you up. You're my problem for three days."

If anything, that combination of remarks deepened my frown further. "Your share of assignations?"

Was he just marking bedpost notches with Mayhem?

Rather than a quip, Ezra cut a look at me. "Yes."

"And would Lainey qualify as one of those?"

His expression tightened, instant tension hardening his mouth into a firm line. "She is many things to me, and I respect your interest—"

"Do you?" I didn't bother to wait for whatever bullshit he wanted to shell out. "You show up, you fuck her, then you leave. Somewhere in there you hurt her."

He said nothing.

"Now, you've done it again. Don't tell me what she isn't," I told him. "Tell me what she is and why I shouldn't break both of your arms."

His knuckles went white on the steering wheel. "She's everything."

Well, that was a lot better than the earlier answer.

"And I don't really have a good reason for you to not break my arms."

Surprise ballooned through my aggravation.

"I made her a promise, and then I didn't keep it." Dislike for himself seemed to shadow the words. "I wanted to keep it. Then I didn't. I'd rather explain the whys of that to her, and not you."

Not that I could blame him.

"So…in the interests of making up for my choices to her and to you, I've got a job for you for the next three days." At my lack of response, he smirked. "Right, actions speak louder than words. Get ready for a lot of shouting."

I shook my head, but it wasn't long before he was navigating through Manhattan. The snow here had been much lighter, or they'd cleared it already. There were hints of it here and there. The roads were slick, yet he kept his speed respectable and didn't slip or slide. It wasn't long before I recognized the location.

"We're…"

"Going in the back way," Ezra said as he pulled into the garage. "I still have keys, and so do you. This is also the least likely way of getting in and out without being recognized." Once parked, he was out of the car and I stared at him as he stalked toward the elevators. When I didn't follow right away, he turned around to glare at me.

After unbuckling the seat belt, I pushed the car door open and climbed out. "Why?" The cold air in the garage seemed so much chillier after the heat in the car.

"Why do you care?" Ezra asked. "I'm giving you three days with her when you haven't seen her in weeks. When she hasn't seen you in weeks. What you should be saying is, 'Hey, thanks, Ezra. Aren't you going to get it from King over this?'"

"Except that's not what I'm saying. I'm asking why because if King finds out, it's not just us he punishes."

And I wouldn't risk Mayhem *or* her sister.

Blowing out an aggrieved breath, Ezra stomped over to me. "Pay attention. He won't be doing anything for the next three days except whatever piece of ass he has coming to visit him. He didn't even have a job for me to give you. He just stuck me with you so I'd keep you busy. This is how I keep you busy."

I frowned. "You're taking a lot of this on faith."

"No, I'm taking it on experience. You may be getting to know that piece of shit, but I have known him for a while. Since we found out who he is, I've learned a lot more. None of it I like. The point is—this is a gift. Take it. Enjoy it. Make her happy."

That rocked me because the last three words *mattered* to him. It was also the most honest he'd ever been with me.

"What are you going to be doing?"

"Other shit that I need to do. None of it matters to you. I'll have a cover story for you before you go back. I'll make sure you show up with me, and I'll take any heat he decides to deliver. The only thing you have to do is keep your phone in airplane mode while you're here."

"If he tries to reach me?"

"I said, I'll deal with it. Me being a shit he's used to, and you're supposed to follow my orders, remember?"

This was insane, and at the same time...

I pivoted to return to the car, he popped the trunk and I pulled out my bags. No wonder he hadn't really cared what I brought with me.

"Let's be absolutely clear on one thing... if this goes sideways and she gets targeted—"

"I'll offer myself up to you to beat bloody," Ezra said. "When I said she's everything, I meant it. She is. She deserves a hell of a lot more than I've given her. Today—I'm going to start fixing that."

With me.

He was giving me to her and as much as he irked me, I had to admit I wanted this weekend. As I stepped into the elevator, I fixed him with a look. "This doesn't make us friends."

"I never believed it did," he told me as he swiped a card and entered a code for the elevator. "Just call us enemies with benefits. "

I snorted, but I didn't miss Ezra's faint grin.

"Better than the alternative." Upstairs, he let me into Lainey's place and I disarmed the alarm. She hadn't changed my code. No one was there, but there was a tree and it was quiet and dark.

"She's not here."

"She'll be back in a few hours," Ezra said, as he checked his phone. "She was at Tally's for Thanksgiving, then at her grandfather's. She'll be back in the city this afternoon. Get comfortable. I'm sure there's food in the kitchen. Don't leave. Don't get seen. Have a good time—and well, don't do anything I wouldn't."

I stared at him.

"Too soon?" He smirked.

"How have you survived this long?" Because the man seemed to have a permanent death wish.

"Ask myself that every day," he admitted and then the door closed behind him. Four hours later, the elevator dinged outside and I was on my feet. I'd not left the living room. Not for a moment.

One glance at the camera revealed Mayhem arriving —alone.

I didn't bother to wait for her to get her keys out, I threw the door open and drank in the sight of her.

Fuck she was beautiful, and then she was in my arms.

CHAPTER
TWENTY-SEVEN

LAINEY

The lock of Pretty Boy's embrace threatened to crush me and I was there for it. His mouth seemed to devour mine, sucking the air from my lungs even as he gave me life. Tongues dueling, he deepened the kiss even further. Elation and fear collided when it registered he was *here* in my apartment. Was he in—

I jerked my head back and stared at him. His eyes were dark, intense, and filled with scorching heat. "Milo..."

"Pretty Boy," he corrected in a rough voice that turned my legs weak. Thank fuck, I didn't have to stand on them because I was wrapped around him.

"Pretty Boy," I said, dragging a hand up to cup his face. "You're here."

"You noticed." The tease was another stroke to the fire he'd ignited in me. "Can I go back to—"

Before he could press his lips to mine, I put my hand over his mouth, earning me raised brows.

"You're *here*—what about King? What about—"

His teeth scraped deliciously over my palm before he huffed out a breath. "Fine, you need details. Understood." With that, he turned and set me down. I wasn't proud of the fact I nearly staggered or that he put a hand on my hip to make sure I was steady before he returned to the hallway and retrieved my things. "Where do you want these?"

"I honestly don't care," I admitted.

He nodded, set them down, then closed and locked the door. A minute later, he armed the alarm system before pivoting to face me. I swore I couldn't look away. I was terrified this was a delusion and he would just vanish. Even as the thought occurred, I licked my lips.

I'd missed him.

I *missed* him so fucking much. "You're really here?"

"I'm really here—Ezra said he was gonna leave you a note."

A half-laugh, half-sob bubbled out of me. "He said he left me a present to make up for—you know that part doesn't matter. You're my present?"

All at once, Pretty Boy's whole expression gentled into a smile that bound up my willing heart and shackled it even more firmly to him than it had already been. "I got the boot from King for three days. He sent me to Ezra to work." With a half-shake of his head as though he still didn't quite believe it, he continued, "Ezra brought me here. Told me to stay out of sight."

"So it's safe for you to be here?" Relief spilled through me and Pretty Boy's eyes softened as he held out a hand to me.

"It's safe, Mayhem. You're stuck with me for three days." His shoulders dropped a fraction. "I wish I could promise you lo—"

Closing the gap between us, I damn near threw myself

at him. He caught me easily enough. In between tongue-stroking kisses, he tugged at my clothes, and I tugged at his. I wish like hell I'd worn a damn dress. As it was, he managed to unzip my boots as I got my pants undone then he was tugging my sweater up and over my head.

Laughter escaped me at the frantic nature of our actions. One of the buttons on my shirt shot away, plinking against something.

"Sorry," Pretty Boy murmured in between kisses. At least, I thought he did.

"Don't care," I gasped before yanking his shirt upward. Getting it off of him meant he had to let me go, so he dragged it up and off before he stared at me. "What?"

He gripped the shirt and broke another button off of it as it went flying. "You don't care?"

The rawness in his voice sent ripples through my whole system. "Not even a little bit," I promised. His slow, sexy grin had my pussy clenching as he pulled my shirt wide. The buttons flew like popcorn and scattered.

Laughter broke through the wild tension as I shrugged off the shirt.

"Pants off, Mayhem."

"Yes, sir," I murmured and enjoyed that possessive flash in his eyes. "Yours too."

"Oh, they're coming off, and then you're coming..."

The delicious heat his kisses had ignited began to uncoil at his words. Need and want were both vibrant demands within me. Licking my lips, I enjoyed watching him pull off his belt before he unbuttoned his jeans.

"I missed you," I whispered, gazing up into his eyes.

"I need you," he answered, echoing the same demand in my soul.

When I peeled down my leggings, he went still. I would

have complained but there was something all-consuming in the way he looked over me. As I straightened, I swore I could feel every inch of skin his gaze touched as it skated over my flesh. The bra and panties weren't special; they were more functional than anything else. Soft, black cotton, but I almost wanted to preen under his observation.

"Pretty Boy..." I beckoned, putting a hand on my hip and soaking up his attention. There was so much affection tangled with pure lust in his whiskey brown eyes as he dragged his gaze up to mine. It assuaged a hunger I barely recognized, filling up those starving parts of me that had begun to waste in his absence.

"Mayhem."

How did he do that? How did he encapsulate everything about me in that one word? It was a summation of my feelings and my desire wrapped in my need for independence and safety. I swore he saw me in a way no one else did, and I wanted to be that person, free of everything society demanded.

With Pretty Boy...

"Catch me if you can," I dared him, laughter exploding out of me as I spun on one heel and darted up the stairs. 'Cause if we fell into each other down here, I didn't think we'd ever make it to the bed.

If we had three days? I wanted every second of it with him in that bed that had already started to grow cold from his scent. His laughter chased after me, and he caught me at the door to the room. With one move, he spun me around and then we were tumbling onto my bed. His mouth dropped down to mine, swallowing my gasp, and like magic, he slid his fingers right into my panties and speared two of them inside me.

"You're already soaking for me," he said against my mouth and I arched my hips as I fisted his hair.

"Don't keep me waiting," I demanded, retaliating as he curled his fingers to stroke that spot inside of me that made my eyes cross by wrapping my hand around his cock. It was thick, the vein below it throbbed, and there was already pre-cum on the tip. I'd missed this—the connection, the closeness, the contact.

His groan answered mine as he thrust his tongue in time with his fingers. I stroked him from base to tip, teasing that hot, velvety skin as he began to rock against my hand. I had no idea who was teasing whom. Frankly, I didn't care —I just wanted more.

All at once, he pulled his fingers free as he yanked his head up. When he sucked them into his mouth, I damn near came from the pleasure on his face. "This isn't going to be slow," he warned me. "Or gentle."

"I don't need either of those..."

Then he gripped my chin and glared at me. Everything about him demanded my attention. "You *deserve* everything, Mayhem. No one gets to treat you poorly, not even you." I stilled my hand on his cock. "I want to make love to you for hours, and I very much intend to."

All the moisture in my mouth fled.

"But I need you right now, and I need you to know how badly I want you." Tears burned in my eyes at that single declaration. "And just how much I love you."

Something hot splashed on my cheek and that devastating demand in his eyes softened.

"I love you," he repeated. "I've been holding onto those words for weeks—but you deserve them."

I opened my mouth, only he didn't let me speak as he kissed me and I forgot words. I forgot everything as he pulled my panties aside, lined himself up and slammed into me. Nothing mattered except all of that muscle and strength driving into me. Every stroke threatened pain with its force as he stretched me and offered only pleasure.

Digging my nails into his shoulders, I clung to him as he pushed a thigh higher and bottomed out repeatedly. The slap of his balls against my ass just encouraged me. Our kiss was both a fight and a dance. Then he teased my clit with his fingers and I detonated.

The orgasm took me by surprise as I sobbed against him, but he didn't let up, slamming from the first, right into the second, before his pace stuttered. The liquid heat filling me up had me writhing. My awareness of him was heightened. Everywhere his skin rubbed against mine, sending off another ripple of sensation.

Then we were shuddering together. My inner muscles clamped down on his cock and he swore as he buried his face in my throat. The nip of his teeth along the column of my neck demanded awareness, but I wasn't sure I could move.

With stealthy fingers, he peeled away my bra and cupped one of my breasts. "Mayhem," he whispered hotly against my ear. "I'm nowhere close to done with you."

That sent another shudder through me and he moved, locking his lips around my nipple as I fisted his hair. He wasn't kidding. He spent the next half hour, or maybe it was an hour, torturing me with his lips, tongue, and teeth. My nipples were almost pained from the attention, and I wanted more.

When he flipped me over and dragged me backward, I was ready to be impaled all over again. The slap of skin on skin was almost as intoxicating as the praise he rained down on me.

"That's my girl," he whispered. "Fucking take every inch of me. You are so goddamn beautiful, Mayhem. So fucking perfect for me."

It was like he was intent on driving me mad, and he succeeded. We broke only for water and a shower before he pressed me up against the wall and ate me out until I damn near blacked out from the pleasure.

A nap, wrapped around each other, was perfect. Even better was opening my eyes before he did and swallowing his cock to wake him up. When my cunt was so sore, he had to bring me an ice pack, I laughed. Marlene had arrived at some point and left again. We never saw her.

Probably good. We were hardly quiet. It was the perfect bubble: my pretty boy and me. I forgot about parties and business meetings. Charities could wait. So could planning and plotting. Even my phone was somewhere downstairs. If it were a real emergency, they'd call the apartment.

I didn't want to miss one single moment. Pretty Boy even helped me decorate the tree before he took me apart beneath the lights. We slept down there for a few hours, and I woke when he lifted me up to carry me upstairs.

Our time together was going to end soon, and that awareness stole sleep from me as I lay there watching him. I didn't want to look away. We'd barely discussed...

"Stahp," he whispered, and those impossibly long lashes of his parted to let him look at me. "I can hear that fantastic mind of yours churning out all the possibilities."

"I don't want you to leave," I admitted, giving in to the selfish need I had to tell him. "I love you."

Surprise flickered across his face.

"I love having you here. I love being with you—I hate when you're gone." Even more, I despised the vulnerability; it opened me up to possible injury. Revealed a weakness that I couldn't contain, didn't want to contain. Yet, he deserved to know.

The warmth of his palm shaping against my cheek made me smile. "Love you too, Mayhem." The sleep-roughened notes in his voice just made the repeat of his declaration all the more potent. "I hate leaving you. I love that we can message, but..."

"We have to be careful." It had been like that with Em, for totally different reasons.

"I'll find a way to see you again. King barely lets *me* out of his sight. I don't want to risk him looking too closely at you."

"I hate that you have to do anything for him."

"We're going to fix this," Pretty Boy promised. "One way or another, we will take him down. This will end."

I licked my lips. I wanted to believe that—I did believe that. "It's just so damn hard."

"I know, now—tell me about Ezra."

I didn't want to talk about him, not in our finite amount of time together. Then again, Ezra also made the past couple of days possible. Blowing out a breath, I said, "Not all of it is my story, but...I will tell you as much as I can." So I told him about Ezra coming to see me, the talk, the revelations he'd made, and the fact that he promised not to run.

"But he did?" Milo lay there, studying me. No judgment lived in that question. He genuinely did seem like he wanted to understand.

"Adam showed up and—"

"They fought." He sighed.

"Yes and—no. There's a lot of unresolved resentment and feelings there."

"Reed doesn't want him anywhere near you." Pretty Boy

wasn't wrong. "But he doesn't get to make decisions for you —that said, Ezra doesn't get to hurt you."

"I think we may all end up hurting each other, but…If we want to make any of this work, I think we need to."

He nodded once. "Tell me about Bodhi."

"Oh." Somewhere this weekend, I'd mentioned going with Bodhi to Philadelphia. So I told him what I could.

"Some of it is his secret," Pretty Boy finished and I gave him a small smile.

"I trust you with my everything," I promised him. "Anything I can tell you, I will. But their secrets have to be safe too."

"Just like you will protect mine." It wasn't a question.

"Yes."

"As much as I hate to say this, I'm with Ezra and Adam. You need to stick with one of them or with Bodhi as much as you can. I don't trust King. I don't trust any of this shit that's going on, but I need you safe above all else, Mayhem. Promise me?"

"I don't know if I can trust any of them with everything… Ezra needs things from me. Adam—"

"He wants you. The man is in love with you."

That flat declaration caught me off-guard. "He says I'm his. Claiming me as a possession isn't the same thing as love."

Pretty Boy chuckled. "To a man like him? Yes, it is. Maybe it's a shitty way of saying it." When he rolled onto his back, I curled up against him and rested my head against his chest while I traced the tattoos inked there. I loved the ivy and the dancer—the one I knew was Emersyn. Even from far away, he'd inked her on his skin at different ages so he could feel close to her.

I half-wondered if he'd ink me somewhere to keep me

close—but I never wanted him to feel so far away as to think that was the only way to be near me.

"I don't necessarily like the choices they've made," Pretty Boy said. "But I've been getting to know them these past few weeks—your Adam and Ezra."

I lifted my gaze to meet his. "And?"

"Ezra has a death wish and Adam wants to control everything."

"Succinct."

"They both would die for you, though," Pretty Boy continued. "Which means sticking close to them will keep you safe."

"And Bodhi?" He was my friend. A good one.

"You two have a history?"

"I'll tell you someday."

"I'd like that."

"I'll see if I can spend time with him too—there's always Karagiani." Even as I said it, I made a face and Pretty Boy chuckled.

"Being cosseted annoys you."

"Yes," I admitted. "It does."

"Thank you for letting us do it, then."

Us. He was aligning with them, and that—was a lot. "Be safe for me?"

Because, soon, I was going to have to say goodbye, and it was the very last thing I wanted to do.

"I'd do anything for you, Mayhem."

And I'd do anything for him.

Anything.

TWENTY-EIGHT

BODHI

Arriving for the board meeting had been a choice. Of course, my father calling for a board meeting two weeks before the holidays was *also* a choice. Phillip Exeter Cavendish III. The family's need to self-fellate by naming subsequent generations after them used to baffle me. Now? It was just another kink. Not mine, though they were welcome to it.

My arrival, timed to leave less than thirty seconds before the doors closed and the board came to order, allowed me to take a seat and the meeting called before my father noticed my presence. Phillip was not pleased.

So sad...

Moving on.

Collin glanced at me from across the table, his lips twitched. The board of directors for Cavendish Pharmaceuticals was not comprised of multi-billionaires appointed or recommended by other board members. No, it was comprised of Cavendish family members.

There were exactly eleven of us who had reached the right age and stock maturity to take our seats. Mine had been secured before my eighteenth birthday. However, I wasn't allowed it until my twenty-first, at my age of majority per the stipulations in the corporate by-laws and family trust.

Phillip stared at me from where he stood, at the end of the table, his knuckles pressed against the wood as though he'd intended to knock—then had forgotten how. Next to him was Aunt Mara—Mara Cavendish Strong, Phillip's sister. To her right was their younger brother, Michael Cavendish, Collin's father. Michael's wife Lara sat to his right. Her position on the board was purely superficial, she had no right to vote outside of his block.

Collin sat next to her. To his right and at the opposite end of the table from Phillip sat Winthrop Cavendish II, my great-uncle. His son, Winthrop Cavendish III, passed away four years earlier, prompting Winthrop to begin attending again. The fourth Winthrop was in elementary school at Blue Ivy Prep in Connecticut.

To my right was Eliza Cavendish Monroe, Winthrop's eldest child and daughter. She also despised my father. That made her my second favorite at the table. To her right were Jay and David Cavendish-Frank; they were also cousins on my father's side but from one of his other female cousins. I'd lost track.

Maybe I didn't care.

Jay and David often voted as a block but didn't control a large percentage of stock. The last member of our little group sat to Phillip's left, Sophia Carsters-Cavendish. If Eliza and Collin were my favorites based on personality, Sophia was the one I respected the most. She was the only surviving member of my great-grandfather's generation, having married into the family when my great-grandfather was in his forties and she was barely nineteen.

Sophia came into the family a trophy wife for all intents and purposes. Still, she wielded considerable corporate and familial assets since my great-grandfather left a sizable chunk to her despite the fact they had no children. She was the one person in the room Phillip refused to upset, which meant she was leverage just by her very presence.

My family.

How I wished most of them were dead.

Or at least several thousand miles away from me.

"I see you decided to join us for a change, Phillip," Phillip the elder said in the chilliest of tones.

"I'm just here for the snacks," I assured him. "Dive right in."

His eyes flattened as neither Jay nor Eliza could hide their chuckles. Collin was far more circumspect. We were in agreement on how Phillip coordinated these meetings in his attempts to circumvent family oversight; I didn't need to observe his reaction.

One would think he'd give this up, but no—he was determined to ram something through. Since I was in town and I could spoil his day, I showed up. I also wanted to have a word with Eliza about Julius King. Except that was for *after* the meeting.

"Do you need to be briefed on the past few meetings you didn't grace us with your presence?"

"For the love of god and money, Phillip, do get on with it." The snap in Eliza's tone drew blood. "Your son is more than capable of reading the reports just like the rest of us, and I have no doubt he's more than adequately prepared, and if he hasn't..." She sliced a hand through the air.

My thoughts exactly.

"Fine," Phillip said, straightening with a seething expression tossed in my direction before he began to address the rest of the room. "As per the by-laws, I've called this meeting because we've been approached with a very lucrative offer that will benefit all of us with the vision to appreciate the impact."

He spent the next thirty minutes shoveling shit with a golden spade as if it would convince the majority to agree to allow an outsider access to the board and any kind of actual vested interest in the company that would enable him access to the board. The family trust existed for a reason.

"Why the hell did you call us all here for something you know we're going to say no to?" Sophia demanded when Phillip wrapped up his presentation. Despite the faintest tremor in her hands, she wore a steely expression, and it would be a mistake to think she'd lost even an ounce of her razor-sharp wit and intelligence.

"Forgive me, Aunt Sophia—"

"I will not," she told him sternly. "And don't take that tone with me. You know damn good and well the terms your great-grandfather placed on the family trust. You are also *not* the executor of it, no matter how you try to play it."

"I agree, that's why I invited you here," he told her, his tone actually gentling as if he were the supplicant, not a role he enjoyed—clearly. "This is the kind of deal that doesn't come along every day and it would benefit all of us —" He swept a look around the table. "Particularly the generation not as interested in pharmaceuticals." The last was a jab at me.

Not that I cared.

"No, you didn't *invite* us here to share this so-called 'brilliant' idea. You are required to bring the trust up to date and involve the board in any decisions. You also need more than a simple majority to make it happen. A simple majority you don't have." With that, Sophia rose, and I was on my feet a heartbeat before the other men, except my father, who just glared at her. "Don't do this again, Phillip. It's rather beneath you and makes you look like a fool and I do know how important your appearances are."

With that, she turned to leave the table and I abandoned my place to open the door for her. Sophia paused when she got to me and her smile held a gentle rebuke.

"I know," I told her. "I need to come for tea."

"You do. I haven't seen you in several months. I should be very cross with you."

"Mind if I bring a guest?" We were speaking quietly as my father glared at us, but he couldn't escape from the others demanding their own hissed explanations. Sophia controlled enough of the trust to stop anyone from doing anything she didn't like.

"Will I like her?" Sophia asked, arching her brows.

"Could be a him," I pointed out.

"Could be but isn't." She patted my cheek. "Bring her to see me. I'll tell you if she's a good match."

"Not why I'd be bringing her."

"Won't stop me," she teased, then she spared a glance back at the room. "Foolish man with stupid ideas he knows no one will accept."

"To be fair, the only two here who definitely disapproved are us, and if we weren't here..."

"True." She grinned, a wicked twinkle in her eyes. "It's a good thing we were here. Call me."

"Yes, ma'am," I said, bowing my head once as she swept out. Her assistant and escort both rose from where they'd been waiting. She had a well-trusted collection to keep her safe, and the bodyguards I'd handpicked made sure no one else in the family helped her along.

Pivoting back to the room, I found Eliza studying me. I raised my brows and nodded to the door. The relief on her face was palpable. She gathered her bag and left the others without a word. I opened the door to let her out then followed.

"Not yet," she said to the man who rose as she came out before she glanced at me. "Where do you want to chat?"

"There's another conference room," I said, leading her down the hallway. Phillip would expect us to go upstairs to the offices or somewhere else. Just another conference room wouldn't occur to him.

It was quieter inside and a little chillier. I checked the thermostat to nudge it upwards as Eliza rubbed her arms. "What is your father up to?"

"Probably a fast capital scheme to turn some assets liquid since the trust keeps an iron grip on the rest of the profits." It wouldn't surprise me. "Collin said he's been seeing someone."

Her nose wrinkled. "Gold digger?"

"If you had to spend time with him, you'd want a payout too." I leaned back against the table.

"You have a point." She sighed. "Sophia can only road-block him for so long. He's already floating a competency hearing."

Unsurprising.

"We'll deal with it. Besides, Sophia is more capable of taking care of herself."

"And surrounded by security you vetted."

"This is also true. You should check into yours," I reminded her. "Sophia's never declared her heir or the final terms of Phillip the First's final edict with regard to the trust because that was only given to her."

"I can take care of myself. Now, you didn't want to talk to me about this."

"No," I said. "But it's good to know where we stand."

"Directly in your father's path." She folded her arms. "Now, what can I do for you?"

"What do you know about a man named Julius King?"

Her lips flattened and her nose crinkled. "I've heard the name. New money. Unsavory type. Does a lot of—investing to divest. Corporate raider behavior. Tries to act like an angel investor or venture capitalist. Moderate success, not a Ponzi scheme as far as I know, but...not our type."

Which meant he didn't travel in these circles as often.

"There were rumors, of course," she continued.

"Rumors?"

"That he was a long-lost son or one born on the wrong side of the marriage. The outsider who isn't."

"But only rumors."

"Yes. Only rumors. Though he very much wants to be our type, and to be one of us," she said. "Almost too much. Avarice is a harsh mistress; when one desires something to the exclusion of all else, it can make one's choices questionable."

I didn't disagree.

"Any idea where the rumors started?" Cause sometimes, rumors could play in the favor of the one they were about.

"Darling, I have no idea. You know how much attention I pay to gossip."

Eliza had been amongst those in charge of social calendars for the elite for so long, I rather doubted there was anyone she didn't know. In this case, she probably just didn't care.

"What's your interest in him?" A fair question.

"Not certain, entirely. He's involved with associates. I want to know if I need to shelter them or not."

"Well, I probably wouldn't be opposed to a small investment, though I certainly wouldn't be inviting him to supper."

Which meant, he might be a curiosity but otherwise not worth the time.

"Anything else, dear?"

"Margareta Waldemar."

"Oh, now that's a name. Charming woman. Very charming. East European, I believe. Aristocrat. Definitely more our kind of people but—insular. She doesn't seek out approval."

Which meant Eliza was dying to know more about her. "Any idea what business she's in?"

"Oh darling, I can't imagine it's anything too scandalous. Probably railroads or transportation. There's every chance it's real estate—why?"

"Curiosity."

"You are being quite the cat, young man."

"Well, I have nine lives to spend, I might as well have some fun doing it."

Her expression softened and she chuckled. "I suppose that's true, but I worry about you. It's well past the time you settled down and started on the next generation before your father tries to disinherit you."

"Settling down and children are not currently high on my list, nor will the family ever be the reason I do it."

"No, too much of your mother in you." The genuine affection populating her tone made it a compliment. "I understand, but I think it's time I started directing a few fine young ladies in your direction."

It might be time to get committed again. I shook my head. "I wish you wouldn't," I said. "But I will allow you your fun." I pressed a kiss to her cheek, and she halted me with a hand on my arm. She searched my face with a narrow-eyed gaze.

"You have found someone."

"Hmm?"

"Don't play coy with me. You only let me have my fun when you know it won't matter... who is she?"

"It's always good to see you, Aunt Eliza," I told her, keeping my own counsel. "If you hear anything on the others... let me know?"

"I will," she said, her word a promise. "And I'll discover this woman's identity. She must be special if you're guarding her so close."

I chuckled. "Enjoy yourself. You do like puzzles."

"I do," she admitted. "Now I'm not sure if there is a girl or if you're just teasing me."

"And that's half the fun."

Shouting came from the original boardroom, and I turned away to head for the elevators. Collin could brief me later. Eliza's opinion about King intrigued me.

Possible insider? Or was that his game to build relationships?

Now I really was curious.

CHAPTER
TWENTY-NINE

ADAM

The club was the best place for this lunch. It was public, nothing to hide, and we both had reasons to be there. Well, to be fair, I wasn't sure Hardigan even had a membership, but his association with King should net him access. If it didn't, I somehow suspected Lainey still had him on her plus-one list.

The knowledge didn't burn as much as it might have once. Still... it aggravated. No amount of truce-making or peace-building would change that fact. Ezra avoided me, and Hardigan wanted to do lunch. Both men were inextricably tied up with my girl.

Mine.

Possessiveness fisted in my gut. I arrived nearly fifteen minutes early. I'd booked a table in the art gallery. It was quieter than the main lunch area, but we'd definitely be on display. The placement of the tables, however, accommodated a different kind of privacy option.

The weight of the gun under my jacket offered a small

comfort even as the feeling of eyes on me kept my head on a swivel as I took my seat and ordered for one. The reservation was actually for one. Hardigan entered the dining room below as the waitress brought me an iced coffee and an appetizer of breadsticks.

A cold snap had officially closed its fist around us and dropped the temperatures to bitter levels. More ice than snow filled the forecasts. An inconvenience, although stores and restaurants still remained open along with most forms of transportation. I kept an eye on it to make sure Lainey wasn't trapped in the city alone if the weather turned truly bad.

Hardigan appeared in my periphery as the hostess guided him toward a table near my own.

Showtime.

I rose to my feet. "Hardigan," I said by way of greeting. His steps slowed as he fixed his gaze on me.

"Reed."

The neutral tone didn't suggest any enjoyment in my presence. It was almost funny.

Almost.

I extended a hand and he eyed it for one second too long, just enough to make it appear he wasn't a fan before clasping it in a brief handshake. We each had our roles to play.

"Meeting someone?" The question from him suggested only the merest of polite veneers.

"Actually," I said. "No. Dining alone. You?"

He grimaced. "Same."

"How unfortunate for us." Etiquette, of course, dictated I invite him to join me. For my part, Waldemar wanted me to make friends. A goal, in all honesty, I hadn't been avidly pursuing.

"Unfortunate?"

"Yes, we're both dining alone, which means I should invite you to join me." It was almost like putting on some cheap pantomime for the eager audience that was the hostess. She was likely on someone's payroll; she netted a nice sum from me when she provided me with Lainey's scheduled reservations, so... I could hardly fault her.

"Should," Hardigan said with the merest hint of humor. "We should do a lot of things. I don't see any reason why *should* or *could* means we have to."

I chuckled, then gestured to the table. "We'll likely keep eyeing each other and trying to assess what the other is up to. Might as well be at the same table while we do it and save ourselves some time."

He sighed. "You know, we don't like each other. We barely tolerate each other in social situations where it's required. Why force it if we don't have to?" There was playing a role, and then there was roasting me over a fire.

Dick.

"Because never let it be said, I can't handle a challenge." I met his gaze and held it. Message sent.

The corners of his mouth tilted upward. "I don't back down." Message received and he volleyed back his own.

"Then join me," I invited in a slightly more civilized version of *prove it*.

He made a show of leaving me hanging for a few seconds longer than necessary before he glanced at our audience, the hostess. "I'll be joining Mr. Reed." Then he put his hand on the chair with its back to the wall. It left us seated more like a V than across from each other.

"Of course, Mr. Hardigan. We'll get a second setting for you right away." She snapped her fingers and my waitress hurried over with a second setting and the place was set before he'd even taken a seat.

"What would you like to drink, sir?" The waitress asked.

"Beer. Something domestic and in the bottle," Hardigan told her. "Then whatever Mr. Reed is having for lunch."

"Of course," she said, then glanced at me. "More coffee, or would you like to choose something different?"

"I'll stick with my coffee for now." I didn't want any alcohol to muddy the waters. She left us, and Hardigan snapped out his napkin before draping it over his lap. The clothing suited someone who belonged at the club; nothing else about him did.

"Problem?" He barely looked at me as he turned his attention to the room below. It hadn't escaped my notice that his gaze never rested, even if his head didn't swivel. I suppose it would be difficult to relax in this atmosphere.

"Always," he said. "Isn't that why we're doing this?"

His lips barely moved and the pitch of his voice wouldn't carry past the table. Our waitress returned with his beer—in the bottle—and a glass of water. She also brought more breadsticks.

Once we were alone again, I reached for a breadstick and broke it in half. The smell of freshly baked bread filled the air. "Any trouble getting away?"

"Nope," he said, tipping the beer bottle up for a long drink. "He took a weekend to himself and sent me off with Ezra."

I shifted to sit forward, wiping my fingers on the napkin to cover my surprise. I wanted to ask how he was doing. I needed to leash that desire, firmly, but at the same time—it was Ezra. "What does King have him doing?"

It was a guarded response and Hardigan just shook his head. "Your guess is as good as mine. He left me at Lainey's for the weekend. To be fair, I know it was partly to make up to her, but it was also to get me out of the way."

Goddammit, Ezra.

"He's fine," Hardigan continued. "As far as I can tell. No bruises or open wounds."

That was something, I supposed.

"He was feeling pretty cocky, too."

I snorted. "That's just Ezra. He can stare a man with a gun to his head right in the eye and crack a joke or insult without a fucking care in the world for whether he pulls the trigger or not."

"Brave or stupid?" Not an unfair question.

"I don't think there's a distinction some days."

The food arrived shortly. I'd gone for clam chowder. They made it very thick. I could order a club sandwich to go with it if I were still hungry, but the breadsticks and the soup were enough. I preferred to keep it light.

"Then why do you let him run like a loose cannon?" The question caught me off guard. Hardigan studied me briefly as he took another drink before resuming his study of the room below us. I almost wanted to ask what he was looking for, but I kept that thought to myself.

"I didn't have much of a choice," I said after a long moment.

"That's an excuse," Hardigan challenged me again. "Not a reason. Anyway—" Before he could continue, his eyes narrowed, and I kept it natural as I followed his glance.

Fuck.

"He didn't have reservations," I warned. I'd checked. King wasn't even supposed to be in the city today.

Shifting his hand to the inside of his jacket, Hardigan pulled out his phone. "He was supposed to be on a flight..."

"He's heading this way." I took a long drink of the coffee

and had my expression schooled before King approached. The scant few seconds of warning afforded by the view definitely did us a favor.

For his part, Hardigan's expression didn't shift. His poker face was impeccable.

"Gentlemen," King said as he approached with our hostess. "I didn't know you two were dining together."

Hardigan shrugged. "I came here to work and ran into him. He invited me to eat."

"So I heard," King said, but his gaze wasn't on Hardigan anymore. No, it was fixed on me and there was nothing friendly in those eyes. If he could get away with it, I didn't doubt that he'd pull his gun and shoot me where I was sitting. "What's your excuse?"

"I don't need an excuse," I told him with a faint smirk. "Emersyn and I are close, remember?" His eyes narrowed. "She's a very dear friend. So is Liam. This is her brother and one of his best friends, of course I'd look out for him."

The pleasant mask slipped for a spare few seconds. A reveal behind the curtain that let his malevolence shine through. "So that's what you're going with?"

"My friendship with Emersyn has been worth the price I had to pay." Was I baiting him? Absolutely. His fury at me would keep Hardigan in the clear. We were still working out the trust between us. The fact King targeted Andrea hadn't been lost on me. Nor that Hardigan had taken the hit for *my* sister.

Reminding King I had a better relationship with his daughter than he did? Well? That was just a perk. The waitress showed up with another setting and King took the seat opposite me.

"You should care about what you choose to aggravate me with, Reed." The warning in King's voice wasn't subtle, nor was he making excuses for it. "You've been allowed a lot of rope. Don't mistake the leniency for forgiveness."

"I'd never make that mistake with you. Just as you shouldn't think that your position affords you any conditions that I'll continue to respect. Our social contract ended when you gave that order."

"Maybe we should—"

"Don't try to cover for him, son. Your sister may care about him, but she doesn't need him. She would get over it."

I snorted. "You keep telling yourself that."

"I don't have to—" King glanced at the room below and a faint smile touched his lips. "There are so many other ways to make you suffer."

Leopold Benedict entered with Lainey. Her cheeks were red and flushed, as was her nose. The heavy sweater dress she wore, along with the boots, was an elegant look, but she was noticeably still cold. They were guiding them towards a table next to the fire.

During the time it took them to move across the room, the waitress returned with a drink for King and Hardigan's neutral expression had turned to one far less friendly. King, though, he watched *me*. Did I get his point? Did I see exactly who he would target?

"What do you want?"

"From you?" King chuckled. "You know what I wanted, but now...you've created a new problem. You know how I feel about problems."

"You know how I feel about threats against what is mine." He'd targeted her once before. I could pretend I didn't care all I wanted, except he'd used her as leverage from the beginning. "There is no gain for me in you continuing to survive."

Right now, it might be worth the jail sentence if I just stood up and executed him. I could practically picture it.

"Yet, any move you make against me might cost you far more than you think—and even more than you'd be willing for her to pay."

Threat. Counter-threat.

Move. Counter-move.

Did he have a nuclear option? A failsafe? It was the one thing we didn't know. But we would figure it out.

"You know, you can only use those threats so often before someone calls you on that bluff." I rose to my feet and dropped the napkin into the seat.

"Are you feeling lucky?" King challenged.

"Enjoy the rest of your lunch, Hardigan. I'll give your regards to Emersyn when I call her later."

Was I planning on calling her? No. But King's whole expression tightened. Neither of us was blinking, and neither of us was getting off this track.

And he'd just threatened Lainey.

Again.

With that, I left the two and headed downstairs. I needed the excuse to walk away or would have just shot him and to hell with the consequences. Across the room, Lainey leaned forward and smiled at something her grandfather said to her. Her gaze tracked to mine for a split second, and her brow tightened.

I shook my head.

Not now.

Not here.

But I would see her soon.

Her and Ezra both.

It was time he stopped fucking running.

CHAPTER
THIRTY

LAINEY

The brutal cold had turned even more frigid. Ice had become a daily addition to the view, even from my high-rise apartment. A sheen of glittering frost kissed the city surfaces. It made me cold simply looking at it, yet business didn't halt because city transport was closed.

Zoom, email, text messages, and Slack allowed meetings to occur at every level. Creatives enjoyed the chance to work from home. The admin staff could clear most of their tasks in the morning and then enjoy some downtime in the afternoons. It wasn't the perfect situation, but it allowed us to touch base with operations and associates around the globe.

While Benedict had amassed wealth and influence from the late 1700s onward within the continental United States, investments and agreements actually linked us to a half a dozen other countries for various operations. While a dozen more courted us to bring in the dynamism of our engineers and more.

"Mr. Benedict," John Dryden, the current vice president overseeing development, spoke up on a call he'd remained silent throughout. "I think there are some benefits to expanding our interests. There are fewer regulations we'd have to worry about, but we could also take advantage of the need for new roads, railways, and transportation in order to structure deals and tax breaks that are more beneficial to us. We would have to build it into the contracts—"

"And we can discuss it next year," Grandfather said, his tone brokering no disagreement. "Anything else?"

No one offered up a peep of argument.

"Finish up your projects, enjoy the holidays with your families. We'll meet again in January." With his pronouncement, the executives fell off the call one at a time until it was just the two of us and his secretary. "Thank you, Johanna. Enjoy your holidays."

"You too, Leopold and Lainey. I will see you both in January." Then she ran off, leaving us alone.

I didn't say anything; I just waited. The video call gave me a solid view of him, and his expression was grave. Something held his attention, so I let him pull the threads loose he wanted to pursue.

"Lewis," he finally said, focusing on me. "Thoughts?"

"He's shopping elsewhere. He has no intentions of finishing out the next fiscal quarter if he can help it. He's bored. Feels under appreciated. Thinks we should be asking more from him and, according to him, more power."

"Worth keeping?" His absolute lack of disagreement with my assessment didn't make me smile. I knew what to look for. Grandfather had spent years training me with these types of exercises.

"No," I said. "In fact, Martinez in his division does ninety percent of the job now for far less pay and zero accolades. He does it because he cares about the work and the people who work for him. I'd be shocked if Lewis could name anyone in his division that isn't a direct report."

Grandfather chuckled. "Martinez... bootstraps. Got his business degree at night school. Started on the factory floors and worked his way up."

"He appreciates the work, but more, he respects the people he works with..." I'd only met him twice, but I'd read all of his reports.

"Wagner," Grandfather said, moving on.

"She's—difficult."

"Explain."

"She's having an issue with someone else in her direct report line—although I can't tell if it's a power imbalance from below or above. She's not happy, though. Her work isn't suffering yet, but—"

"But." Grandfather didn't elaborate. "I want you to meet with her in the New Year. Find out what is happening with her. You're young, you're female, she'll see you as a chick to take under her wing and benefit from her experience."

"You want me to maintain the power differential?" Because, at the end of the day, I worked directly for one man in our company and reported to one man. Everyone else reported to us.

"You decide," he said after a long, thoughtful moment. "If she won't tell us what's going on, there's more than a power imbalance, there's a lack of trust."

"Don't be so stubborn," I said. "She's one of three women, not named Benedict, who have achieved the level of success she has. Women don't achieve that level by complaining about the men around them..."

His expression shifted and I was suddenly the focus of all that attention. "You think she's being harassed?"

"I don't know. But I can't dismiss it. I also can't dismiss that she might be the harasser. This is all supposition at the moment. I don't doubt her loyalty, she isn't looking to leave us. However, I don't believe she would ever willingly confess to any issues within the company to anyone."

"She'll take care of it herself."

"I would." Those two words earned me another sharp look.

"If any man in this company—"

I raised a hand. "Grandfather, I'm fine. More than capable of looking after myself."

His expression darkened. "Expand."

"No," I told him, and his eyes narrowed, but I didn't yell, argue, or complain. I just told him, 'no'. Finally, he let out a harsh chuckle.

"Stubborn girl."

"I am who you raised me to be."

That earned me a snort and a look of affection. "Calling me stubborn?"

"If the appellation fits." I grinned and he chuckled.

"Are you coming to Der Sonne for Christmas?" It sounded more like a command than a question, but I understood.

"Yes, for some of it. But I'm also going to Waltham Corners for Andrea."

Dislike filtered through his expression. I met his gaze evenly. This was a very old argument—one of the few where I'd held my ground and never retreated. Andrea was my sister. Her last name didn't matter to me. She needed me, and I would damn well be there.

He huffed out a breath. "Invite her over."

I raised my brows. "You don't have to do that."

"You were planning on inviting her anyway," he retorted, the disgruntlement almost disguising his smile. "I noticed the new horses."

"She loves them," I reminded him. "Apparently, Harper was selling her favorite, so Adam bought her and had her delivered to us."

Honestly, that revelation seemed to sour him further. "Invite her over the day after Christmas. You'll want to see her for a couple of hours on Christmas Day. Have her come to the house for Boxing Day."

"Will you join us?"

"Don't press your luck," he scolded.

"That's not an answer." I would never understand how he could cut her off for her last name alone, and I wouldn't pretend to understand. She was his granddaughter every bit as much as I was.

"Where's that Hardigan boy? Will you be bringing him?"

"Unfortunately, he is otherwise committed for the season." It didn't matter that he was making a deflection or a distraction. "Maybe in the new year."

He eyed me for a moment. "I'll join you for lunch with the girl if you tell me what is going on with Reed and Hardigan."

"That's an opening volley," I said. "Let's discuss it over drinks next week. We'll see if we can come to terms."

Now, a genuine smile chased away his earlier concern. "That's my girl. Keep me on my toes."

"I'll see you soon, Grandfather. Love you."

"Love you, darling girl." Then the call ended and I sat back. Exhaustion wore on me. Grandfather had mentioned Pretty Boy a couple of times, more subtly, but he couldn't be happy with my responses if he was coming at me directly.

I checked the time and picked up my phone as Marlene appeared with more coffee. "That was a long meeting."

"End of the year ones tend to be." Executive bonuses were going out and that would soften the sour grapes for those who had to table their agendas until later. Meetings were always exhausting. "What about you? When do you leave to go see your daughter and your grandchildren?"

Marlene gave me a stern look. "Not for another week. Are you so eager to be rid of me?"

"Absolutely not. I'm going to have to fend for myself and just heat the magnificent meals you leave me. Don't think I'm not aware of your plans to fully stock everything *before* you go and that you've already called out to Der Sonne to make sure they do a delivery before I come back from the holidays."

"I would never presume to tell you such stories," Marlene said with a great deal of affection. "Finish your coffee. You have that appointment for alterations on the dress since you've lost weight."

Oh, there was the scold.

"Wood and Mr. Karagiani are on their way. They will ring up when they are here. You also said you wanted to set up another hair appointment before the holidays. She can't come until Monday, but if you want to go to her, she can fit you in on Thursday."

"I don't mind waiting, but I also don't want her coming here if the weather is terrible, so can you let her know we'll play it by ear? If I have to, I can see Jewels when I'm at Der

Sonne. That's more than enough time to get everything done before the party."

"I'll take care of it. Drink your coffee." She took the tray of half-eaten food away with just the barest look of reproval. My lack of appetite the past couple of months had been remarked upon more than once. She was not a fan. Today, I'd simply gotten caught up in the meeting and forgotten to eat.

Now? I was thinking about everything else. I glanced at my phone now that I was alone and opened the app. There was a message from Pretty Boy waiting for me and a shiver went through my whole body.

Pretty Boy: *What do you want for Christmas, Mayhem?*

I almost snorted aloud. That was so easy.

Me: *You.*

I somehow didn't think he'd get to escape from King again anytime soon. I still owed Ezra a thank you for helping us make that happen. Still...

Me: *What do you want?*

I stared at the messages. They wouldn't vanish until he read them and his was already gone. Missing him had become a permanent part of me. Forcing myself to close the app, I sent a message to Ezra asking him to call me.

A part of me wanted to invite him to come see me, but chasing wasn't working. It was time to start luring. I flicked a look to the flowers on the table near the door. It was a stunning arrangement, including a card with a date and a time.

The fact it was only signed A wasn't lost on me.

They were all making me crazy. Although there was one I hadn't heard from, so I sent a message to Trouble. A check-in. I wanted to make sure he was also alright. His search with regard to his mother left me with a lot of questions. Then Tally and Andrea seemed to take turns blowing up my phone with their talk of the holidays, presents, and shopping.

Honestly, it was probably the distraction I needed.

An hour later, Wood picked me up in the garage rather than out front. Karagiani met me in the lobby and took the elevator down with me. Dress loaded, I climbed into the back.

"Are you sure we're okay with the weather?" The ice and snow had added freezing rain to the rather miserable mixture outside.

Wood flashed me an easy smile. "It looks a lot worse than it is. But we've got this. It's a few blocks, and we'll take our time."

"Thank you, Wood."

Once I was settled in, seatbelt on, Wood headed up and out of the garage. He wasn't wrong about it looking worse. From above, it had a frosted city effect. From down here, it was more icy hell. There weren't many people on the sidewalks. Some stores were open, but not all of them.

Delivery drivers seemed to be out and even one guy on an electric bicycle. That just could not be pleasant, even all bundled up. I was in a coat and gloves and in the back of a warm car, and it was still giving me the shivers. If I didn't need the dress taken in a little, I would have skipped this. However, we weren't going to have much time with so many preparing for the Fire and Ice party that was just a week after Christmas.

As promised, Wood went slow. Except more than once, there was a sensation of sliding as we took a corner. Even focusing on my breathing didn't keep me as calm as I would have liked.

Wood was a skilled driver, he could handle it. I didn't

need to be the one behind the wheel. He clearly had more experience than I did...

I chanted that on repeat as we slowed near the next light, but it turned green. Wood didn't speed up or hit the brakes. Yet the blow from the back knocked us forward. Metal shrieked, and then we drifted, literally sliding sideways, and I forgot how to breathe.

The accident dominoed as one vehicle after another slid into each other. The echo of crunching metal and jolting force resounded until we came to a sudden and abrupt stop. The impact had me scraping my tongue on my teeth and blood filled my mouth.

THIRTY-ONE

MILO

Another tedious day in hell had gotten worse. During one of the breaks, I'd gone to comfort myself. King was distracted, and I needed a minute. Today's meetings weren't just business as usual. Nor were the other people in that conference room self-aggrandizing blue bloods. I didn't know those men. I'd never met any of them personally before, but I knew their type.

Violence was their business. Blood was their currency. They were here negotiating *terms* with King. Terms of a possible partnership. A street read told me I didn't have enough information to pick a side. Nor had King seen it fit to inform me who called the meeting, just that we had it.

I was missing a lot of pieces. It was also the first time in weeks that something looking like leverage had fallen into my lap. Then I opened the app to see if she'd read my messages to find her responses. The first two were fine, but the third damn near erased them from existence.

Mayhem: I'm all right.

That was it. Three words.

My stomach dropped and my spine went cold. I threw caution to the wind and called her, but the call failed to connect.

Three times.

Liam was my next call.

"Easy," he said when I gritted out the words. "Take a breath, give me five minutes before you lose your shit."

"Just find out she's okay—for real."

"Then what happened," Liam said, understanding underscoring every single syllable. Why else would she send me the assurance before I'd even heard anything? What the fuck was there to hear? "I got this. Hang on. I'm not hanging up."

That—helped. Liam's assurance kept me focused and breathing, as the murmur of his voice carried. Though he asked for five minutes, it took an eternity and under three for him to come back.

"She's at the hospital in Midtown."

I forgot how to breathe.

"There was a car accident. She's a little shaken up—" He paused. "Yes, I'm talking to him now. Let me brief him. Just stay right there..."

"Are you talking to her?" I asked.

"Contact at the hospital. They have eyes on her. She's fine, shaken up."

"If she's *fine*, why is she at the hospital?" I tried to picture the geography of Manhattan in my head. What hospitals were in Midtown?

"Her driver is hurt. She has another guy with her, he has a cut on his forehead but refuses to separate from her. Contact thinks he's a bodyguard."

Relief had my shoulders drooping abruptly. "She's really alright?"

"Far as they can see. You want me to talk to her personally? I can call Hellspawn, if you want the cover."

I wanted to be the one who spoke to her. I blew out another breath. "No, that's good, she's okay. I'll get a message to her."

"Okay, what else do you need?"

"What's happening?" Kellan Traschel's voice filtered in from the background. Liam must be at the Clubhouse, or maybe they were at the garage. There was some comfort in picturing them in the home they'd all built, the businesses they'd had to rebuild, and the town the Vandals claimed as territory. As far as I knew, King had pulled his interests from Braxton Harbor.

King.

Even as I listened to Liam fill Kellan in, I wasn't focusing on them so much anymore.

Car accident.

"When I was eight... I was in a car accident. It wasn't pretty," Mayhem said. "I had nightmares for months about it. But Grandfather was right there, and he helped. I got over it and then...I guess I just haven't thought about it in a while."

"Okay," I said slowly, studying her. There was an intensity about her as she recounted the accident. It was as though she was reliving that moment. "What happened?"

"I always thought it was just an accident. Car ran a light and t-boned the car I was in; there was a lot of noise, broken glass, and a horn that never seemed to stop blaring, though they said it cut off at some point—maybe I heard it in my head. Anyway, the driver died and it took them hours to get me out of the car."

That sounded horrific.

"Today, Ezra told me that accident wasn't an accident."

"What?"

"It was leverage—Julius King, as in The King, had made his approach to Adam about tapping him for Bay Ridge Royals. Bringing him into the society, and utilizing him. Adam apparently wasn't interested, and the king warned him that bad things happened that could have been prevented."

"Then you were in a car accident."

She lifted her shoulders. "I had no idea it was related. They were fourteen? And I had no idea...but that was how he got them to agree. To keep me safe, and I honestly don't even know what to think about it."

Was King capable of having an eight-year-old killed? No doubt existed within me. But Mayhem struggled with the idea that she'd been used as part of the method to keep Adam and Ezra under control and loyal.

And even more, she struggled with the fact the idiots had punished her by pushing her away so she wouldn't look like leverage. Being an asshole to save someone seemed great on paper, but it was absolute bullshit in practice. If nothing else, finding Ivy with the Vandals proved that point to me. I'd been so focused on getting her away to where I thought was somewhere safer, I didn't realize how hard I was shoving her away from all of us.

Thankfully, Ivy and Mayhem seemed made out of the same stubborn stuff, and my baby sister pretty much told me to go get fucked. I'd thank her for it, but she was already too cocky. "Their choices are theirs," I told Mayhem, wrapping her up in a hug and pressing a kiss to her temple. "I know you hate what they did, but given the same set of options, I know you..."

Her little sigh answered me. Yes, she would have done the same.

So would I.

I still would and had. Mayhem was in a car accident *again* just a handful of days *after* King dropped into my lunch with Adam? The implied threat he'd set on the table hadn't been lost on me or Adam. The test of whether King would find out about the "casual" lunch had reaped greater results than either of us anticipated.

We were being watched. However, his concern made him change his plans to return to find out what we were doing? To make sure we knew he knew? The stink of his machinations was on everything.

Now Mayhem had been hurt.

"Keep me updated," I said to Liam abruptly. "I have something I need to take care of."

"Raptor," Liam warned. "Think before you act."

"That's my line," I reminded him. "I have thought." With that, I hung up and shoved the phone into my pocket. Leaving the bathroom, I strode down the hall toward the conference room. I'd ducked in there just for the privacy. The women's bathroom had been empty since there were no women at this meeting or even on the damn floor.

I wanted a place to check where I wouldn't be observed. The lack of other employees on the floor wasn't suspicious. King's security, never far away, were stationed at the elevators along with our "guest's" security. I didn't slow as I walked right into the conference room.

King was locked in conversation with Carmine Bruni. The anger threading through me refused patience. I crossed the room, ignoring everyone else. My approach captured both men's attention and King shot me a look.

"Excuse me, Mr. Bruni," I said, my tone as polite as the boiling for violence in my blood allowed. "I need a word with Mr. King."

"It can wait," King said, but I cut him off with a shake of my head.

"No, it can't." I fired all three words like bullets, which snared King's attention and his frown.

"Take a moment," Bruni said generously. "I need to make some calls. If you don't mind leaving us the room."

King was not thrilled but he nodded. "Of course, you may sweep it for surveillance if you like, but I did turn it off."

"As you stated, and as you have offered the information freely, to question it would be to question your honor." Bruni gave him a bland look. Just because he said it might, didn't mean he wouldn't do it.

"I never look at pragmatism or good business as anything to do with honor." King nodded. "We'll keep this brief."

Then King motioned for me to lead the way. I was more than happy to oblige. I stalked out of the conference room, not that he followed *immediately*. Instead, he strolled out like he had all the time in the world. After he closed the doors to the room, he turned to me, shaking his head.

"I have an office on this floor." Then he walked away and it forced me to follow him. Fine. Whatever. Once we were in the room and the door was closed, he faced me. "You better have a very good reason for that interruption, son. We were on the cusp of a profitable deal and could have lost momentum now."

"I don't give a shit about your deal," I told him as I stalked forward. "I want to know what the fuck you were thinking with the accident."

He pulled out a handkerchief from his pocket and dabbed at his face almost casually before giving me a puzzled look. "You'll need to be a little clearer, son. What accident?"

It was like throwing gasoline onto burning coals. "Lainey Benedict's car accident. She's at the hospital. What the hell were you thinking?"

"I wasn't thinking anything at all…" King said, pocketing the handkerchief like we were at a casual lunch. "Accidents do happen, son. Is she well?"

"Like you care."

"I'm not the one who brought it up." The casual ease in his manner and the bland delivery just pissed me off more. "So, I take it she is well if she called you about an accident."

"She didn't call me," I corrected him. "I heard it from a friend. Why do it? Why lash out at her? Adam walked away when you issued that threat, and you and I have a deal."

"We do," King agreed with me. "And frankly, with the weather outside, I imagine there were a great many accidents. Maybe Miss Benedict shouldn't be venturing out into dangerous territory."

For some reason, that comment lit the final fuse, detonating the last vestiges of my patience. The smirk on his face and the absolute lack of care on display left a red haze over my vision, and I gave in to an urge that I'd had for months.

Years, really. Years since the bastard looked me in the eye and told me to get my shit together and follow him.

Years since he walked out.

Years since he abandoned us.

Years since he'd begun to actively try to destroy my life.

I didn't think it was possible to hate this man more.

Then Mayhem said she was all right after another fucking car accident. I lashed out, and he tried to block my fist as if he expected it, but my left was followed by a much faster right, and I knocked him on his ass. The satisfaction of pain in my knuckles from where they smashed into his jaw was miserable compensation for the years of hell this man had inflicted.

"Well, well," King said, pulling out that handkerchief again to mop at the blood escaping the new split on his lip. "There's my boy. All that raw fury and rage. I knew you had it in you..."

"Fuck you," I said. "Why did you hurt her?"

"I have no quarrel with Lainey Benedict," he told me as he stood. His smirk returned as he studied his blood on the handkerchief then looked at me again. "Accidents do happen, Milo. They happen because of bad weather, poor choices, and even trusting the wrong people."

I flexed my hands.

"Our agreement was you come to work for me. You come to learn the business. You become a Royal and you walk away from her. You've upheld that end of the bargain, haven't you?" The last was a challenge. "Unless there's something you're not telling me about her. If that's the case, son, you and I have a much larger problem than why is she in the hospital."

I wanted to hit him again.

I wanted to hit him until he didn't get up again.

Fisting my control and not my hands took every ounce of effort. King seemed to study me for a moment and when I finally spread my fingers and backed up a step, he narrowed his eyes.

He seemed determined to project an air of non-involvement. The problem was, I didn't believe him. "If anything happens to her, if she so much as catches a cold, I'm going to think you were involved. You're not a subtle man. You're nowhere near as refined as you pretend to be. So between you and me," I said, grinding out every word in as level a tone as I could manage, "our deal included her safety. You don't get to use her as leverage or to send a message, ever again, clear?"

"Be very careful, son," he told me, all traces of civility gone. This was better. This kind of honesty. It was like staring into a darker, more twisted mirror of myself. "If I wanted to punish you, I have plenty of ways to do it that don't involve accidents. Maybe you need to be reminded of your place."

"Keep your hands off of her." I didn't care about his threats. "I don't give a shit what Reed or Graham do. I don't care if your coffee is too cold in the morning. Don't even look in her direction."

"That's your final word?"

Fuck it. "Yes, because next time, I won't be talking."

I'd just kill him, and to hell with the consequences.

THIRTY-TWO

LAINEY

The hospital was busy. The ice storm had caused numerous accidents. The couple in the car that hit mine was also being treated here. I'd called our lawyer to ensure we covered all of the medical expenses. The police had been through and there had been questions. I'd ridden with Wood in the ambulance, though he'd complained the whole time.

Karagiani stayed with the car until it could be collected. Though we'd been in the emergency room for a few hours, Wood seemed to be in good spirits. At the moment, we were just waiting for his—

"Where is she?" The demand in that voice carried across the busy emergency room. Curtains were all that separated each bed in a nod to privacy. They did nothing to block the sound. If someone didn't answer him...

I was already on my feet when Karagiani pulled the curtain aside to let Ezra charge in. His hair was violently askew and damp, his cheeks red, and his lips shiny. There was a wildness in his eyes that made me want to soothe him. His clothes, like his hair, were also damp. Even the hems of his pants were wet and he had on dress shoes.

"Where is your coat?" I managed to get out before Ezra wrapped me in a fierce hug. The chill of his shirt against me tightened my nipples to hard points. His hands were like ice where they rested against my back, invading the otherwise warm cocoon of my sweater. Rather than pull away, I hugged him more tightly.

Because Ezra was shaking.

I caught Karagiani's eye over Ezra's shoulder and flicked a look to the curtain. He dropped it closed immediately, giving us the illusion of privacy. That was all it was too, an illusion. Wood lay in the bed just a couple of feet away, and there were numerous patients and medical staff moving around us.

Conversations hummed, rising and falling, against a backdrop of machines beeping, intercom calls, and the swish of electronic doors opening and closing. The sounds washed over me as Ezra's arms flexed, threatening to crush me. I ran my hand up his back.

"I'm here," I murmured. "I'm fine." When I would have pulled back to show him, he dug his fingers in to keep me still as if he couldn't bear to release me. I returned the ferocity of his hug. If he needed this, then I would be there.

I hadn't seen him in weeks. Not since he fled. Here he was, bursting into the hospital, because I was here. The touch of his lips to my throat was feathering and light as he traced a kiss to my jaw. "Kotyonok," he damn near whispered the word. Frankly, I wasn't sure if I *heard* it or if I just felt it. I slid my hand into his hair, then fisted it. The tug did what my words didn't manage. He lifted his head and the storm raging in his eyes struck me.

"I'm fine," I told him. "I don't think I even got bruises. If I did, I don't really feel them." The cut on my tongue still stung, but it wasn't bleeding anymore. The seatbelt had snapped tight against my chest, keeping me in place. But that wasn't important right now.

His trembling wasn't from the cold, though I wanted to bundle him up. His eyes were almost too bright.

Finally, he raised one hand to my cheek. The caress was barely there, like he just had to make sure I was real. I'd been there. If he weren't so upset, I'd give him hell right now, but I couldn't bring myself to do it. I could yell at him later.

Another shudder passed through him before he dipped his head. The whisper of a kiss to my lips was like the ones he'd pressed to my throat. Gentle as a butterfly's wings. So much temptation wound up in that light touch. I stroked my nails against his scalp as he sealed the kiss, stealing my breath and sucking so deeply on my tongue that I had to relent and thrust it against his.

Despite all the pleasure sparking through me, awareness of where we were was inescapable. We were in the emergency room. It was like kissing him for the first time. Finally, I bit down on his lip. I didn't want to hurt him, but I needed him grounded in the here and the now.

With a grunt, he drew his head back to stare at me. The storm in his eyes seemed to ease, and then he pressed his forehead to mine as the trembling lessened. "Karagiani called me."

Not really a question I'd had. "Then you should have known I was fine. He was there with the car when I left with Wood. He followed us as soon as the vehicle was secured."

"Probably," Ezra admitted, then gave me a faint smile.

"To be fair, I didn't hear much beyond the words car accident and what hospital you were at."

"There you go, being impulsive again." The remark did what I wanted it to; it widened his smile.

"You make me crazy," he said without an ounce of irony.

"Not a very long trip." I wasn't sure whether it was the dry delivery I went for or the actual words themselves that made him laugh. But he was almost not shaking anymore. The mad dash of his heart calmed and I rubbed a slow circle against his chest over his heart as his grip on me loosened.

"No," Ezra agreed with me. "Not really." Then he flicked a glance past me. "Wood."

"Mr. Graham," Wood said in the wryest of tones. "Forgive me for not giving you both more privacy."

I bit my lip.

"Not a problem," Ezra told him. "I kind of crashed your party."

"Not at all, sir," Wood retorted in the most droll of tones. "That was the three other vehicles and some black ice."

I turned to meet Wood's gaze and the good humor reflected there decried the pain he'd been in. The neck collar kept his head still. They wanted to do X-rays and more, but he wasn't considered a "critical" case, so we had to wait our turn.

"Maybe you could convince Miss Benedict to go home, or at least somewhere more comfortable for her."

Before Ezra could grapple with that, I snorted. "Miss Benedict is fine right here. I told you I'd leave when you did."

"This could take a few hours," he chided and I lifted my shoulders.

"Sick of me already?"

He chuckled. "Not at all. I just don't feel like you should have to wait. We can call as soon as we know something."

"Wood, do you have someone I can call to get here for you?" I wasn't really sure if he was dating. His parents were in New Jersey and he had a sister at school in Pittsburgh.

"I wouldn't want anyone coming out in this weather. I'm just fine to wait. I'm not even in that much pain."

"Why don't we give it a few minutes then," Ezra suggested. "I can get you both some coffee or—can you have anything?"

"Coffee would be amazing," Wood admitted. "And they didn't say I couldn't have any food or drink." He shot a look at me. "Right?"

And that alone was enough to make me continue to stay right here until he was ready to go home. If necessary, I'd make arrangements for him to go out to Der Sonne, where someone could look after him until he was on his feet.

"Yes," I told him, then half-twisted, tilting to glance up at Ezra. "I'd love some hot cocoa or a mocha if they have it. I feel the need for chocolate."

"Oh, do you mind if I change my order?" The note of hope in Wood's voice made me grin and Ezra just nodded.

"I'll take care of it." Then he brushed a kiss to my forehead, before another to my lips. "You're really alright?"

"I promise."

Another shudder went through him. "Good. Okay, hot cocoa. Food—of some kind—any food allergies?" He wasn't asking me.

"No, sir."

"I'll be back shortly." Then Ezra's gaze locked on mine. "You'll be here?"

"Yes." I didn't scold him for the demand laced in that

question. Ezra didn't want to go, yet he was making himself because he wanted to help. "Right here." I spread my fingers against his chest. The mad staccato beat of his heart had begun to calm.

One more kiss to my forehead and then he pulled away. The ripple of transition went over him as he straightened, packing away the shuddering, trembling man with the fear and worry in his eyes to be replaced by the cool, sardonic asshole I knew so well. It might surprise others, but not me.

He gave a curt nod to Wood, then he was gone, and it was Wood and I again. When I faced him, arms folded, he wore the tiniest of smirks.

"Don't start," I warned him and that smirk widened to a full-fledged grin for a brief moment.

"I wouldn't dream of it, Miss Benedict."

No, he was far too polite. Didn't mean he wouldn't think it. Ezra was not the first man Wood had seen me with, but that was all an issue for another day. I trusted his discretion. Thankfully, it wasn't long before a nurse and a tech stepped in to get Wood to take him down for X-rays. I remained in the cubicle to wait.

He'd been gone about thirty minutes when Ezra returned. "I got the hot cocoa, coffee, and sandwiches. Not a lot of options in this place. They need to add some better amenities."

I accepted the Styrofoam cup gratefully and Ezra set aside Wood's before he dragged another chair over to sit next to me. "It's a hospital, I'm fairly certain their focus is more on their patients than on the people who just come to see them."

He snorted. "Good food and good coffee should be requisites for any facility dedicated to treating others." He wasn't himself yet, but he was doing an admirable job of pulling himself together.

"Well, I'm not on a charity for this hospital, but I could look into it."

"Let me know, and I'll make sure to write a big check." He grimaced after taking a sip from his cup. The look told me all I needed to know. The hot cocoa was watery, the chocolate a suggestion, and there wasn't even a hint of whipped cream or marshmallows. That said, it was warm and it hit the spot. "Will you tell me what happened?"

I half-wanted to tweak him about next time listening to his spy if he was going to get reports from him, but Karagiani *wasn't* reporting on me. He'd notified him of an accident and Ezra already said he'd stopped listening after those two words.

"Not much to tell," I said. "We were on the way to the seamstress. I didn't want her coming out in this weather, and I needed to get some slight alterations done to my dress. If she had any openings next week, I'd have put it off, but the Fire and Ice Gala is soon and I needed to make sure it was ready."

I blew out a breath and took another drink of the hot cocoa as he pulled out two of the saddest-looking sandwiches I'd ever seen. They were sealed in a plastic container with a pull-tab layer over the top. When he showed them to me, they were both chicken salad, so I just took one with a smile.

"Anyway, we were getting ready to turn—Wood was being very careful, you know how he is, when someone collided with us from the back. Then another car hit them and it dominoed. Several were involved in the accident, but I don't think there were any serious injuries, just some damage to the vehicles. Poor Wood—the whiplash appears to be the worst of it, but I want to be sure because his airbag deployed and his face is already red from the burn."

"Makes sense," Ezra said. He was picking at his sandwich as though it were some kind of alien substance. I didn't expect fine cuisine and I wasn't remotely disappointed. The bread was stale, the sandwich was dry, and the chicken salad seemed more a suggestion than actual content, but it satisfied the gnaw of my stomach.

"Thank you for coming to check on me," I murmured when I found Ezra studying me.

"I'm sorry I've been gone," he said, and I reached over a hand to rest on his leg. He covered my hand with his. "I'm back now."

"Yeah?" I tilted my head.

He nodded. "When we're done here, I'll take you home."

It wasn't a question, and for once, the high-handed decision-making didn't bother me. I wanted Ezra there. I wanted to see him.

I needed it.

"We'll talk?" I asked it as gently as possible because we had much to discuss.

Rather than shy away from it, Ezra locked his gaze on mine. "I'd like to."

It wasn't an agreement, but it would do.

For now.

THIRTY-THREE

EZRA

I t took hours at the hospital. I was glad Wood wasn't hurt worse, but the way they triaged meant it took forever to get him cleared. After having a driver take him and Karagiani home, I packed Lainey into my car. I'd driven the Range Rover. It wasn't sexy, but it had better traction and was built like a tank.

Accident.

Every single one of them said accident. Even Karagiani said it was an accident. I trusted the bodyguard, but at the same time...

No, I shook my head. Trust was for the foolish. King had arranged an accident for her before. This one hadn't been as severe, but did it need to be to send a message? All the way to the hospital, all I'd pictured was her injured. Again. Because of us...

Thank fuck she seemed fine, if concerned. The worry for everyone else, the fact she'd gone to check on the other victims of the same "accident." I'd seen the one Karagiani said was driving the car that hit them in the first place. The man—an accountant—seemed more dazed and apologetic than anything else.

It wasn't an assassination attempt.

No matter what it *looked* like.

King had been in a mood the past few days. Twice, he'd interrogated me about Adam. Twice. There was no attempt to cover his fury about Adam's recent actions. Though the part that worried me—was the glint in his eyes each time King brought up Adam's "survival."

For the first time, I was glad he seemed to truly want something from Emersyn, 'cause Liam's marriage to her kept *Liam* safe. Somehow, I suspected, there would already have been death threats or attempts. Worse, I kept waiting for him to give me the orders.

Lainey laid her hand against my thigh, which calmed some of the tension thrumming through me. At the traffic light, I slanted a look at her. She wasn't paying attention to me. Her gaze was a thousand miles away as she worked her lower lip with her teeth.

All that did was make me want to bite down until it was lush and swollen from the contact. Not the time, however, so I placed my hand over hers. "How are you, Kotyonok?"

"Tired." The admission tugged at me. Lainey was a force of nature. For all that she looked fragile, she was a fierce wind, a powerful storm, a raging tide... "Not how I pictured spending my day."

It was dark outside. The day had passed into evening before we left. Hours spent in the emergency room. A couple of hours where I bullied her into getting checked out by one of the doctors even if she didn't want to. Her "I'm fine, Ezra" didn't ease my concerns. She didn't want to take away from the actual patients, but the doctor finally said sometimes patients can feel fine even if they do have something wrong.

I could have kissed the man.

Her absolute exasperation transferred from me to him, and she eventually conceded. With Karagiani staying with Wood, I went with them to a different room while she put up with the exam, answered questions, and got a few X-rays. When it was done, the look she favored me with said I wasn't totally *off* the hook, but the doctor seemed satisfied.

"We'll have you back to the apartment soon," I promised her. "Unless you want me to take you somewhere else?"

I could drive her to her grandfather's. I didn't want to go out there, but if it made her feel better...

"The apartment is fine," she said, smothering a yawn. "I need a shower, a change of clothes, some food... and you promised to talk to me."

"I'd offer to cook," I told her in all seriousness. "Except the last time I made you food, I ended up wearing it."

Her sudden burst of laughter was exactly what I wanted. The island held many memories, and the food fight was probably my favorite.

"That was so undignified," she said in between little huffs of laughter.

"Worth it," I told her and she shook her head.

"You just liked following me into the shower to finish the argument."

"Not going to lie, I might have enjoyed that a little more than the fight itself." I wasn't going to argue, either. "Still, I think my favorite part of all was you relaxed."

For the first time since I scooped her up from Braxton Harbor, brought her back here, then stole her away to the island. She let go of the tension.

She let go of all of it.

It was the beginning of three incomparably perfect days.

The flash of her smile warmed me and then I focused as I turned into the garage beneath the building. I used the card to get in, and her exasperated sigh made me grin.

"I still can't believe you two."

The mention of Adam sent a flash of unease through me, but at the same time... "We care," I reminded her, and I was proud that my voice held true. "Is that so bad?"

She didn't answer, yet the affection in her eyes didn't vanish, so I'd take the win. I drove down to the private parking area and set the Range Rover into a corner, backed in. She didn't say a word as I made it easier to get out of here later—if we needed it.

"Stay put," I ordered before hopping out and walking to her door. The arch of her eyebrows reminded me she was perfectly capable of handling everything herself, yet she waited. "Thank you," I said, opening her door. She allowed me to take her hand as she climbed out and I didn't for a second miss the evidence of stiffness as she moved.

"First time I've really sat still today," she admitted before I could comment.

"Hurts?"

"Doesn't feel great," she admitted. "Seatbelt got me."

I pressed my lips to her temple. The seatbelt did its job. "But they said the x-rays were good?" Yes, I was confirming it because I needed to feel better.

"They did."

Her phone vibrated as we headed to the elevator. She let me wrap an arm around her shoulders and leaned into me as we walked. The fact she let me take care of her was everything. Once inside, I used my card key and the code before I pressed her floor while she pulled out her phone. She didn't pull away so I could see the screen.

"Trouble?"

"Yes," she answered, cryptic as ever, not that she attempted to hide the series of messages flashing onto the screen.

Trouble: *Are you all right?*

Trouble: *What happened?*

Trouble: *Say yes or Y if you just want me to come by.*

I eyed those messages. It didn't read like Hardigan. Adam wouldn't ask; he'd just show up. The fact he'd made no appearance told me he didn't *know* about the accident yet. Not that he wasn't coming.

She typed her response in.

I'm fine. Just a car accident. Weather to blame. Wood hurt, but he will be fine. I'm home now. Planning to stay here.

Trouble: *Someone with you?*

Yes, I'll call you tomorrow unless you need me.

I was almost holding my breath waiting for the answer.

Trouble: *Tomorrow is fine. Call me sooner if you need me.*

Then she hearted the message before she lifted her gaze to mine. The elevator doors dinged open. "I want to ask," I told her, bracing the doors so she could step out ahead of me.

"But you're not?" Was she teasing me?

"No," I admitted as she led the way to her door. She still moved with care and I kept a close eye on her. "I am, but— trying not to demand."

She unlocked the door and opened it, then moved to reset the alarm before glancing at me. "How is that working out for you?"

I stared at her. I hated this. Her lips twitched. "You're being mean to me," I pointed out before closing and locking the door behind us. Then I reached for her coat as she eased it off.

"I can be meaner," she said, turning to me as I shrugged off my own jacket.

"Is that a threat or a promise?"

She chuckled. "I'm going upstairs to shower." Then she looked at me. "What are you going to do?"

That was a very wide door she'd just thrown open. "Am I invited?"

"Do you want to be invited?" It wasn't a coy question at all. It was a flat-out challenge. "Because normally you charge in and get all bossy."

"I didn't get bossy today—" Then I sighed. "Much."

"Much," she agreed. "Although you did charge in."

"I was worried about you."

"I know," she murmured. "It's why it didn't bother me."

Oh, that meant I still had some latitude.

"But I also meant what I said, I want to talk. I want you to talk."

I took a deep breath. "About what happened with Adam." The immediate thud of my heart was a sudden, loud thumping.

"Yes, I would like to know if you are willing to share. I'm also more interested in what happened with you—why you bolted? Why you've avoided us?"

Us. She knew I hadn't spoken to Adam, which meant she had.

"And to say thank you."

I frowned. "For what?"

"For my present. I really needed to see him."

The urge to swoop over and pick her up was right there, so I shoved my hands into my pockets. Bad manners, but still... "Let's go up. You shower, I'll sit with you and I'll talk."

"Okay."

Just—that. A simple okay. Acceptance wrapped around me like the embrace I didn't know I needed. "I'd offer to give you privacy," I said as she led the way up the stairs and I trailed after her. "But I have a feeling if I sit down here alone with my thoughts, I'll take off."

At the top of the stairs, she glanced at me. "That's honest."

"It's cowardly," I admitted.

"Not if you didn't feel safe." The warmth in her eyes held me hostage even as those few words shackled me. It wasn't recrimination or doubt. Just—acceptance. I did not deserve her.

None of us did.

"Come on," I said, shuttering away how exposed I felt to nudge her down the hall. I'd never been up here with her. The bedroom she entered was so Lainey though, down to the cream covers and soft chocolate bedspread. It wasn't just "earth tones," but warm and earthy. There was a pile of pillows on the bed and a pair of lamps that cast a warm glow. The windows overlooking the city were floor to ceiling and I found myself staring out at them.

There were a couple of chairs opposite the bed with a small table. A perfect spot to read or to just sit. I didn't see a television in here, and yet I was soaking up every part of the room. It was just—peaceful.

I was still staring out the window as the shower turned on. The rustle of clothing told me she was stripping. Turning, I moved toward the bathroom. As eager as I always was to drink in the sight of her, I also needed to make sure she was all right.

The bruise across her chest held me riveted.

"I'd say it probably looks worse than it feels," she told

me with a faint smile. "Though it's pretty damn uncomfortable."

I dragged my gaze up to hers as I closed the distance between us. I needed to not crowd her. But even as I told myself that, she opened her arms and I scooped her up carefully. Cradling her. "Thank you for being safe."

She buried her face against my throat and I shuddered. The feel of her warm skin under my hands was *everything*. Even more, the steady thrum of her heart. I fixed my gaze on the falling water in the shower while I held her to me. Her arms tightened like they had when we'd been in the hospital.

I was supposed to be taking care of her, and she held me with such pure strength that I wanted to lose myself in her.

"I'm sorry I left," I whispered, ripping open that barricade. If I took down the door, it was all going to come out. "I shouldn't have. I know I promised to stay. I promised and then Adam..."

I licked my suddenly dry lips.

"I love you, Kotyonok," I admitted, voicing the words that were never supposed to be allowed out. Burying them deep in my mind had been an act of will. I'd kept them there, under lock and key, but chain after chain fell away. "I love you so goddamn much. I've only ever loved two people in my life the way I love you."

Half-braced for the rejection, I rushed forward and kept my gaze on that water and how it hit the tile. The steam rising up would begin to cloud the mirrors, obscuring everything. I could do this. She needed to hear it. I needed to tell her.

"The truth is—I love you, and I love Adam." The last few words broke me and I shuddered as they spilled free.

"I've loved you both for so long, I forgot what it was like to not love you. Even when I hated you both, I loved you."

My voice broke as the words got jammed behind the lump in my throat. When she pulled back, I dropped my chin and let her go. Shame slithered in through the cracks. Shame, self-doubt, and self-loathing. She deserved so much better...

"Ezra," she whispered, but it wasn't a request and I was as helpless to disobey that command as I'd been to not shatter the glass between us. It had been cracking forever. So many little places where it spider-webbed out, distorting everything. "Look at me."

I dragged my gaze off the water, but when her face wavered, I realized that the shower wasn't the only place where tears were falling. Concern filled her eyes and her fingers were so soft on my face.

"It's okay."

The world tilted heavily and I blinked. "What?"

"It's okay to love us," she whispered.

"I love—"

"You love Adam," she said, and her smile held not an ounce of recrimination or rebuke.

"And you."

"I heard that part too," she whispered. "I adore you."

Adore.

Hope was the most vicious of emotions; it threatened to rip out my chest.

"You love us both."

I nodded. "But..."

Then she touched her fingers to my lips. "You love us both. That's why you kissed him."

I shuddered, and then she was holding me steady and I leaned too much into her. "I never meant—"

"It's okay," she told me as a hot tear hit my cheeks. "It's okay, Ezra."

I buried my face against her hair as she kept me on my feet. "You don't hate me?"

"I could never hate you..." she whispered. "Even when I wanted to kick you in the balls, I didn't hate you."

Laughter broke through my tears and I dug my fingers into her as I held on tighter. I was supposed to be taking care of her and, instead, I was clinging to her like the broken man I was, and she was my life raft in the storm.

"I have you," she whispered. "I have you."

CHAPTER
THIRTY-FOUR

LAINEY

E zra followed me into the shower and I had to help him shed his clothes. The fact there were bruises littering his chest gave me pause. "What—"

"Don't worry about them," he said, cupping my face as he dipped his head. Then he sealed his mouth to mine as we slipped under the hot water. It was hardly our first shower together. Yet it was the first time he'd even been in this bedroom with me, or this shower.

When he trailed his fingers up my spine and to my scalp, I groaned. The thrust of his tongue tangling with mine kept my desire sharp in opposition to the soothing stroke of his fingers through my hair. When he turned me to face the water, I sighed as I leaned back against him. He mouthed kisses along my shoulder before he reached for my shampoo.

"I can wash my hair," I reminded him.

"I know," he agreed, dropping another kiss against my

jaw as he poured the shampoo into his palm. "But I want to take care of you."

Everything inside of me went low, hot, and tight at those words. Leaning my head back against his shoulder, I stared up at him and he didn't look away or make a joke. Instead, he continued the slow massage of my scalp as he worked the shampoo into my hair.

"You make me crazy when you get like this." The admission cost me nothing since it's the truth. Ezra had been driving me crazy for years.

"Can't handle my tender loving side?" The barest echo of fear danced through his eyes as I fought to keep mine open. I forgot how good he was at the scalp massage. He was good at a lot of things. The thing was, I couldn't let him distract me. No one wanted to be rejected, and the expectation in him that I would do that twisted me into knots.

"Ezra," I said, forcing myself up and turning, but closing my eyes as he tipped my head back. With care, he rinsed my hair clean. More worried he might try to slip away or put up those barricades between us again, I spread my hands against his chest.

However, I was also worried about those bruises. The dark lividity against his skin said they were deep. Considering how tight my chest was from where the seatbelt snapped me, I could just imagine how bad his were.

When he eased me forward and leaned past me for the conditioner, I blinked the water out of my eyes. "Don't run away."

"I'm not," he said, grunting at my arched eyebrow. "I'm right here, Kotyonok. I'm trying to be open with you, baring my body and my soul."

The thickness of his erection pressed against my leg, a reminder that he was also turned on. Considering the slickness between my thighs had very little to do with the water pouring down around me, I trailed my fingers over him. He worked the conditioner through my hair as I teased his skin with my nails.

"I know you are—and I adore you for it," I told him. "I hate the idea of anything hurting you."

"Yeah? Except when you want to kick me in the balls?" It was so wry I had to smile.

"I still hate the idea that it will hurt you." I pushed up on my toes as I looped my arms around his neck. "Especially since it means I'll be the one doing it."

He hesitated. "Accepted."

"I'm worried about you..."

"I'm fine."

"No," I told him. "You're not." But he pushed me back under the stream again. As manhandling went, it was gentle as hell. After my hair was rinsed, he passed me the loofa and body soap. Then he was washing his own hair as I studied him. "Ezra...I'm here for you too."

The hesitation that marked his response earlier reappeared as he raked his fingers through his hair. He turned those dark, tormented eyes on me and I tracked my gaze over all of him. He was a beautiful man, but the scars that marred him—along with the bruises—told a story he liked to keep from everyone else.

Those bruises were very fresh.

Too fresh.

Someone had hurt him.

It made me want to go for the jugular. Wrestling that response, I spread the soap over my arms and chest, then spun to wash him. He frowned but leaned into the contact, and I sighed when he passed a whisper of a kiss to my lips.

"I know you want to protect me, Kotyonok, but that's not your job."

As arrogant as that sounded, I understood the words. We were still tangled together after we had fully rinsed, and I slid my hand into his hair as he wrapped his hand around my nape.

"But it's your job to protect me?"

"Yes," he said, flatly. "This isn't sexism."

"No?"

"No." He shut off the water then reached for one of the larger fluffy towels and wrapped it around me before he nudged me out of the shower and followed after. Taking charge, he soaked up the moisture from my hair with one towel before he skated another over him. When I snagged the lotion to do my arms and legs, he tugged me out of the bathroom and prowled toward my bed.

"Then what is it?" I demanded when he nudged me toward the bed.

"Who I am...who Adam is." He groaned, and when he gave my ass a gentle, barely there slap and looked at the bed, I rolled my eyes. I crawled up onto it, very well aware of the image I gave him and the low sound he made. Only instead of gripping my hips or getting playful, he began to warm the lotion up on his hands and then spread it out over my back.

"Talk to me," I said, wondering if the fact I couldn't see him would help. Sometimes, secrets were easier to confess when you didn't have to read the reaction in someone else's eyes.

"Adam has loved you for as long as I can remember," he said, pressing a kiss to the back of my shoulder as if to punctuate the sentiment. I frowned at the statement as he began to work the tense muscles in my back. "I never could compete with him," he continued and I groaned. "I know, it's just—you're the one person he wanted, and I wanted you for him. Then—he went missing and everything changed."

The confession shredded me.

"I love you," he whispered. "I loved you at first because of him. But now I love you for you. Balancing my world between you two has never been a challenge before. After he disappeared, and I couldn't find you at first, it was— hell." My heart broke all over again at the rawness in him. "He's my best friend, Kotyonok, and I don't know if I fucked that all up or not."

Enough.

It was too much. I rolled over beneath him and Ezra froze as he stared at me. It was right there; he was waiting for me to reject him. I grabbed the lotion from his hand and pushed it away before I reached for him.

Fisting his hair, I tugged and he collapsed into me, his mouth crashing down against mine. I wrapped my legs around him as he fought to keep his weight from crushing me, but I wanted the pressure.

I wanted him. When I wrapped a hand around his cock, he groaned and then electricity surged through our kiss as he thrust his tongue against mine the way I wanted his cock. We angled him together as I dragged him against my pussy, and he hissed out a breath.

"So wet," he whispered against my mouth, never once pulling away, like he couldn't bear to be apart from me. And I needed him right there. When he trailed an arm down to hook under my thigh, I pressed him against my entrance.

I don't know which of us moved first, but he surged into me, filling me with one hard thrust that had me seeing stars. The piercings lit me up. Every time I thought I was used to how they felt, it was like experiencing it all over again for the first time.

"I need you," I told him and Ezra's whole body shuddered. "I need you, Ezra." I yanked at his hair as he began to rock his hips. He dragged his fiery gaze up to mine. "I need you and I want you."

Every word seemed to slice through the tension holding him captive and then his mouth was savage as our lips fused together. There was nothing except the hard slap of his skin against mine as I dug my fingers into his back. He raked his hands down to my hips, and then he rolled over, and I was on top.

He didn't let up, bracing his feet flat against the bed as he began to thrust into me. The steady cadence threatened to drive me mad, because there was no slow build or teasing grind. He kept the pressure intense, striking my G-spot with every deep push. The orgasm didn't climb, it crescendoed and I threw my head back. His lips closed around a nipple in a hard suck.

The scrape of teeth added pain to the pleasure, edging me, and then he was trailing his fingers from my hips to my ass. I was coming and all I could do was hold on for life as I fisted the comforter and his shoulders. Then he flipped us again, only he pulled out of me and I let out a gasp before he rolled me onto my stomach, pulled back on my hips and then he fucked right into me again.

"Hold on, Kotyonok," he ordered and I had no choice. The sudden pressure of his thumb against the rim of my ass startled me and he pushed into me even as he dragged me along the length of his cock. My vision hazed as he added a second finger. The burn had me bucking. Did I want it? Did I want it to stop?

I couldn't catch my breath and I swore there was an

explosive release that soaked my thighs as he bit down against my shoulder.

"You can do it," he whispered, barely slowing his pace. Holy shit, he was going to kill me.

"No," I said, squeezing the word out,

"You can," he whispered, and then he scissored his fingers as he slammed all the way inside me. The bruising pleasure had me blacking out and I was pretty sure I screamed. Time elongated as I floated. The burn intensified distantly and then eased as he slid his fingers free. "So perfect," he whispered and I shivered. When he eased his cock from my pussy, a whimper left me along with a gush of release.

His low laughter was a stroke against my senses. We'd been talking, and then fucking, and now—I drifted. Something warm dribbled along my ass and I tried to lift my head. No, it wasn't dribbling, it was a cloth. Warm, and damp. It eased the soreness there. Boneless, I couldn't move, and if he hadn't rolled me over gently, I didn't think I'd have had the strength to do it.

The smile on his face was somewhere between angelic and devilish. "You look happy," I murmured and the grin he wore pulled his lips wider and gave me a flash of teeth.

"You came over and over again, Kotyonok. You blacked out while soaking my cock. I am happy."

That—filled my chest with this sudden warmth that extinguished even the suggestion of a chill. His lips brushed over mine.

"So wet for me," he teased, dragging a cloth between my legs. I groaned. It was almost too sore, but I found my hips lifting to chase the contact. "And still so eager... Do you have any idea how beautiful this cunt of yours is? It's soft, pink, and swollen..." He bit down on my nipple, just a hint of pain that forced my eyes wider. "Full of my cum and I want to fill it up some more."

He wrapped my hand around his cock. It was wet, just like he said, and already stiffening.

"This is what you do to me," he continued in that languorous tone that threatened to drug me. "I know I should leave—"

That snapped me out of the haze. "No."

He frowned. "Shh, I've got you. Go back to that happy place."

"Don't leave," I ordered him, fighting away the lassitude invading all of me as I clung to him. "Please."

"I'm not going to leave," he said, settling down to lay beside me. "I just—I don't know. I shouldn't have pushed this and at the same time, I never want to let you go."

"You can care about more than one person, Ezra," I reminded him. "Me caring for you and for Milo, it doesn't diminish my feelings for Adam." Or Bodhi. That little voice whispered from the back of my mind like the errant little troublemaker it was—he was, and at the same time. I raised a hand to cup Ezra's cheek and he leaned his face into my touch. "You can care about me and about Adam— although it doesn't mean you can only care about one of us."

"I don't—I don't know if I can face him, Kotyonok. Having the feelings. That was one thing. I had no idea how deep they were until he went missing, and then—I've been trying to put them back where they belong, but he—"

I summoned a smile. "He's infuriating and careless about his own life."

"Yes," Ezra said with a grunt that had me reaching up to hold him. He shifted, shifting us away from the wet spot to the other side of the bed, and then he tucked me up against him. "He makes me insane."

"Not a long trip," I reminded him, and he gave my ass a light tap. However, he didn't disagree with me. "Ezra—whatever else happens between you, you have to talk to him." I rubbed my cheek against his chest.

"I—I don't know how."

"Well, I'm sure yelling and punching will be involved. But you have to talk to him and you have to let him talk to you." This was important and even as exhaustion wrapped me up almost as tightly as Ezra did, I couldn't let this go. "Running from him won't solve anything."

"What if—"

When he didn't finish the thought, I pushed myself up so I could see him. The pensive expression said it all.

"He's your best friend," I reminded him. "Trust that, if nothing else."

"What if he doesn't want me the same way?"

"Then you'll know." My heart twisted for him. "And you won't be sitting here tearing yourself up wondering. But one thing I know for certain, the not knowing is so much worse."

He sighed. "We did that to you."

"Yes," I said slowly. "You did."

"I'm sorry, Kotyonok."

"We can't change the past, but I'm here now and so are you...don't run. I'll have your back."

His lips turned down and then he hauled me to him. "I'm supposed to be looking after you."

"Letting me take care of you is looking after me," I told him.

We lay like that for a long time, and his sigh held so much loneliness that tears burned in my eyes. But I didn't let him go. Instead, I just massaged my hand over his heart as he rubbed my back. I hadn't forgotten about either of our bruises. Still, I fought sleep. If I closed my eyes—he might leave.

"Sleep, Kotyonok," he whispered.

"I don't want you to go..."

"I'll be here in the morning. I promise." Then, before I could comment, he said, "Even if Adam shows up to punch me."

"I'll kick him in the nuts."

He chuckled.

"I did it once for you. I can totally do it again."

"When did you?"

I opened my mouth to tell him, but all that came out was a yawn, and then he chuckled again. Another kiss.

"Sleep. Tell me in the morning."

I could do that.

In the morning.

ADAM

The past week had been a grueling series of meetings and hours spent taking apart a series of shell corporations. I'd been so fucking buried, the fact Lainey had been in a car accident didn't reach me until the following day. Only because her driver reached out to let me know he could not keep me apprised of her schedule for a few weeks.

If he hadn't prefaced the whole interaction with the knowledge that she was *uninjured*, I might have lost my goddamn mind. Even returning to the meeting with Margareta Waldemar and the lieutenants she had gathered wasn't enough to distract me from my concerns.

King had *just* threatened her. Yet, Wood assured me that Lainey was not injured. He also informed me that Ezra had poked his head up from wherever he had been hiding. That was enough to make me consider leaving to head directly to her apartment. Though I'd fought to maintain my neutrality and distance throughout the briefing, Waldemar kept her eye on me.

"Stay a moment, Adam."

Those were not the words I wanted to hear following the dismissal, but I settled back in my chair while she bid the others goodbye as they trickled out. Until all that remained were the two of us—not even her guards.

"Tea?"

"I'm fine, thank you." I glanced to the tea service that had been set out. "Would you like me to pour your cup?"

"Thank you, but I have it. What has you so distracted today?"

"Nothing that will impact my work for you," I assured her. "I know what you need. The best time to move on it will be right after the New Year. The Fire and Ice Ball the Grahams throw is a good cover to make contact with a few of these leads. Everyone attends, even people who hate them."

Which had always pleased Wallace Graham far too much. He liked nothing more than entertaining the people who loathed him most because *they* needed him, not the other way around.

"I'm not concerned about the impact on your work for me," she said as she poured her tea. "Your work has been exemplary. I know you've reached out to Milo Hardigan and have made the first overtures of an alliance. You have identified several key insertion points in King's empire..."

His empire. Though, the more I broke it down, the more fascinated I became. He'd structurally built a damn near impenetrable fortress around his *personal* interests by using shell corporations, businesses, and more. Finding what was *actually* his and what was just another smokescreen had been one of the more challenging puzzles to unravel.

At the same time, the deeper I went, the more irked I'd grown. He'd hidden so much beneath our own business interests, using almost gossamer-like connections as legal and ethical shields that, once pierced, may bring down far more than him.

Talk about a house of cards.

"I'm concerned about *you*," she continued as she carried her cup of tea over and claimed the chair just to my right rather than returning to her position at the head of the table. "Talk to me. What's preoccupying you?"

"Thank you for your concern, but I assure you, it's nothing."

"Hmm." She took a sip of the tea, then settled back in her seat to give me the firmest, most direct, wordless expression of *bullshit* one might exhibit in polite company. "My understanding of the accident involving Miss Benedict was that it was *only* an accident."

Discipline kept me from reacting as I raised my eyebrows. "You were looking into the accident?"

"I like to be kept apprised of a great many things. Miss Benedict is an intriguing young woman, strong-willed, determined, and very intelligent. She's also a source of some leverage over several notable figures surrounding the King. And I would imagine King himself has his own ideas about a girl who is the sole inheritor of a thirty billion dollar empire in her own right."

"I can understand that."

"Perfectly neutral." Margareta chuckled, her smile growing. "Well done, Mr. Reed. As generous and upfront as you have been in our deal, how long would I survive if I suggested a threat directed in Miss Benedict's direction?"

"It depends," I said, maintaining my neutrality.

"On?"

"A great many things."

Her laughter grew. "Well done." However, her amusement did not last. If anything, her smile diminished as she studied me. "You care a great deal about your stepsister."

That didn't require a response, so I merely observed her. "If you have a question, ask."

"Why are you so worried?"

"There are any number of answers to *that* particular question. We're in the process of waging a war that has any number of consequences for multiple players against a man who has made it very clear he has no issues hurting *children*."

Her lips compressed.

"If you would care to be more specific about your question, I will do my best to answer it."

"Is he threatening Miss Benedict?"

"He has threatened her for well over a decade at this point." I wouldn't pretend otherwise.

"And you are the only reason he hasn't approached her about this society of theirs?" This was the most direct she'd ever been in her probing about Lainey.

"Arrogance aside, I think he's uncertain of making her grandfather an enemy. As far as I can determine, Julius King and Leopold Benedict have no contact whatsoever. Leopold has never suffered any fool, no matter how powerful they think they are, and he would strike back if he perceived such a threat to her."

"Yet, he didn't where her mother was concerned."

Melissa.

"I can't speak to that. His relationship, or lack thereof, with Melissa has existed for as long as I've known her, and I am assuming longer than I was aware of it."

"You have theories?" Margareta folded her hands in her

lap. We could have been discussing anything from her posture.

"No," I said. "While not entirely true as you would see it, it's an area I don't care to speculate in. Melissa Benedict Reed and her father are not friends. He disinherited her before Lainey's birth—I believe—but I have no actual evidence to support or disprove it. They have minimal, if any, social contact even when in the same location."

"Yet, he allowed her to continue to see the younger Miss Benedict, even though I know for a fact he severed her custody."

So did I. "Not a subject I will discuss with you. Miss Benedict is off-limits."

That earned me raised brows. "Indeed. Do you want to place your cards on the table?"

"I don't have to." This much I'd already ascertained, Margareta Waldemar did not ask questions she hadn't already answered for herself.

"No?" Her amusement returned.

"No."

"Adam," she said with almost a happy sigh. "I do enjoy these chats."

"No," I repeated. "You don't. But you do enjoy seeing how far you can push me because while I am useful to you, and you need some of the information I am providing, you do not care for the fact that you do not own my loyalty."

That was something else about Margareta Waldemar. She appreciated rebellion and respected dissent, and sometimes demanded the debate. Yet, she preferred loyalty above all three, no matter how she had to secure it.

In my case, the pursuit continued to intrigue her, and what I brought to the table made it worth her time. If and when that changed, I held no illusions about how long I may last. Fortunately, that wasn't the problem today.

"You enjoy baiting me," she said as I rose from my seat.

"Not particularly, though a man does like perks."

That earned me another laugh and then she waved me off. "Go. I'll speak with you later. Call me if anything changes."

I nodded, then showed myself out. While she didn't turn to track my departure, I didn't doubt for an instant she was aware of my movements. Just like I didn't discount her ability to protect herself. Margareta Waldemar was a fascinating mixture of Old World charm, European sophistication, and cold-blooded killer.

Only a fool would ignore any of those facets.

Two hours later, I parked near the barn at Der Sonne. I could have just gone to Waltham Corners, but I promised Andrea I would check on both her sister and her horses since she was still a few days away from the Christmas break that would bring her back to Long Island.

Lainey would likely make more appearances at Waltham Corner as well. She always did when Andrea was home. No matter what distractions occupied her time, she put Andrea first. I'd changed before I made the drive, but I had to reach into the trunk to retrieve my boots. A couple of the stablehands nodded to me as they went about their duties.

When I shut the trunk, I came face to face with Leopold Benedict. This confrontation hadn't been on my schedule.

"Sir," I said, inclining my head before shifting the boots to hold under my arm and offering him a hand.

He eyed it briefly, the extra second or two a blatant repudiation before he grasped it in a single shake. "Reed. My granddaughter is not here."

I didn't react to that. He had two granddaughters. The only one he acknowledged, however, was Lainey. Andrea barely rated a mention. "I'm aware," I told him, keeping my tone cool. "I promised the younger one I would check on her horses for her."

If he took umbrage with that reminder, it didn't reflect. The old man was harder than a diamond to read. "And hoped that my Lainey would be here for you to harass?"

Chuckling, I pocketed my keys and headed for the stable interior. This was the larger of the three show stables built on Der Sonne and the only one with an interior riding arena, perfect for working the horses when unfortunate weather struck.

"You think harassing my granddaughter is funny?"

"I think you believing that my attention toward Lainey is harassment she doesn't enjoy and isn't quite capable of slapping me down on her own is entertaining, yes."

He said nothing as I held the door open for him, but he finally stepped inside. While he didn't quite stomp, he moved with such deliberate purpose, it wasn't hard at all to believe he was a giant.

A dangerous giant.

"Let's put our cards on the table, shall we?" He didn't wait for my response as he faced me. Ten feet away, one of the stablehands slipped out of the stall he'd been cleaning and headed down the aisle and away from us. He wasn't the only one.

The staff was clearing out.

"You aren't good enough for Lainey. You will never be good enough. I know what you want from her. I've watched you watch her for years. She will never be a Reed. You are never taking her away."

"That's your final word?" For all his gruff, Leopold

Benedict wasn't a fool nor a man who spouted off without deliberate thought or purpose. He'd never pretended to like me or my family.

"No, my final word is to leave her alone. You don't want me as an enemy."

"You sound very certain about the last part."

That earned me a narrow-eyed glare. "I am certain. You may be young and foolish enough to think that I am incapable just because I've never done anything."

I would never make that mistake, but I said nothing.

"Leave Lainey alone, Reed. Your father did enough destruction. I won't let you do that to her. She's not a toy or a plaything or a prize."

There are three things I would likely gut another man for, save for the last: Lainey was a prize. She was the highest of prizes, one *no man* deserved. Except he'd forgotten something very important.

She was also mine.

"Your concern is noted," I told him as respectfully as I could muster. "However, just to assure that we're both being brutally honest here—I'm going nowhere. You don't make decisions for her, and the only reason you're talking to me at all is because she is. As long as she wants me—I'm here. So do your worst, *sir.*"

With that, I nodded then moved around him to head down the aisle. He didn't follow. When I glanced back, he was gone.

War with Leopold Benedict wasn't on my to-do list before today.

But I'd make time for it.

For Lainey.

Period.

CHAPTER
THIRTY-SIX

LAINEY

Christmas came and went in a rush. As promised, Ezra didn't bolt from my apartment the very next day after the car accident. He actually stayed for two days. Unfortunately, he had to take care of some things. As much as he didn't want the holidays with his parents—that was where he would be. He left me with a kiss and a promise to see me at the party, if not before.

I hated the dark look in his eyes as he walked out the door. Especially when I'd tried to get him to talk to me about what was going on.

"I want to tell you," he said with a long sigh.

"You don't," I countered, not really wanting to argue. Only the way he would look away said a lot more about where his head was.

"No," he admitted. "I don't. Kotyonok, I've done a lot of shit that I'm not proud of—that you wouldn't be proud of, and I know you want to help me—but you can't. Not with this. I've got a plan and it's going to work out."

"But you still won't tell me." It wasn't a question and the look in his eyes practically begged me to simply accept it. *"Ezra... you're not alone in this. If I can help, I will."*

"I've got this," he said, but it sounded more like a hope and a prayer than assurance.

Still, he wouldn't bend and in the end, I had to let him go. I saw Adam only briefly over Christmas. Andrea was home for two days only, and then she was off again. A skiing trip with friends in St. Moritz. The fact Adam didn't protest or even give her any side-eye had me cornering him.

"What do you know about her trip that I don't?" For as grateful as I was that she wouldn't be here, I missed her. I didn't want us to grow apart because she was always gone. Being at Waltham Corners was bad enough. Harper had been all too happy to see me, whereas my mother had just wandered off with barely a word beyond a flippant good afternoon.

"I know a lot of things," he said, sliding his hand up to rest against my throat. We were away from the others, tucked into a corner in the shadowed halls. *"But primarily that the trip really is just friends from her school hosted by two sets of parents, both European, and the girls are staying at the villa of one of them in the Swiss Alps."*

"You background-checked them?" At his bland look, I closed my eyes and fisted my temper. *"Indulge me. Your overprotective side knows no boundaries. So make me feel better about—"*

His lips were cool when he closed them over my mouth and swallowed the next sounds. His grip on my throat tightened as he used his thumb to nudge my head back, and then a soft sigh escaped as he thrust his tongue against mine. Hands against his chest, I savored the heat rolling off him and the steady thrum of his heart which seemed to increase its pace alongside my own.

The wall was colder at my back as he crowded me into the corner, and then his kiss turned deeper, almost drugging as he demanded my response, and I dueled with his tongue. Artful and sweet, I wanted more and when he pressed a leg between mine, I shuddered. The kiss lingered but then he nipped my lower lip.

"I want more than a quickie in the corner," he whispered against my lips. "And yes, I am confident in the people she is staying with, the girlfriends she is hanging out with." Another kiss and then he bit down gently behind my ear. "The body-guards I hired will also keep an eye on them on and off the slopes."

There it was and I wrapped my arms around him. He gave the briefest of shudders at the contact then curled his arms around me and half-lifted until I could bury my face against his throat.

"We can't stay here," he warned but he made no rush to let me go.

"I know," I admitted. "But thank you for telling me."

"I will always protect her," he promised. "Just like I will you."

"Adam..." The reluctance to scold him was new, even as his soft chuckle teased my senses. "We need to talk..."

"We are talking," he murmured. Yet, when I leaned back to gaze up at him, he sighed. "I suppose it's a good sign that you aren't pushing me away?"

It was the first time he'd asked me a question like that. Usually, he dismissed the concerns, changed the subject, or, of late, just kissed me again. "I don't know what it means," I told him honestly. "Except we're all moving in different directions. I know you're up to something, like I know Ezra is..." And Bodhi. He'd been messaging me daily since the accident, sometimes a funny remark, but always the same thing—did I need him? Was I alright?

And Pretty Boy? We were spending Christmas apart, but it

didn't stop me from getting him a present or sending him a message.

"We need to work together."

"It's going to be okay," Adam said, lifting his hands to pull mine from his neck and holding them between us. "I promise. When I can tell you—I will. Before you get mad and think I don't trust you, this isn't about trust."

"No?" Seeing as I didn't believe him there.

"It's about choices we all made at different times, choices I made...but yes, I do want to talk to you too—at length, and maybe with far fewer clothes between us."

Heat scorched through me at the suggestion and he chuckled at my expression but the humor dried up almost immediately.

"You've seen Ezra?" The concern he downplayed was right there in his eyes.

"I have," I told him and my heart still twisted for him.

"He's still avoiding me," Adam said.

"I'm surprised you're letting him."

"I'm not—" He paused, then gave me a look as his mouth flattened. I just raised my eyebrows. Dipping his chin, he lifted my hands to kiss them. "Sometimes, I have to let him come to me even when I'd prefer to just drag it out of him. Based on every-thing that happened—this is one of those times."

I believed him. "He needs to know you don't hate him."

When his grip on my hands tightened, I flexed my hands around his.

Still, I gave him a moment to consider it all before I asked, "What do you need?"

A week later and, I was still turning his response over in my head.

"You're not ready for my answer."

Nothing I said changed his mind, so what the hell did that mean? Considering how often he said, *you're mine*, I wasn't sure what to do with his new reply. Had he changed his mind?

No sooner did that thought take purchase than I dismissed it wholesale. The kisses he gave me were not remotely platonic. If anything, they seemed fiery as ever. Still, I was so over the idea of the men in my life trying to "protect" me by telling me nothing.

The night of the Fire and Ice Ball was here, New Year's Eve. It was going to be a wild party. Extravagant, over the top, and filled with everyone and anyone. The exclusivity of the list was not limited to just those in the immediate circle or even New York society. Guests came from all over the world when the invitations went out. Enemies and allies alike.

Rumors of debauchery, orgies, and drunken revelry were as much a part of the ball's mystique as anything else. A quick knock on the door to my room before it opened had me turning to see Tally sticking her head inside. "Please tell me you're not decent," she teased and I laughed.

"Oh good, you're not dressed yet." Tally, however, was, as revealed when she pushed the door inward to walk inside. The icy blue and silver dress she sported looked positively painted on.

An ice princess come to life and it contrasted perfectly with the deep golden tone of her skin and the streaks of blonde she'd added to the pile of dark hair that turned it into a crown around her head was just the icing on top.

Literally.

A sun goddess wrapped in ice.

"Tally, you look..."

"I know," she said with a wide smile, then did a little turn so I could take in the whole dress. "Killer, yes?"

"Beyond killer, you're stunning." I was still marveling at

how gorgeous she was when she held up the bottle of champagne. "Getting the party started early?"

She threw her head back and laughed. "Yes, and because I've missed you this month. After Thanksgiving, I thought we'd have time to do more stuff but you've been so busy."

"I wasn't the only one," I pointed out as she beckoned to one of the maids to bring in the tray with the glasses. "Thank you, Molly."

"You're welcome, Miss. Do you need help with your dress now, or did you want to finish your drink first?" I'd already had my hair and cosmetics done, I literally just needed to put on the dress.

"Give us a few minutes?" I asked. "A couple of glasses and she'll calm down."

"Ha," Tally said, then pointed at me with a chuckle. "I had a glass earlier, so I challenge your premise."

Molly hid a smile as she slipped out and I shook my head as Tally walked toward me. I welcomed her hug though, and she pressed a noisy kiss next to my ear but not on me. Her lips were gleaming a slash of vibrant red.

"You're in a mood." I studied her as she poured our glasses. The champagne had definitely been popped else-where but it was still bubbly. Based on the temperature of the Champagne when she passed me my glass, it was still very cold. I waited until she set the bottle down and held her glass toward me.

"I'm—in a wonderful mood," she said after a moment. "I think I'm in love."

"What?" Shock rippled through me. Tally loved men. She loved to dangle them on a string, play with them, and then move on. To my knowledge, the problem was she loved the chase, and she loved when they chased her. For a while, the capture was fun but she got bored.

"I'm in love," she told me before she raised her glass. "I have my best friend. I'm ready to start the new year, and I'm in love. So, to us and kicking everything off right."

"Who?" I demanded, and at her impatient look, I tapped my glass to hers to finish the toast.

"Not sharing that yet," she told me after she took a drink, then shot me an apologetic look. "It's—I don't want to stare too closely. Because..."

Sympathy rolled through me. "Because it's too new." I loved Pretty Boy and he loved me. Ezra told me he loved me and while I hadn't said the words back exactly—I wasn't lying to myself. I'd loved him and Adam for a very long time. It was just so... "Complicated."

"Complicated," Tally said, grasping onto the word like it was a life raft. She moved over to the fainting couch that occupied the corner of my suite here at Der Sonne. It was where I used to read when I was younger. While the little sitting area also boasted a fireplace, it wasn't lit. "That is such a good word for it."

"But you love him?" While I used to tease her when we were younger about how fast she fell into and out of love, this was different.

Tally was different.

"I do, Lainey—I have never felt this way about anyone. It's like—obsession." She stared at me. "Do you know what I mean?"

Obsession? Pretty Boy's face had lived rent-free in my memories for years before I met him again. The conflagration of passion and emotion he provoked—yeah, I have an obsession. I got it with Ezra and with Adam...and while I wasn't sure about a lot of things, I did know that my feelings where Bodhi was concerned were also very complicated.

"Yes," I said, moving to perch on the end of the fainting couch before I took a long drink of the champagne. It was cold, crisp, and the bubbly tickled my nose. The effervescent feeling helped, and so did the hit of alcohol to my system. "I understand."

"Is it like that with you and Milo?"

I sighed. "It's complicated," I told her. "So complicated. I mean...I can't see him right now and I miss him."

"Why can't you see him?"

"Long story, just—he has things he has to do. He got away for a weekend right after Thanksgiving and it was—amazing. But I haven't seen him since and worry about him." I looked at my champagne glass, then over at Tally. "I miss him."

"Will he be at the ball tonight?"

I hoped so. "I don't know..."

"Okay, if he's there, you give me the nod. We'll find a way to sneak you two some time." She drained her glass and then reached for the bottle. "You need someone to kiss at midnight, you know?"

I laughed. "I think I'm going to abstain." So no one got stabbed. The guys were all a little territorial there.

"Where's the fun in that..."

"What about your guy?" I was still sipping my champagne so I shook my head when she offered to fill the glass. "Will he be there?"

"Maybe," Tally said, dipping her eyelashes coyly.

"Oh, Tally...please tell me he isn't married." Older men were her thing. Older married men had been a phase I truly hoped she'd grown out of.

"He's not," she said almost too easily, and at my look,

she gave an exasperated huff. "He's not married, engaged, separated, or about to be divorced. He's just—very private."

Private.

I frowned.

"Don't look at me like that," she scolded. "Just be happy for me. As soon as I can, I'll introduce you."

"Hmm...understand I reserve the right to geld him if he hurts you." I also wanted to make sure he wasn't using her for her money or anything else. That was the problem with secrets; they hid motives and agendas.

"Because you're the best," Tally said, her smile undiminished as she reached out to grasp my hand. "Now, let's get you dressed while I think of the best way to get you time with your pretty boy..."

The hopeful little flare in my chest was right there. It was the first time since the masquerade we'd all be in the same place—if Milo came. He hadn't mentioned it but then he had to know Ezra and Adam would be there as well.

"C'mon," Tally coaxed as she rose. "No more melancholy for either of us. We're going to be too stunning for anyone to ignore tonight."

If only it could be that easy.

THIRTY-SEVEN

BODHI

"Good evening, Mr. Cavendish," the silver-haired butler said as he accepted my embossed invitation. "Welcome to Harrows Park. If you'll simply follow the lighted path through the courtyard, you will find the ballroom."

I nodded as I stepped inside. I'd turned my car over to one of the valets and tucked the claim card into the inner pocket of my jacket. The car was clean. Anything Graham's people tried to lift from it would disappoint them. I'd rented it specifically for this event. Last check, there was something like seven hundred and fifty names on their guest list.

The number didn't include plus ones.

My path took me through the foyer, past two wide double doors into a courtyard garden. The snow had been cleared away. Heat lamps offered respite for guests along the various benches that lined the pathways with the Greek statuary. Some of those pieces were originals, valued far more than the property they occupied.

Still, it was an ostentatious display of wealth that guests were treated to as we followed the line of others heading to the doors on the far side that granted entrance to the ballroom.

The interior courtyard was surrounded by balconied pathways connecting the front building to the back. Security maintained a discreet yet visible presence. Graham brought the wealthy to his door to sup at his hands and provide him with information, blackmail material, and more.

The number of scandals making their debut at this event had tipped off most of the major players. Still, some people would sell their kidneys to be included on the guest list. After all, the value of being seen at the annual Fire and Ice Ball was worth the possible future divorce or child support payments.

The couple ahead of me were already in the midst of an argument based on the icy glares and stiff shoulders. I paused as they took their first steps into the ballroom. Wallace and Dinah Graham waited to greet them and receive their homage. I gave it a beat until they were both preoccupied and then just walked right past them all and into the main room itself.

Ice sculptures decorated the room at intervals, interspersed with ice sculpture torches. Blue and red lights spotlighted various areas. Tables lined the huge ballroom while a live band performed at the far end. The marble floors gleamed. There were three—no, four separate bars. Above the ballroom, balconied areas surrounded us where food appeared to be served.

As events went, it was still early. I doubted there were a

third of the people here who were on the guest list. The car line to arrive had stretched out behind me so I made my way to the nearest bar. While there were ice sculpture torches at this end, the other boasted a massive fireplace with crystals dancing above it.

Between the decorations and the flowers, there had to be a cool few hundred thousand on display. Drink ordered, I found a good place to settle in and watch. There were a few names that I wanted to observe.

One of them now strode across the ballroom floor, his face a mask of barely restrained fury. Ezra Graham's palpable anger seemed to eddy the air around him as he slowed, his gaze firmly on his father. Only there was a constant stream of guests being welcomed by the Grahams.

I took a single sip of the vodka, enjoying the ice-cold fire as it made its way down my throat. Graham gritted his teeth then turned and his gaze clashed with mine. There was something—deeply unsettled about the man. He started to take a step toward me, which had me straightening.

Before he could complete the thought, a young woman hurried up to him. She wore a pale blue shimmering gown that sported more than a few diamonds. Upset filled her expression and she captured all of Ezra's attention. Whatever she said to him distracted him entirely, because he guided her back the way he'd come and disappeared out of another door.

I didn't recognize her.

I knew most of the families. Who she wasn't, however, was Lainey B. So what was Graham up to? For the next hour, I kept a mental tally of the arrivals. Margareta Waldemar. Claudette and Oliver Marlowe. Imogene and Trevor Adley, along with their irritating son, Christian.

Nicholas Clifton made an appearance, his parents not far behind. The Reeds were here in force from Harper and his second wife Melissa to Jason and his wife Sable. The scum-sucking middle brother was also present, but he arrived alone and had gone out of his way to avoid his brothers.

Adam Reed bypassed the Grahams on his way in and headed over to the bar I'd settled near. I half-expected he'd be with Ezra somewhere. Didn't those two usually have each other's backs everywhere?

Then again, maybe that dynamic shifted with Ezra's interest in Lainey B. I wouldn't doubt it.

"Cavendish," Adam said as he joined me at the high-top where I stood with my drink.

I spared him a brief look. "Reed."

Then I resumed my study of the room. There he was, Julius King had arrived and he had Milo Hardigan with him. King and Graham were shaking hands and exchanging pleasantries while Hardigan studied the ballroom.

No, he was searching it. But she wasn't here yet.

I'd been watching for her too. There were easily eight hundred people present, if she was waiting to make her entrance, this would be a good time.

"You planning on mingling?" Reed asked after standing there, ignoring his drink for the last thirty minutes.

"No."

When Reed checked his watch for the fourth time, then reached for his phone, I spared him a look. The room was packed. The band was in full swing. Dancers moved around the ballroom floor and the temperatures soared. The doors to the exterior had been thrown open around the room to let the colder air in.

It was just nine when I caught sight of her stepping

inside. She was with Tally Marlowe. They were the perfect mix of fire and ice. Marlowe greeted the Grahams warmly, but Buttercup swept her gaze over the room before she turned to take Wallace Graham's hand.

The barely there polite smile suggested she wasn't a fan of whatever the older man was saying. Greetings done, she turned to face the room fully as she strode forward and I drank in her appearance.

"Fuck," Adam said, and I had zero doubt he'd noticed Lainey B's arrival. It would be damn near impossible in the red, gold-burnished black, strapless number that rippled like it was on fire as she walked. The slit bared almost all of her left leg as she moved, revealing a pair of back stiletto heels.

She moved with the kind of casual confidence of a woman who knew exactly how much she was worth. Power. Confidence. Beauty. She had it all. There wasn't an eye in the house that didn't track her movement.

From Hardigan across the room, who was as aware of her as she was of him, to Adam Reed standing next to me, to the other players. The Reeds and the Adleys. Wallace Graham left his position at the door to enter the ballroom properly. Lainey wasn't moving alone, Tally Marlowe drifted with her and while Lainey was all flame, Marlowe wore an icy body sheathe in silver and the palest of blues.

The contrasts were almost visceral, and yet it was Marlowe who pulled the first real smile from Buttercup. Adam knocked back his drink then strode away from the table. Like Graham and Hardigan, he circled Lainey B in a gradually decaying orbit with all three on a collision course.

The problem was the fallout threatened *her,* and I found myself disliking that intensely. At Adam's approach, she smiled and I relaxed with my drink. She wasn't making him leave her alone, so I allowed the interaction while tracking the reactions throughout the room, from King's less-than-benevolent expression to Waldemar's almost amused one.

Schemes.

Plots.

Scandals.

Rumors.

The party had populated with them before guests even began arriving. Movement near the entrance to the ball-room drew my attention from where Reed guided Lainey out to the dance floor. Cavendish Senior had arrived.

Wonderful. I scanned to see who he was with, but he didn't appear to have brought a plus one. Instead, he was focusing all of his charm on Dinah Graham. Their famil-iarity suggested a long acquaintance, although I doubted she was his type. She was too attached to her husband.

My father preferred lower-hanging fruit.

Younger too.

As if summoned by the thought, Tally Marlowe sidled up to me after claiming a drink from the bar.

"Phillip," she said in a warm tone.

"No," I told her as simply and politely as possible while keeping track of the players in the room. I sipped my vodka. Just allowing the taste to touch my lips, enough to savor it and nowhere near enough to begin inebriation. Too much to do tonight.

"You don't even know what I was going to ask." She practically pouted with her words.

"Don't need to know," I said. "But I don't want to dance. I'm not bored. Nor am I looking for a companion. Chase down Adley if you want some entertainment. He's thick, yet obedient."

Dead silence greeted my words and when I cast a glance

at her she stared at me. Her struggle seemed real so I left her to it until she finally said, "I don't know whether to be insulted or amused."

"Whichever it turns out to be, would you mind doing it elsewhere?" If necessary, I would move, except this was a perfect position. Lainey and Adam had done three songs so far, and he was very engaged in talking to her. While I didn't think it was an argument, it did seem intense.

I wasn't the only one watching her. Hardigan stood not far from the dance floor, watching her while not watching her. As hard as he attempted to look casual, it wasn't working.

"Maybe go ask Hardigan to dance so he'll relax," I suggested to my current nuisance.

"Oh," she said. "That's an idea." With that, she left me. I bid him a mental apology, but if he wanted to keep King's gaze off Lainey B, Hardigan should really stop staring at her. Tally Marlowe made a beeline across the ballroom just as Ezra Graham finally reappeared. Despite the suit and the tie, he appeared—

Something was wrong. He'd raked his hands through his hair and it seemed to be standing on end. Still, he made his way around the ballroom with one goal. The air around her shifted as Graham tapped Reed on the shoulder.

I could almost hear the snark. The looks being exchanged by all of them were hard to interpret. Though reluctant, Reed surrendered her, and she moved to dance with Graham. When I thought Reed was heading back here, he was intercepted by his own father.

That was a conversation I could skip. Still, the energy in the room was off. While scandals were typical, there was something else going on.

Hardigan was on the dance floor with Tally Marlowe

and even as she seemed to keep up a constant stream of chatter, he wasn't that far from Lainey B and Graham. Would he attempt to swap partners, or would he keep his cool?

The music halted abruptly as a speaker played some feedback. It was a record-scratch moment, yet it wrenched everyone's attention to the band where Wallace Graham stood in a bit of a spotlight with a microphone in hand.

"Good evening, everyone, welcome to Fire and Ice. As you know, Dinah and I love hosting this event every year. It's the perfect way to close out the year, burning up the old and setting fire to the new, as it were. No one ever likes to be left out in the cold. This year's Fire and Ice is a very special event—Ezra and Dinah, do you want to join me up here?"

Graham had gone stiff and then he left Lainey B to head up to the dais. His mother also made her way through the crowd, leaving my father. Speaking of whom, he'd already begun working his way through the gathering to where Lainey B stood. I left my drink and got there first. I met his gaze and he faltered a step before angling away from her.

"Hey, Buttercup," I said, as I took a stand next to her.

"Hey, Trouble," she replied, but there was nothing light in her tone. Instead, she was very focused on the dais, her expression guarded.

"What's wrong?"

"I don't know," she confessed. "Ezra was trying to tell me something..."

Then his father called him up there.

That couldn't be good. I settled a hand at her lower back as I moved a little closer. It gave me a better vantage at who was watching her and making sure they understood she was not alone. Adam was not far from the dais, his expression cold and furious, with his father standing beside him. King had approached Hardigan where he stood with Tally and she excused herself.

Maybe she thought to move this way, then again—maybe not.

"There we go," Wallace said as his family joined him. Wrapping an arm around Ezra's shoulders, he said, "Tonight, we're not just getting rid of the old and getting ready to welcome the new—we're going to be growing our family and welcoming a new Graham as we truly look forward to the future. Dinah and I are very proud to announce the engagement of our son Ezra to Oksana Dovzhenko. May their union be as powerful and happy as Dinah's and my own."

Surprise rippled through the crowd. Lainey B jerked and I shifted my arm to wrapping it around her rather than just resting against her. Ezra was expressionless, but as a light swung to a young blonde who looked both startled and flushed at the attention, he pulled from his father.

Spontaneous applause broke out as she walked toward them, and it was impossible to miss the rock on her hand. It was the girl he'd left the ballroom with earlier. Somewhere, a part of my mind cataloged the various responses from the players present, but my attention wholly focused on Lainey B as the bride-to-be reached her new fiancé.

When he dipped her into a kiss, Lainey leaned into me heavily.

"Chin up, Buttercup," I told her as I kept my arm firm around her and pressed my lips to her hair to keep anyone from lip reading. "Lean on me, we're getting the fuck out of this circus."

"I—"

"I got you," I told her as I captured her hand in mine. As

the crowd surged around us, cheering and applauding as they sought to congratulate the happy couple, I angled Lainey B out of the ballroom and away from the madness.

Hardigan was ready to kill, and Reed's expression was equally thunderstruck. Ezra wore a smile as he glanced down at the woman in his arms. I filed all of that away for later.

Right now, Lainey B needed me.

∿

The Royals will return in Wicked Surrender.

AFTERWORD

So... I was told this could have been worse. And I mean, they're right. It could totally be worse.

Will it be worse in Wicked Surrender?

Anything is possible.

Anything.

You guys are the best!

xoxo

Heather

P.S. Yes, I am heading right back to my corner! We added a coffeemaker and some great cushions.

Reader group:
facebook.com/groups/heatherspack
Spoiler group:
facebook.com/groups/teammadatheather

WICKED SURRENDER

BAY RIDGE ROYALS BOOK 4

Every moment of my life was planned out before birth...

Family legacy dictates everything from type of education to suitability of friends to eligible marriage opportunities to the type of business I'm expected to go pursue. It's more than just DNA, it's also about birth order, gender, and unfortunately—the family name.

I was born a Reed and the weight that carries isn't limited to the doors that it opens, but also the ones it bars shut. When I was tapped for the Royals, I saw my first way out—but it only proved to be a deeper trap.

Every single move I've made has been to tear us all free from King, from our parents, from our families—but there is no way out. There is only through.

We can't break away, we have to take over.

Lies, betrayal, family.

The only woman I've ever loved is a the center of the board, courted and pursued on all sides by new players and old. There can be no truce.

My best friend? He's lost his damn mind, avoiding me, and agreeing to plans he swore had long since fallen by the wayside.

Yet here we are. He's surrendered.

I refuse to accept that.

I refuse to accept it for her, for him, or for us.

If the only way out is to destroy everyone in our path—then that's exactly what we're going to do.

BENEDICT FAMILY

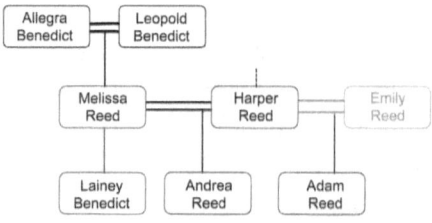

HARDIGAN FAMILY

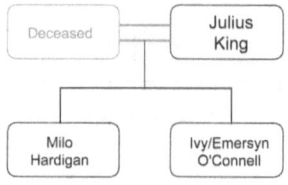

REED FAMILY

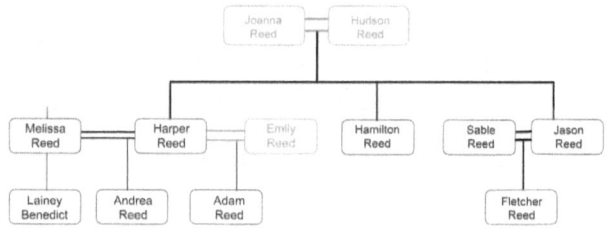

GRAHAM FAMILY

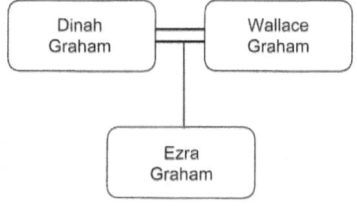

CAVENDISH FAMILY

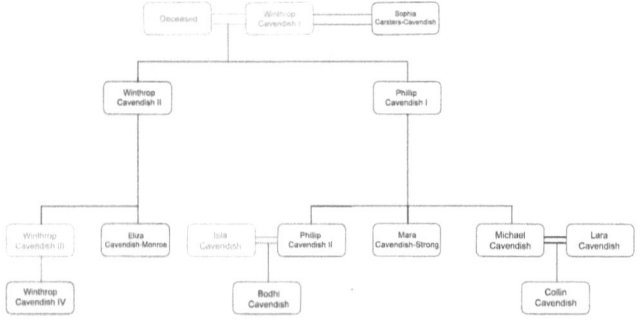

MARLOWE FAMILY

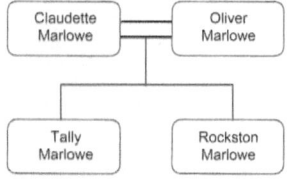

About Heather Long

I *love* books. Not just a little bit, but a lot. Books were my best friends when I was growing up. Books didn't care if I was new to a town or to a class. They were always there, my trustiest of companions. Until they turned on me and said I had to write them.

I can tell you that my own personal happily ever after included writing books. I've always said that an HEA is a work in progress. It's true in my marriage, my friendships, and in my career. I am constantly nurturing my muse as we dive into new tales, new tropes, new characters and more.

After seventeen years in Texas, we relocated to the Pacific Northwest in search of seasons, new experiences, and new geography. I can't wait to discover what life (and my muse) have in store for me.

Maybe writing was always my destiny and romance my fate. After all, my grandmother wasn't a fan of picture books and used to read me her Harlequin Romance novels.

Follow Heather & Sign up for her newsletter:
www.heatherlong.net
TikTok

Also by Heather Long

82nd Street Vandals

Savage Vandal

Vicious Rebel

Ruthless Traitor

Dirty Devil

Shamelessly Loyal (Novella)

Brutal Fighter

Dangerous Renegade

Merciless Spy

Reckless Thief

Fierce Dancer

Bay Ridge Royals

Shamelessly Loyal (Novella)

Battle Lines

Deceptive Truce

Wicked Surrender

Blue Ivy Prep

Problem Child

Mad Boys

Party Crashers

Money Shot

Bravo Team Wolf

When Danger Bites

Bitten Under Fire

Cardinal Sins

Kill Song

First Chorus

High Note

Last Word

Chance Monroe

Earth Witches Aren't Easy

Plan Witch from Out of Town

Bad Witch Rising

Fevered Hearts

Marshal of Hel Dorado

Brave are the Lonely

Micah & Mrs. Miller

A Fistful of Dreams

Raising Kane

Wanted: Fevered or Alive

Wild and Fevered

The Quick & The Fevered

A Man Called Wyatt

Heart of the Nebula

Queenmaker

Deal Breaker

Throne Taker

Lone Star Leathernecks

Semper Fi Cowboy

As You Were, Cowboy

Shackled Souls

Succubus Chained

Succubus Unchained

Succubus Blessed

Shackled Souls (Omnibus)

STANDALONES

Kiss of Fate (w/Blake Blessing)

Taste of Karma (w/Blake Blessing)

I'll Be Home... (w/Tate James)

Untouchable

Rules and Roses

Changes and Chocolates

Keys and Kisses

Whispers and Wishes

Hangovers and Holidays

Brazen and Breathless

Trials and Tiaras

Graduation and Gifts

Defiance and Dedication